Also By Brenda Hasse

<u>An Afterlife Journey Trilogy</u>
On The Third Day
From Beyond The Grave
Until We Meet Again

<u>Adult</u>
A Victim Of Desperation

<u>Young Adult</u>
The Freelancer
A Lady's Destiny
The Moment Of Trust
Wilkinshire

<u>Picture Books For Children</u>
My Horsy And Me, What Can We Be?
A Unicorn For My Birthday
Yes, I Am Loved

The Cursed Witch

~

Brenda Hasse

The Cursed Witch

978-1-7347786-6-3 (pbk)
978-1-7347786-7-0 (ebk)

To the innocent victims who were falsely accused,
may they rest in peace.

Chapter 1

The clip-clop of the horse's hooves on the cobblestone echoed throughout the deserted main street. The driver of the flatbed wagon kept the mare at a slow pace. Sitting next to him was his partner, who scanned every close and window for someone who may be awake at the late bewitching hour of the night.

Flickering candles on windowsills illuminated colorful glass witch balls and hag stones protectively dangling from ribbons, warding off evil spirits. For tonight, the thin veil between the seen and unseen allowed spirits to roam freely amongst the living. At least the superstitious resurrectionists believed the pagan legend to be true.

"Glad he rented us the horse and wagon. Makes the job easier, ye ken." Martin encouraged the chestnut mare down a side street and pulled on the reins to bring the horse to a stop.

"Aye, the guard's been paid, right?" John's short legs reached down to the street as he descended from the seat and grabbed a shovel from the flatbed. He looked up at Martin, who was a head taller, and awaited his reply.

A black cat darted beneath the wagon with a dead rodent dangling limply from her mouth.

Martin looked down as the ebony feline scurried across his boots before it disappeared into the shadowed darkness. Slow to react, he took a skittish step backward and kicked his foot toward the feral. "Damn cat!" He made the sign of the cross on his body, praying the feline was not a bad omen. Martin picked up the second shovel from the wagon bed. "Aye, he told us the guard has been bought off. Can't you remember anything, John?" He sighed, lowering the volume of his voice to a whisper. "We should be in the clear as long as a constable doesn't stroll by the kirkyard." Martin looked up and down the street. "He said this one is young and hasn't been dead long." He flashed his partner a grin of blackened teeth. "We should get near £10 for her."

John's empty stomach grumbled. "Maybe we can get a meat pie for each of us. I do like meat pies. You do too." He patted his abdomen before retrieving the lantern from a hook on the front of the wagon. "Do we need this?" He held the glowing light up for his partner to see.

Martin cringed, waving his arm in a downward motion, encouraging John to lower the lantern. He looked at the full moon, another ominous sign. The bright orb shed ample light on the crowded city of Edinburgh, but he feared the grave of the young woman may be overshadowed by a stone wall or another gravestone. "Aye, bring it. Keep it near your body and cover it with the blade of your shovel, so its light isn't seen."

Withered leaves swirled in the wind crossing their pathway as if warning the men of impending danger. They crept along the iron fence of Saint Cuthbert's kirkyard.

John looked at the spear finials topping the barrier and wondered if its purpose was to keep trespassers out or the restless spirits within.

The wind whistled through the nearly bare branches of the trees freeing a broken limb. It fell to the ground with a resounding thud. Assuming the noise was a heavy footstep, the men froze in place and listened.

John's heart pounded like a drum in his chest. His rapid breathing appeared like wispy clouds in the chilly night air. Even though he and Martin were homeless, living within various closes with other poor vagabonds, he knew if they were caught, a speedy trial would ensue. The magistrate may rule to put them on a convict ship with a one-way trip to Australia. On the other hand, if they were accused of murdering the woman, their crime would be considered grievous, and they would be hung in public. He preferred neither option.

The men stopped before the tall iron gate and looked about. Assuming they remained undetected, Martin exhaled, relieved he saw no witnesses. He looked at his superstitious partner, whose previous comment caused doubt to seep into his mind. "Let's hope he is true to his word, and the gate is unlocked. Otherwise, we may have to scale the fence, ye ken."

John held his breath as he watched Martin grasp the latch and lift it cautiously. He cringed, fearing the hinges were rusty and would squeak. He exhaled as it swung open silently.

Pulling the gate just wide enough for them to pass, Martin jerked his head toward the opening, signaling John to go before him. Once they were both inside the kirkyard, he pulled the gate closed, leaving it unlatched for their escape. He turned and nearly bumped into John, who had yet to take a step onto the hallowed ground. Exhaling like an angry bull, Martin stared down at the back of John's head. "She's buried in the northwest corner." He nudged his partner's shoulder, encouraging him forward, but John's feet were planted solidly as he scanned the gravestones within the kirkyard, uncertain which direction he should go.

"You know I'm not good with compass directions. Which way, left, right, or straight ahead?"

Martin pressed his lips together to control his temper, looked heavenward, and grabbed John by the forearm. He glanced up at a lit window in the tower as they passed by it, ignoring the silhouette looking down at him, and headed in the direction of the grave with his friend in tow.

The guard watched the men, assuming they were the ones he had been expecting. Typically, Angus would tour the graveyard paying careful attention to the recently buried, stopping to listen for the sound of a bell from the dead ringers. If he heard an alarm, he would dig up the survivor who was saved by the bell. His responsibilities also included deterring resurrectionists and grave robbers during his long graveyard shift. Tonight, however, he was paid to ignore the men for a few hours it would take them to retrieve a body.

Within the past two days, three bodies had been added to the kirkyard. Two of the deceased were men of wealth. They received a proper burial, including a bell tucked under one hand before their caskets were sealed. In addition, their families had paid for expensive iron mortsafes to enclose the casket, ensuring their loved ones remained safely in the ground to rest in peace.

The third, a young woman, who had yet to reach twenty years of age, had died under mysterious circumstances. She was not given a bell, nor was her casket enclosed in a mortsafe. Many in the city did not want her body buried in the kirkyard, for they knew she was the seventh daughter of the seventh daughter, thus cursing her as a witch. When she was born, those in her immediate family refused to step forward as her godparent. Finally, a person outside of the family was kind enough to assume the role. Her godmother, ever-present yet always unseen, guided her goddaughter from afar. She remained hidden in the shadows of the kirkyard during the funeral, loyal to the end.

The haunting call of an owl echoed throughout the kirkyard.

John scanned the treetops, his panic welling within him. "An owl? In the city? It's a sign and a bad one." He was pulled past a gravestone embellished with an hourglass, skull, and an angel with her wings outstretched. Fixated on the hollow eyes of the sculpture staring back at him, he wondered if the soul within the grave was at rest. He looked from gravestone to gravestone, silent sentinels, as shadows as black as ink danced between them, or was it just his imagination?

As the pair neared the corner of the kirkyard, Martin slowed his pace as he searched the ground for freshly overturned soil. "Here it is." He pointed with the handle of his shovel at the mounded rectangle of dirt.

John set the lantern on the ground and looked at each narrow end of the grave. "No marker. What end do you think they placed her head?"

Martin looked for a nearby grave for comparison, but there were none. The kirk had isolated the woman's body far away from the others. "A good question. They may have buried her in the opposite direction to make sure she never rises."

"He told us she wasn't given a bell, so the guard won't know to save her if she wakes, and she can't get out of there, especially not that far down in the ground." John reasoned.

Knowing the townsfolks presumed the girl to be a witch, Martin warned, "Don't be too sure. She may possess the power to do so even in death."

John looked at one end of the grave, then the other. "Let's start at this end," he guessed as he set the tip of his shovel in the loosened soil, "and hope I'm right."

They pushed their shovels into the soil and dropped the dirt in a pile beside the grave. Even in the cool temperature of the night, the men unbuttoned their never-washed overcoats and wiped their brows with the sleeves to sop the dripping sweat from stinging their eyes. They continued to dig until the tip of Martin's shovel collided with something hollow and wooden. He looked at John and smiled. John grinned in return displaying his missing front tooth.

They widened the hole, exposing the narrow end of the casket made crudely from repurposed wood.

John retrieved the lantern and held it above the hole. "A few more shovelfuls at each corner should free it enough to bust the end and get her out."

Martin licked his lips as he thrust his shovel into the hole. "I can taste that meat pie already." He dumped a shovelful of dirt onto the pile. "With the colder weather, her body hasn't had a chance to rot much. She'll be a fine one for Knox's students to watch as he cuts her apart."

The men finished clearing the end of the casket, used the tip of their shovels to pry it open, and saw thick, wavey scarlet hair lying within.

Martin looked at his partner in crime. "Looks like you guessed right."

John nodded as his chest puffed up like a proud rooster. "Let's get her out." The men tossed aside their shovels.

Martin, being quite muscular and robust, lay on his stomach on the grave and grabbed the corpse's head. Placing his large hands on the cranium, he pulled on the body and exposed the young woman's face. Her eyes were closed as if she was sleeping. He reached into the casket and grasped beneath her arms. "Here she comes." He yanked and thrust the body upward into John's waiting hands.

"Got her." John dragged the body out of the hole as Martin continued to push it upward, stood, and grabbed the ankles as the body was exhumed. They dropped the corpse on the ground. Both men looked at it, breathing heavily and pleased to have the worst of the task done.

"Aye, she's fresh, alright. No stench whatsoever," Martin confirmed.

A gust of wind swayed the treetops. John scanned the kirkyard. A chill ran up his spine as he imagined the restless souls' watchful eyes staring at him, judging him and his partner for their wrongdoing. "Let's grab her and go."

"Don't be daft. We gotta fill the hole first." Martin picked up his shovel. John sighed and retrieved his as well. They each threw a shovelful of dirt back into the hole.

"Ahh-chew!"

"Bless you." The resurrectionists said simultaneously. They looked at each other, pausing with their shovels in their hands.

"I didn't sneeze," John said as he stared at Martin, who stomped the tip of his shovel into the pile of dirt.

Martin pushed his shovel into the pile of dirt and looked at John. "I didn't sneeze either."

The men stood staring at each other as a moan echoed from behind them. They looked over their shoulders and watched as the corpse sat up, its head turned, eyes wide, staring at them.

Tales of witches rising from the dead and bestowing curses on those who betrayed them were well known.

John's mouth opened. He became saucer-eyed as he tried to scream, but no sound came forth.

The color in Martin's face faded to pasty white. He broke out in a cold sweat.

Transfixed by the living-dead woman, John dropped his shovel and took a blind step forward, falling into the open grave. Abandoning his shovel in the dirt, Martin took a giant step into the loose soil of the grave, twisted his ankle, and tumbling into the hole on top of John, who screamed in terror. Martin used John's shoulder like a stepping stool to get out of the grave. He turned and grabbed his partner's pleading arms that reached toward him for help and yanked John out of the ground. The resurrectionists darted from the kirkyard with their unbuttoned overcoats flapping behind them.

Chapter 2

Anna blinked her emerald eyes to clear her blurred vision, and stared at the fleeing men, who faded into the shadowed darkness. She scanned her surroundings to see gravestones of various heights before wincing in pain. The swollen bump on her head throbbed with each beat of her heart, her only source of injury. Perplexed, she tried to piece together the fragmented memories scattered in the thick fog of her mind.

The list . . .she recalled.

Lachlan, her brother, had given her a list of items her mother needed for the next day, and the errand needed to be done immediately, or so she assumed from the tone of her brother's voice. Apprehension twisted her stomach as she looked at the grandfather clock, which indicated the hour was late and close to closing time for the general store. Scanning the list, some of the items were strange and quite odd. She wondered if everything would be in stock. Walking the distance in the rising moonlight on the evening before Samhain caused gooseflesh to rise on her arms.

Donning her overcoat, she placed the list in her pocket as she stepped out the front door of their house and descended the steps. Her head turned like a loose shutter in the wind as she looked from one side of the street to the other, astutely aware of every imagined shadow cast in the moonlight as she walked. Neep, squash, and pumpkin lanterns with their flickering mocking faces stared at her from the stoops of households.

Footsteps echoed behind her, but when she turned around, no one was there. Anna tried to avoid the crowded closes where the homeless huddled around buckets of flickering firelight for warmth. Hearing the footsteps again, she darted into a darkened street to avoid whoever was following her. She turned around to confront the person and saw the back of a shovel in the moonlight before it collided with the side of her head. Her vision faded to black as her body crumbled to the ground.

Looking at the abandoned pair of shovels before her, she wondered, "Was it all a bad dream?" Still dressed in her overcoat, Anna sat on the cold ground. She reached into the pocket of her regency garment and pulled out the list of items she never purchased. It was indeed written in her mother's hand.

The rapid clatter of a horse's hooves and wagon wheels outside the kirkyard drew her attention. She saw the silhouettes of a pair of men on the wagon seat and assumed they were the same two who had unearthed her and ran away.

Anna stood and staggered a few steps as a wave of dizziness overcame her. When her vision cleared and she regained her balance, she brushed off her full-length Regency overcoat, picked up the lantern, and looked down into the hole at the open casket. "They assumed I was dead." Anna looked at each of her wrists, but nothing was tied to either of them. "They didn't give me a bell?" She imagined lying within the confines of the wooden box, trapped, withering like a flower without water, and dying. A shiver ran up her spine. She would have suffered a slow and lonely death.

Home. She needed to go home. Running her dry tongue over her cracked lips, she planned to drink several cups of tea and hoped the cook had a tin of freshly baked scones designated for breakfast. Anna planned to eat several of them smothered with butter and jam.

Her legs trembled as she walked toward the kirkyard entrance. Another wave of dizziness caused her to sidestep. Anna leaned against the nearest gravestone for support. Inhaling the cold evening air while resting a moment, she looked up at the shadowed figure in the tower staring down at her. Scanning the kirkyard, the familiarity of her surroundings became apparent. She held the lantern before the headstone and read the inscription. "Oliver Stewart." She sighed, displaying a slight grin. "Hello, Dad. Even in death, you are propping me up."

Her father passed away several years ago while at sea. Since she was on the ship when the accident occurred, people believe his death was brought on by Anna's curse.

"It's comforting to know I was at least buried near you." Regaining her balance, Anna avoided treading on the occupied plots as she went to the entrance and passed through the open gate.

With the lantern in hand, Anna stepped onto the vacant street. She looked right and left for a coach. There were none. Turning toward home, she began to walk but soon realized the sound of her hard-heeled shoes echoed on the cobblestones. The noise would draw the attention of the homeless. Pausing, she veered to the center of the street to distance herself from their prying eyes as they peered at her from a close. Anna prayed she would arrive home unmolested.

She looked up at the full moon, its placement in the night sky, and estimated the time was a few hours past midnight. Her family would be asleep, except possibly Lachlan, who usually enjoyed a late evening at a local pub.

A movement to her left caused Anna to turn her head quickly and look at the opening of a close. Several people were huddled together for warmth, covered with blankets that resembled cheesecloth. They sat around a bucket with their hands extended over the flickering flames. Their hopeless eyes staring over their shoulders at her as she looked away, breaking eye contact. She lengthened her stride, hurrying her steps, and wondered if her mother would be surprised to see her.

Anna approached a stone building, four stories high, which housed several families. The waling of a baby resonated from an upper floor, and she looked up to see a lit lamp in the window.

Footsteps echoed behind her. Anna turned around, walked backward, and saw a gentleman dressed in a dark overcoat with tails and a beaver top hat stagger from the pub. He collapsed onto a nearby bench to sleep off whatever he had over consumed. Two other men resembling workers from the harbor emerged from the establishment and helped the semi-unconscious man to his feet. She assumed they would escort him home or to the nearest boardinghouse.

As she turned around, Anna stopped short, nearly slamming into an elderly woman standing in her pathway. The old crone leaned on her cane with one hand. She was dressed in a ragged overcoat. Her long, thin gray hair framed her face, and steel-gray eyes bored into Anna, unblinking.

Anna looked down at the woman's side to see her dog protectively standing guard. The black and brown canine stared at her. His massive jowls were nearly as wide as his chest.

Even though the witch trials were long ago, many believed some had escaped and lived among them, hidden in plain sight. The old hag's reputation as a pagan, healer, and conjurer was well renowned. Many believe she was a witch. Anyone who could not afford a physician would visit her to cure their ailments, prescribe a remedy, help with a difficult birth, or asked her to cast a spell for either good or bad reasons. However, everyone knew to never anger or cross her, for they feared she may place an evil curse on anyone who did.

"I'm sorry," Anna apologized. "If you'll excuse me." She sidestepped the woman to continue her journey home.

"There's no excuse for you."

The aged, raspy voice caused Anna to cringe. She stopped and turned around to face the woman, who turned toward her. "I beg your pardon?"

"My dear, do you know who I am?" The old woman switched her cane to the other hand and petted the dog by her side. The vicious-looking beast stepped forward and sniffed Anna's ankles and clothing.

Anna took a step backward, distancing herself from the canine.

"Barret won't hurt you. He's kind in nature unless he is provoked or ordered to protect." Her sharp whistle called the beast to her side.

"I know your name," Anna confessed, answering the old witch's question. She stared at the dog, who obediently obeyed the command.

"Ah, but I'm more than just a name to you."

Anna scowled; she had never met the woman face to face. "How so?"

"I accepted an important role in your life when others would not."

Anna took a step closer. She raised the lantern to see the woman's wrinkled face. "I don't understand."

With the assistance of her cane, the old woman took a step forward, staring into Anna's eyes. "No member of your family would accept the responsibility, so I did. I'm your godmother."

Anna stared into the aged eyes of the woman. She tilted her head to one side, puzzled by the information. "My godmother? As far as I know, I don't have one. At least I was never told I had one." She assumed her mother would verify the old hag's tale. "Excuse me. I'm going home." She turned and took a step forward.

The crone shook her head. "That's a bad idea."

Anna froze and turned back to the old woman. "Why?"

"They may be responsible for attempting to kill you."

Anna's eyebrows raised at the notion. "Kill me?"

"Aye, to rid your family of the curse you possess, a curse blamed for your father's death."

The possible truth hit Anna's stomach as if she had been punched. Did everyone, including her mother and brother, honestly believe she was responsible for her father's death? Her brother often accused her of being cursed. Her mother never uttered the words, at least not to her face. She stared at the aged woman standing before her. A seed of doubt had been planted within her mind. Of all the people in the city to formulate the conspiracy theory, it came from the most credible, all-knowing, and trusted person, the town witch, Haggadah Blyth.

Chapter 3

Anna looked skyward, searching for an answer amongst the stars. "I don't understand." She whispered to herself. "A supposed curse?"

Her mother was the seventh daughter of her parents. With her six older sisters passing away at a young age, she was also the seventh daughter, making her the seventh daughter of the seventh daughter.

She sighed, recalling the hushed conversations of others she had overheard since she was a little girl. "The cursed witch," Anna whispered.

Haggadah walked toward Anna, tapping her cane on the ground with each step. "Aye, the same reason no one in your family would be your godparent." The old witch continued past her with Barret by her side.

Anna turned to face the woman's retreating figure. She stood in the center of the intersection and looked down the street at her house. "Wouldn't a constable have reported my death to Mum? Perhaps he told her who tried to kill me?"

~

Lachlan opened his bloodshot hazel eyes to the darkness of his bedroom, laid still, and listened. His mother's sobbing had awakened him once again. "Must she cry all night?" He rose from his bed, donned his robe, went to her bedroom, and pressed his ear against the six-panel wooden door. He could hear the floor creaking as she paced, whaling in her grief. He sighed, unsure of what to say, but knocked anyway. "Mum?"

Evelyn looked at the portal, recognizing the concerned tone in her son's voice. She dabbed the tiny rivulets of tears streaming down her cheeks with her handkerchief, ashamed her behavior disturbed Lachlan's sleep once again. She could not shut off her mind as it continued to torment her with images of her lost loved ones whenever she closed her eyes to sleep.

Her reputation as a strong woman, capable of handling the direst of situations, was well known. When her husband, Oliver, was out to sea for months overseeing the Stewart Mercantile Shipping Company, she had little choice to be otherwise. Much like a crumbling stone wall, Evelyn began to weaken when she received the news that he was crushed by shifting cargo and died during a storm at sea. After he was buried, she no longer desired the company of others. It was awkward going to social events unaccompanied. Her friends stopped inviting her to gatherings and gala balls, respecting her time to grieve. It was expected that Lachlan would take over the family business, but at seventeen years old, he had little interest. Evelyn employed an accountant, Mr. Corbin Heywood, to oversee the business and ordered Lachlan to go to the office daily hoping he would eventually accept the responsibility.

She exhaled, closed her eyes, and envisioned the constable knocking on the door in her mind. The officer refused to make eye contact as he told her Anna's lifeless body was discovered in a close. The shock of losing her last remaining daughter pushed her grief to despair. During the funeral, she stood next to Anna's wooden casket lying amongst the autumn leaves on the kirkyard grass. A pillar in society, Evelyn displayed a facade of strength, free of emotion as they lowered her daughter's body into the grave as nearest to her husband's resting place that was allowed.

Opening her eyes, Evelyn folded her open robe over her body and secured it with its belt. She dabbed her swollen eyes with her handkerchief and wiped the end of her reddened nose. "Aye, Lachlan."

Evelyn heard the door creak open and her son's footsteps shuffling on the rug as he entered the room. Refusing to meet his askance eyes, she stood with her back toward him, staring out the window overlooking the quiet cobblestone street below. Evelyn stared at the flickering flames of the oil lampposts dotted along the walkway. The illuminated lights danced in the moonlight like trapped tiny glowing pixies within the glass.

Lachlan saw the silhouette of his mother standing in the moonlight of the window. Her long ebony hair streaked with silver, which was usually pinned in place, hung loosely down her back to her waist. "Shall I ring the maid? She can make you a cup of tea or get you a sedative to help you sleep."

"No, thank you. I just need time." Evelyn crossed her arms over her chest.

Lachlan approached and stood behind her shoulder. He resembled his father in both height and facial characteristics. He assumed what was troubling her so. "Dad's death was tragic and unexpected, but so long ago, Mum. I know Anna's death hasn't been easy on you. . .

"Murdered? Only eighteen years old, much too young." Evelyn interrupted.

Uncertain how to comfort her, Lachlan placed his hands upon her shoulders and squeezed them gently. "There are a lot of homeless people, and crime is rampant. So, sending her out into the darkness of the night was unwise."

"I didn't..."

"I'm equally as guilty, Mum. The maid gave me your list of items. I, in turn, gave it to Anna assuming the errand needed her immediate attention. It could have waited until the light of day." Lachlan sighed. "We cannot undo what has been done. We need to be strong and move forward. It's what she would want us to do."

Still refusing to meet the concern in her son's eyes, Evelyn reached toward her shoulder and patted Lachlan's hand. A movement at the end of the street caught her attention. She squinted her eyes, straining to see the disheveled vibrant red hair of a woman walking at a familiar gait. "Anna?" She leaned toward the pane of glass, resting her forehead on its coolness, and watched as the figure carrying a lantern stood in the crossroad. "It's Anna. God almighty, she has risen from the dead. She truly is a cursed witch."

~

The old witch stopped walking and looked over her shoulder. "A constable went to your house when your body was found in the close. Word has yet to reach my ears of the murderer's arrest. If the killer is still in the city and your family announces your return from the dead, then you may be giving the murderer the opportunity to ensure you take a permanent dirt nap. So, it's best if you come with me, at least until the culprit is in custody."

Anna looked at Haggadah, not wanting to believe the old woman, yet afraid not to if she was right. Looking toward her residence again, she knew her family believed she was dead. Would they be pleased if she walked through the front door alive? Anna was certain they loved her yet failed to recall them ever uttering the words.

"Well, are you coming?" Haggadah waited. Barret turned toward Anna and tilted his head to one side as if questioning her too.

Anna looked at the old witch, who turned to face her. Her shadowed silhouette in the moonlight projected an eerie, ghostly appearance. She sighed, conceding to Haggadah's reasoning. "Aye, until I can gather my thoughts and come to some conclusion as to why someone, anyone would go so far as to try to kill me."

Haggadah watched her goddaughter as she approached timidly. "You may stay with me for as long as you like. I'm certain Nero and Barret will enjoy your company." Her gnarled, arthritic hand reached toward the beastly dog's head and patted it affectionately.

~

Lachlan sighed. He suspected his mother was so overwrought with grief that she was delusional, but thought it was best to humor her. "Where, Mum?" He stepped to the window as she took a step backward.

"There." She pointed to the crossroads as she looked away from the intersection and the figure disappeared.

Lachlan scrutinized the empty intersection. "I see nothing." He looked at his mother as she leaned into the window once again. Lachlan shook his head and sighed, unwilling to listen to any more of her ranting. "Here, let me tuck you into bed."

Evelyn pressed her head against the cold glass again, straining her eyes to see her daughter once more, but she was gone. "She was there. I saw her." She looked over her shoulder, refusing to look away from the window as Lachlan guided her toward her bed. Evelyn climbed between the covers, rolled onto her side away from her son, and reached for her husband, Oliver, whose usual place beside her was vacant.

Lachlan pulled the plush covers over his mother's body. "Try to get some rest." If her incessant grieving continued, he feared they would both succumb to an illness. "I need to have a clear mind for tomorrow when I review the ledger with Corbin," he muttered to himself. The accountant had forewarned him of the company's declining revenues. He was not looking forward to the meeting.

Lachlan left her bedroom, pulling the door closed until it clicked shut. He stood in the hallway momentarily to listen. Her sobbing echoed from her room once again. Rubbing his tired eyes, he decided to tell Helen, the maid, to add a sedative to his mother's evening tea to help her sleep.

~

Anna met Barret's stare as she walked toward Haggadah. The dog's jowls were rumored to break the back of small animals and could fracture a man's arm. The canine stood waist-high to the witch, always protective and alert.

Those who spotted Haggadah's cat, Nero, usually saw the feline darting through the city's streets. They described him as enormous too, weighing nearly two stones, with long ebony fur as dark as coal and a rat usually dangling from his mouth. The feline would scurry into the protective shadow of a close and peer out at them with his amber eyes that seemed to glow.

Haggadah turned, tapping her cane on the cobblestone as she led the way to her house just outside of the city. Her old cottage was well known by everyone. A single story, with a loft, was surrounded by a waist-high stone wall and a rickety wooden gate. A flagstone walkway ushered visitors to the front door. Those who dared to pass by her house did so on the opposite side of the street. If the chimney emanated a colorful or fragrant smoke, they avoided going by it altogether. Even though people refused to cross the old witch's path when encountering her on the street, she received many visitors to her cottage asking for help.

Anna fell in stride behind the old witch, who walked slowly but deliberately and with purpose.

"No reason to keep your thoughts to yourself, Anna. It only festers within you, making you ill." Haggadah looked over her shoulder at her goddaughter as she turned down a side street, weaving her way home.

Anna glanced at the profile of the witch, hesitant about confiding her deepest thoughts. However, she needed a second opinion and advice. She touched the throbbing bump on her head. "Do you know what happened to me?"

The old witch gazed into the distance as if listening to a message from someone unseen. "Someone tried to kill you. I see the blade of a shovel striking you. They thought you were dead. Whoever it was, convinced someone to exhume your body."

"Aye, the two men in the kirkyard." She recalled. "But I wasn't dead. So why did they bury me when I wasn't dead?"

"Lack of knowledge, perhaps. They failed to listen for your heartbeat, or maybe they ignored it and declared you dead." Haggadah looked at her goddaughter. "People are superstitious of those who are different. They believe silly nonsense, and their fear can drive them to do the unimaginable."

"Superstitious?"

Haggadah stopped walking and turned toward her goddaughter. "Because there are people who believe you are cursed, born a witch, they live in fear. When you died, their fear was eased."

Anna stopped short. "What?" She recalled the history of the many women burned alive for the flimsy suspicion of being a witch. She put her fisted hands on her hips. "I'm not a witch."

Haggadah grinned, turned, and continued walking.

Anna's jaw dropped open. The old witch had not confirmed nor denied the possibility. She marched toward the woman and came alongside her. "I'm not a witch. I cannot be a witch. I mean, I know of some home remedies for a sore throat and a cough, but cast spells, not me, not ever."

"Stop babbling, child. Even the sin eater wouldn't come to visit you once you were declared dead."

"But the sin eater visits everyone when they die." Anna justified. "They put a slice of bread on the body of the dead, say a few prayers while they listen to a family member confess the sins of the deceased, and then the sin eater eats the bread, thus absolving the sins from the dead. So why did the sin eater not come to visit me?"

"Because she refused to eat the sins of one who is cursed."

"Even the sin eater believes I'm cursed as a witch." Anna sighed.

"Never fear. You will come into your own in due time."

"Come into my own?" Anna raised her eyebrows in question. "Does that mean I am a witch?"

"In due time, aye. People believe we are evil. But in truth, we are healers. You have much to learn, and I'll teach you all I know." Haggadah turned onto another side street. Her cane tapping with each step.

"But what about Mum?" Anna followed. "Shouldn't she be told I'm alive?"

"As long as the murderer or anyone else believes you are dead, then no one will look for you. It'll give us time to discover the truth. Ah, here we are." Haggadah opened the gate within the protective stone wall. Barret darted toward the front door.

Anna closed the gate and scanned the shabby old cottage with its thatched roof and stone walls. She closed the short distance between her and Haggadah and followed the old witch up the flagstone walkway.

Haggadah opened the front door and stepped inside.

Nero, curled on his mistress's bed, lifted his head to see who entered the small house disturbing his sleep.

The old witch took off her ragged coat with its many patches and hung it on a peg on the wall. She went to her bed and patted Nero's head. "Oh, my sleepy feline, do not be rude. I've brought a guest. This is Anna. She'll be staying with us for a while." Haggadah went to the fireplace and stirred the ashen embers with an iron poker. Anna watched the shadowed figure select a thin stick from a bundle on the hearth, stuck it into the embers, and waited until the tip was aflame before lighting several candles on the mantel. The old witch approached the table in the center of the room, lit the oil lamp, which illuminated the interior of the one-room cottage. Haggadah tossed the stick in the fire.

Anna closed the door and looked about the tiny house as the golden glow from the candles and lamp illuminated its interior. A single bed was against a wall on her left with a nightstand topped by an unlit candle. Curled on the bed was a large black cat. He stared at her curiously. The floor was stone with a multi-colored braided rag rug covering a large circle beneath a table surrounded by four chairs. A ladder leaned against what she assumed was a loft above. Looking to her immediate left was an enormous rectangular cupboard next to the wall. It remained somewhat hidden until she had closed the front door. She assumed it contained the wardrobe of Haggadah's clothes but imagined the old witch had very few, so her reasoning did not justify its size. The walls were made of stone, as was the fireplace with its roughed honed wooden mantel. A wooden three-legged stool and a nicely made bench were near the fireplace. The kitchen area had a single cupboard, a water handpump with a washtub, and a working table to prepare food. Various dried herbs and flowers hung in bundles from the beamed ceiling. It was a functional house and perfect for the witch in both size and location. Overall, it was quaint and cozy.

Anna took off her overcoat and hung it on a peg beside the witch's coat.

Nero hopped down from the bed, curious to meet the visitor. The feline approached with his head lowered. He sniffed Anna's shoes, her dress as far as he could reach upward, and looked at her face. Meeting his approval, he rubbed the length of his body against the side of her dress, pressing it to her leg.

Anna reached down and stroked his velvety long, ebony fur. "I've never seen such a large cat."

Haggadah looked at her feline. "Nero likes to hog my bed while we sleep." She smiled slightly. "But he keeps me warm at night, at least on the nights he isn't out hunting for mice."

Barret went to Anna's side. She took a step backward, stiffened, afraid to move.

The old witch sighed. "Let Barret sniff your hand before you try petting him."

Anna had no intention of petting the canine. She liked animals. Unfortunately, her parents never allowed her to have a pet of her own. Perhaps another sign of their silly superstition and fear she may turn the creature against them or change it into a venomous snake.

Timidly, she held out her hand to Barret and waited for the dog's approval.

Barret traced his nose along the palm of her hand, each finger, and the back. He finally looked at Anna and blinked his eyes.

Cautiously, Anna stroked the top of the dog's head. He obediently sat as she continued down his neck. Then, tempting fate, she stroked the dog a second time.

The witch picked up a log from the hearth. "See, he isn't as mean as everyone assumes. Poor thing. Can you imagine people always thinking the worst of you, even though they don't know you?" She tossed the wood onto the embers and grabbed a second log.

Anna looked at the old witch. "But isn't that how people treat you? Don't they assume the worst because you are a witch?"

Haggadah sat on the stool before the fireplace, her only source of heat. A slight smile appeared on her face. "When I was younger, other children wouldn't play with me. Their mothers poisoned them with fear, taught them to stay clear, and told me I would bewitch them if given a chance. Even though we are different from others, being left out hurts, and it cuts one's heart deeply. I guess I have become numb to the lack of friendship over the years."

"You never married?" Anna pried.

"No, gentlemen knew of my reputation and stayed clear."

"Why didn't you leave town? Go someplace where others did not know you?"

"Over time, my skills in healing became known. I was needed here. Even though I'm without friends, other than Barret and Nero, it's good to feel needed. It gives me a purpose." Haggadah peeked into a cauldron of water that hung on a suspended hook over the fire. The crackling flames lifting skyward would warm the water quickly. She looked at her goddaughter. "Care for a cup of tea?"

"Tea sounds lovely, thank you." Anna patted the top of Barret's head before going to the fireplace and sitting on the bench. She traced her hand over the detailed engraving along its edge. "This is quite nice, such craftmanship."

Haggadah rose and went to the cupboard. She retrieved two teacups and a tin of loose tea. "The bench was a generous payment of gratitude. The man couldn't afford to pay me with money, so he made me the bench. His wife ran a high fever after delivering a little girl. He feared she would die and came to me for help." She opened the tea, plunged her aged fingers into the loosed leaves, and pinched a small amount into each cup before returning to the stool.

"So, his fear of losing his wife was more than his fear of you." Anna reasoned.

Haggadah smiled. "You can say so, aye."

"But after helping save his wife's life, do you think his fear has turned to trust?"

"In me?"

"Aye."

"Maybe when the man is alone, he admits it to himself, but in the company of others, he probably conforms to what others think and say." Haggadah carried the teacups to the hearth, set them upon the stone, and peeked into the cauldron of water that had yet to boil.

Nero jumped onto the bench next to Anna.

"Oh, my." Anna lifted her clasped hands from her lap as the cat climbed onto it, laid down, and purred as she stroked his fur.

The old witch shook her head. "Nero, such an opportunist. You would think with his thick coat of fur, he would remain comfortably warm."

"He is so large that he hardly fits on my lap."

"It's his breed, big, hairy, and heavy."

Barret lay on the floor at Haggadah's feet. "As you can see, my accommodations are simple. There is an outhouse out back when your need should arise." She yawned. "I'm usually not awake at this time of night, especially in the wee morning hours."

"Then why were you out tonight?"

"I was waiting for you." She smiled all-knowingly. "If people were superstitious of you before, just think how much they are going to fear you now that you have risen from the dead."

Chapter 4

Anna agreed with her godmother's logic. If the rumor of her rising from the dead should circulate throughout the city, it would only reinforce the abhorred curse and confirm her as a witch.

Steam began to rise from the cauldron.

"Ah, the water is ready." Haggadah took a ladle from the hook on the mantel, dipped it into the hot water, and filled each teacup. She handed a cup to Anna. "Let it steep for a minute or two."

Anna inhaled the rich aroma of the black tea and watched the tealeaves as they slowly sank below the surface of the hot water. She waited as Haggadah, known for her wisdom and advice, sat on the stool and wrapped her arthritic hands around her teacup to warm them. "So, now what?"

"You live with me and learn the various ways of healing." Haggadah grinned. "And maybe a spell or two." She winked before taking a sip of her tea.

Anna grinned, uncertain if her godmother was telling a falsehood. She sipped her tea, scorching her tongue, but was grateful for the soothing liquid which warmed her body. "Since I'm to remain here until we discover who is responsible for my alleged death, what if I'm recognized by someone who visits you for a remedy?"

"I never allow anyone inside the cottage. However, when I answer the door, it's difficult for me to squelch the caller's curiosity. People often peer into my humble abode. We will somehow keep you hidden from their sight." Haggadah looked at her front door. She chuckled before returning her gaze to Anna. "Do you think anyone would believe them if they said they saw you? After all, you are dead."

A genuine smile spread across Anna's face. "But you know how people like to gossip. They could say you conjured a spell, calling me to your side as your assistant. Or perhaps I had risen from the dead on the night of the full moon." The women smiled at the far-fetched ideas. Anna's smile faded. "What if word should reach the ears of the one who tried to kill me?"

"That's why you will remain hidden," Haggadah confirmed. "There seems to be a wicked strangeness about the city. For the past nine months, people, mostly women, have mysteriously disappeared. I believe they were murdered. With body-snatching prevalent, their corpses were most likely sold to Dr. Robert Knox at the college. He dissects them in the anatomy theater for the medical students to observe."

"Sold?"

"Aye, for quite a sum too. Body-snatching is a profitable business, hard work, but very profitable."

"The people who are missing, were they buried and dug up like me?"

Haggadah tilted her head to the side in thought. "Oddly, no. It would be too much work to put the dead in the ground and dig them up again. I suspect they were taken directly to the college after being killed."

"Murder for profit." Anna's eyes widened. "So, I could have been sold and dissected too?"

"Aye, very likely."

"Can you imagine if I was lying naked on a table, surrounded by men staring down at me? What if I had woken when the doctor began cutting me open?"

"An embarrassing situation and quite painful, indeed." The old witch finished her cup of tea and set it on the hearth. "Since you were buried, I believe we can eliminate the culprits responsible for the unfortunate missing as suspects."

"Do you truly believe I know the person who is responsible for trying to kill me?" Anna sipped her tea.

"It is possible." Haggadah sighed. Her eyelids weighed heavily with deprived sleep. "On the night you were killed, how did you manage to be out at such a late hour?"

"Lachlan gave me a list of items to purchase for Samhain. He said the maid found it on Mum's desk, and I assumed the task should be done immediately. So, I left the house after dark. I didn't want Mum to be disappointed. She has been so forgetful since Father's death." Anna stroked Nero's fur, unwilling to meet the inquisitive stare of the old witch.

Haggadah scowled. "His death was an accident."

Anna stared at the flames licking around the log in the fireplace. "I was with him on the ship. We were going to our cabin for dinner when one of the men reported rough water ahead. Dad went below to see if the cargo was secure. As the ship swayed from a rogue wave, a rope snapped, and cargo fell . . ." She closed her eyes, wishing the haunting memory of that day would vanish from her mind. "His passing has taken a toll on Mum's sanity." She sighed, looked at her godmother, and redirected her train of thought to the topic at hand. "With Mum's list in my overcoat pocket, I left the house. I remember rounding the corner onto a street, hearing a scuffling of footsteps behind me, and when I turned around, something collided with my head. I thought I saw the blade of a shovel before my vision turned to black." She touched the lump on her head.

"It could have been anyone, someone homeless, even someone paid to do the deed." Haggadah put another log on the fire. "Your mum had you buried the next morning. I was at your funeral, hidden in the shadows of a large tree. Only your mum and brother were in attendance."

Anna's eyes widened with disbelief. "Mum didn't allow anyone to view my body and pay their last respects?"

The old witch shook her head. "With your mum locking herself away from society and people believing in your curse, who would have come?"

Her godmother was right. "Was there a priest at my funeral?"

Haggadah shook her head. "Aye, he spoke briefly. Your mum appeared unshaken, kept her emotions in check, as did your brother."

Anna looked at the flickering flames once again, seeing them yet not seeing them. Her thoughts turned to her mother, who experienced more than her fair share of grief over the years. "Mum gave birth to six daughters before giving birth to me. All six died at a young age. I only remember two of my sisters. Even after Dad's death, the mercantile shipping business continued to thrive and provide for us." Anna thought of their house, just off the main street. Would she ever be able to go home again? "We have a maid, Helen, and a cook."

Haggadah let her goddaughter talk, even though what she shared was nothing new to her.

"Lachlan, my baby brother who is a pampered brat, likes to drink, gamble, and stay out all hours of the night. Mum expects him to follow in Dad's footsteps and oversee the business, but he has little interest in doing so. Dad must have recognized his lack of desire. When his last will and testament was read by the lawyer, each of us inherited an equal share of the company. I remember the glaring stares I received from Mum and Lachlan and the humiliation when the lawyer read Dad's final statement, 'no man will ever marry Anna because of her curse, so I am seeing fit to her provision.'"

Anna looked away from the mesmerizing flames at her soiled dress. Her disheveled vibrant auburn hair had fallen from where it had been pinned in place. If her mother saw her, she would undoubtedly receive a reprimand.

She lifted a loose strand from her shoulder and rubbed its silkiness between her thumb and index finger. Her hair had been the topic of many family discussions during dinner, where she could not escape the criticism unless excused from the table. Anna was the only one in the family who had the offensive color. Her father said it resembled the flames of Hell.

Haggadah watched her goddaughter, surmising her thoughts. "Do you believe your curse was the motive behind your attack?"

Anna looked at the old witch as she released the strand and let it fall to her shoulder. "Perhaps."

"Auch, you probably have an Irish ancestor in your family. They commonly have your color of hair."

"I don't know much about my family history. It was never mentioned." Warm and relaxed, Anna glanced at the small interior of the cottage. It was old, maybe several hundred years old. Hand-cut wooden beams ran the length of the ceiling with various dried herbs, almost camouflaging them. She reached to her lap and stroked the still purring cat.

"There is a coop with chickens in the backyard. You can gather the eggs in the morning, and we can have them with beans and bread for breakfast." Haggadah stood. "I'm going to sleep. There is a cot in the loft I made up this morning. You may sleep there. As I mentioned, if the necessity should arise, the outhouse is in the backyard at the far end. Just pass through that doorway." She pointed to a windowless door, rose, put her teacup in the washtub, and pulled the quilt back on her bed.

Anna stared at the back of the woman. "How did you know I would arrive tonight?"

She turned and looked at her guest. "I read it in my tea leaves." She smiled. "Goodnight." Haggadah got into bed, pulled the covers over her shoulder, and rolled onto her side facing the wall.

Anna stared down at the pattern of the tea leaves in her cup. It seemed farfetched to predict someone's arrival by the way they lay. Maybe there was a technique of swishing the tea in a cup or turning it upside down and allowing it to drip down the porcelain. She drank the last mouthful of cooled tea. Placing Nero on the floor, she rose, set the teacup in the washtub, and extinguished the lamp and the candles except for one, which she picked up and climbed the ladder to the loft.

Anna stepped onto the wooden floor, stood, and bumped her head on the low ceiling. She touched the rising lump on her head and held the candle upward to verify the height above her head. In her stooped-over position, she looked about the tiny room. A cot with several folded blankets at its foot and a pillow at the opposite end was wedged against the slanted ceiling. A stool was beside the cot, where she placed the candle and turned to view a chest, several woven baskets, and crates filled with various bottles. The stone chimney ran up the wall to the peak, adding warmth to the small chamber. Anna laid a blanket on the cot, sat, and removed the remaining pins from her hair and her shoes. She pulled the second blanket over her as she settled into bed, blew out the candle, and lay down.

After all she had experienced, she was thankful. Thankful for the two men who exhumed her body. Grateful to have Haggadah, who stepped forward when no one else would and became her godmother. The old witch was now her protector and guardian, but from who?

Chapter 5

The slam of a door jolted Anna from her slumber. Shuffling footsteps pierced the fogginess of her mind as she sniffed, inhaling a strange odor. Was something burning? Opening her eyes, the honed beams of the ceiling jogged her memory of her current situation. Was Haggadah awake? She listened to the clip-clop of horse hooves and the clatter of carriage wheels on the street as it passed by the cottage.

A door slammed again. Anna sat up in bed and peered over the edge of the loft. It was indeed daylight.

Haggadah looked at the loft and grinned. "You might as well retrieve the eggs while you use the outhouse and then help me make breakfast." She stoked the fire to heat the cauldron of water and put another pan with dried beans and water to boil on the iron grate within the fireplace.

Anna climbed down from the loft. She saw her godmother standing before the fireplace with a wooden spoon in her hand. "Good morning." Anna brushed the palms of her hands over her skirt to remove the wrinkles and inhaled the strange but fragrant odor. "What smells so . . . different?" She extended her hand toward Barret as he greeted her, his tail wagging rapidly. Anna petted his head and glanced at Haggadah's bed where Nero slept, ignoring her entirely.

"I burn sage every morning to cleanse the house." Haggadah looked at the condition of her long-term guest. Her hair needed combing, and a clean dress was in order. "It's sunny outside." Hinted Haggadah as she stirred the beans. "There is a basket in the next room you may use to gather the eggs." She nodded toward the windowless door as she set the spoon across the opening of the pot and went to the kitchen.

Anna opened the portal hesitantly, as if it were a secret passage, and entered a small room filled with various strange things hanging from the ceiling and nails on the wall. A single window in the opposite door allowed a smidgeon of light into the room. She squinted her eyes, not quite believing what she saw dangling from a string before her. "Crow's feet?" Its toes curled and dried as if it were trying to grasp its soul as it left its body. Anna spied several dehydrated rats with their tails tied together. They hung from a nail on the wood-paneled wall. She wrinkled her nose as she took a step backward. Next to the vermin were several braids of garlic and onions. Propped in the corner of the tiny room was a hoe, shovel, and pitchfork. Facing the portal, she had passed through, Anna searched the various shelves on the wall framing the door until she found the basket.

The wooden floor beneath her feet sounded hollow as she crossed it and exited through the exterior doorway onto a narrow pathway, which divided the garden in half. The backyard was small but rich with various herbs, flowers, and vegetables, many past their peak this late in the season.

After using the outhouse, Anna gathered the eggs from the chicken coop and paused to inspect some of the herbs. She was familiar with a few of them and their medicinal purposes. "My, there's a lot of white sage and peppermint too." A garden section was covered with straw to keep root vegetables from freezing until they were harvested. She stepped to a plant near the protective stone wall, inspected it, and broke off a leaf. Her eyebrows drew together as she contemplated its identity. Anna rotated it between her index finger and thumb as she carried the leaf back into the house. She set the basket on the working table as the old witch withdrew a pair of unmatching ceramic plates from the cupboard.

Anna inhaled the fragrance of the leaf and looked at her godmother. "I could identify some of the plants in your garden, but this one, in particular, has me baffled." She held the leaf before Haggadah, who held out her open hand. Anna dropped the herb into the old witch's palm.

"Ah, you have found my mugwort plant. Its purpose is quite powerful. For those who travel the dream world and this one, it is used as protection."

"Dreamworld?"

"Aye, some believe we travel to other worlds while we sleep. It can be burned before meditation, used in smudging, or worn as a amulet for protection."

"Is it effective?"

Haggadah smiled. "No one has complained yet." She smirked before taking a lit candle from the mantel, opening the door to the small exterior room, lifting the cellar door, and descended the stairs into the root cellar. "Anna, come and take these, please."

Anna accepted two crocks her godmother placed in her awaiting hands. She watched as Haggadah took another from a shelf before climbing the stairs and closing the cellar door.

"Set the crocks next to the eggs." Haggadah followed Anna to the kitchen and placed her small crock alongside the others. After setting the candle on the working table, she took a large cast-iron frying pan hanging from a nail by the washtub, removed the oilcloth covering on one of the crocks, and plopped a scoop of lard into the pan from its ever-present spoon. The old witch cracked five eggs on the edge of the pan and dropped their contents into it. "Anna, set the pan over the fire to cook and stir the beans. If the beans are dry, add some water." Haggadah retrieved a cloth-wrapped loaf of bread from a cupboard, sliced two thick portions, and dipped the knife into the butter crock. She spread a generous layer on each slice and placed each serving on a plate.

Anna sat on the stool and placed the pan of eggs over the fire to cook. She stirred the beans.

A knock sounded on the door causing Barret to rise from his usual place before the fire. He approached the front portal, sat, and waited for Haggadah to join him.

Anna's heart skipped a beat. She stood abruptly, glanced at the door, and then to her godmother.

The old witch looked at the door and quickly detected her goddaughter's distress. "Sit down and stay hidden behind the table. Watch the eggs. They will burn easily. I'll see to our visitor." She placed the plates on the table and went to the front door.

As instructed, Anna returned to her seat and turned toward the fireplace. Curious, she peeked over her shoulder and watched Haggadah open the door just enough to allow the visitor to see her face. The murmured request of the man reached her ears as she stirred the beans and moved the cooked eggs to the stone hearth so they would not burn. She watched as Haggadah closed the door, went to the large cupboard, and opened the double doors to reveal an apothecary filled with numerous shelves containing glass bottles with toppers and tiny drawers. The bottles and drawers were labeled to identify their contents.

Haggadah filled a bottle with several ingredients and took an amethyst crystal from a drawer. She went to the door, gave instructions for the remedy, and received payment for her service, another chicken. She closed the door and turned toward her goddaughter as she rose from the stool.

Drawn to the cabinet, Anna stared transfixed as she stood before the numerous bottles and drawers. "I have never seen such a complete collection of medicinal aids."

Haggadah stepped beside her. "It was passed down to me by another, and I added more herbs, spices, and crystals as I learned more about natural remedies over the years."

Anna's head turned toward the witch. "Passed down? From whom?"

"That story can wait, for now. Take this hen and put it with the others." Haggadah placed the cackling chicken in Anna's arms.

Nero lifted his head and curiously looked at the source of the strange noise. Barret went to the back door, anticipating an opportunity to stretch his legs.

"Isn't the hen an unusual payment for your service?" Anna held the fowl against her body.

"Many cannot afford the medical fee of a physician, so they come to me for help and pay what they can. But, as you can see, I don't always receive money." Haggadah looked toward the fireplace to see the pan of eggs on the hearth. "Go and put her in the coop before our eggs get cold."

Anna watched the old witch close the apothecary cabinet before exiting the room. Her mind raced with questions as she put the hen with the others. She scanned the garden with its many plants as doubt crept into her mind. Would she be able to learn about every herb and spice? She would have to learn the properties of each crystal or stone too. Would she be able to retain the detailed knowledge to safely create remedies for various needs? What if she made a remedy that harmed someone instead of helped them?

Barret pranced beside her as she walked back to the cottage. She looked down at the canine's face staring up at her. He appeared to be smiling, which made Anna smile too.

Haggadah placed a spoonful of beans on each plate and looked at the pair as they entered the room. "Anna, would you like one egg or two?"

"Two, please." Anna scanned the prepared meal and looked about the cottage. Her life had taken such a turn. No longer was she residing in the comforts of her home, but her accommodations were cozy, and she was thankful to be alive. She recalled the flickering candlelight of the carved evil faces placed on stoops the previous night. "Is it still Samhain?"

"Aye, it ends tonight." Haggadah set the pan with the remaining egg on the table. She gathered two teacups, added the black tea from the tin, and filled the vessels with hot water. "Anna, retrieve a fork for each of us." The old witch placed the drinks on the table, sat in her chair, and waited for her goddaughter to join her. "Thank you." She accepted the fork and politely waited to eat until Anna was seated across from her. Nero and Barret gathered at the base of the witch's chair with their askance eyes cast upon her.

"Then tomorrow will be All Soul's Day." Anna reasoned. "Do you think my family will visit my grave to pray for my soul?"

"It would be interesting to know if they, or anyone else does." Haggadah smiled as a plan developed in her mind. She cut the extra egg in half and scooted each portion to the opposite sides of the pan. Using the crust of her bread, she split it in half, sopped up the spilled egg yolk, and put a piece near each egg half. Nero and Barret stood as the old witch placed the pan on the floor. Haggadah looked at her goddaughter. "We shall see what tomorrow brings."

Chapter 6

"As you can see, Mrs. Stewart, the company has taken a downward turn." Mr. Heywood stood in the study beside Evelyn, who sat in the upholstered chair before the fireplace. He presented the open ledger for her to view. She leaned forward as he pointed to the dwindling balance and the column of expenses. "There have been several capital withdrawals as of lately, and expenses have increased." The accountant looked at Lachlan's face for any display of guilt.

Lachlan peered over his mother's shoulder and scowled at the ledger in her lap. He was responsible for the withdrawals and would have to curtail his love for the game of cards and the consumption of whisky at the pub.

Evelyn turned to the first page of the ledger and saw the accountant's handwriting. She nodded in understanding. "We must tighten the budget and decrease expenditures. Do you agree, Mr. Heywood?" She looked at the gentleman for his reply.

"Aye, I do. Absolutely." Mr. Heywood lifted his chin. "I'll return in a week, as always, to update you on the status of the business." The accountant glared at Lachlan, whose face flushed scarlet.

Lachlan took the ledger from his mother's hands and snapped the book shut. "Mum, Mr. Heywood is quite busy and may not have the time to meet with you once a week." He handed the closed ledger to the accountant. "Isn't that true, Mr. Heywood?"

"Oh, I'm certain Mr. Heywood would keep the weekly meetings short." Evelyn reasoned. "After all, I don't want to impose on his time." She grinned at the accountant.

Mr. Heywood nodded in agreement. "Until next week then. Good day to you both." He tucked the ledger under his arm and left the room. The maid handed him his black overcoat and top hat, a necessity against the brisk autumn wind. He glanced toward the study before leaving the house.

~

Each knock on the wooden door synchronized with Douglas's throbbing head. He looked at the window and squinted his hazel eyes to shield them from the brightness of the overcast day. His eyelids fell shut as the sound ceased. Douglas nearly cursed as the rhythmic wrapping began again. "Enter."

"Good morning, sir. You didn't answer when I knocked a few hours ago. So, I returned your breakfast to the kitchen to keep it warm. Would you like it now, or shall I return it to the kitchen again?" The boardinghouse maid wrinkled her nose as she detected the pungent stench of alcohol, most likely whisky. With the tray of food in her hands, she waited by the open door for his reply.

Douglas grunted as he licked his parched lips. His mouth was as dry as a desert, and the woman's uplifting mood gnawed at his patience.

The chubby maid stood for a moment, perplexed by his lack of communication. "Well, I'll just put it on the table for you. If you need anything else, let me know. My name is Fiona." She left the room, closing the door behind her.

Douglas looked at the ceramic pitcher and forced his legs over the side of the bed. He sat for a minute, blinking his bloodshot eyes, and hoped the room would stop spinning. "Why did I ever allow the crew to convince me to go to the pub. You think I would learn. The outcome is always the same." Rising, he walked the few steps to the chair, sat at the table, and poured a glass of water. He drank the contents without taking a breath and poured himself a second before lifting the cover on the plate to see a typical Scottish breakfast - eggs, bacon, sausage, beans, tomatoes, mushrooms, haggis, and toast.

Still fully dressed from the previous night, he was thankful the men had managed to return him to the boardinghouse. He reached into his pocket and withdrew his watch. It was past midday.

His three ships had pulled into the harbor in the late afternoon yesterday. The trip across the Atlantic Ocean was uneventful and smooth. While in Edinburgh, their cargo would be unloaded and reloaded with merchandise before setting sail for Virginia once again. Douglas assumed he would be in the city for at least a week, perhaps two, but would confirm the schedule with his assistant, Mr. Townsend.

Even though he had little appetite, Douglas stabbed a sausage with his fork and took a bite. His body shook as a shiver went up his spine. Even though he had an aversion to physicians, he wondered if the maid could recommend one to prescribe something for his aching head. With a lot on his day's agenda, the annoying ailment would hinder his judgment and slow him down, something he was unaccustomed to doing. Douglas looked at the empty bed with its covers open, inviting him to return to its warmth.

~

"Do not answer the door while I'm away." Haggadah inserted her arm into the sleeve of her overcoat and glanced at Anna, who nodded in acknowledgment as she dried a freshly washed plate from breakfast. "Whatever they need or want, they can return and ask for it when I get home." The old witch fastened the garment, grabbed her cane, and patted Nero, who lifted his head from the mattress, blinked his eyes, and wondered why he was roused from his slumber. The old witch left the cottage with Barret faithfully by her side.

Haggadah smiled to herself as she walked toward the main street. People parted like the Red Sea, allowing a wide berth for herself and Barret to pass. Sideways glances from the strangers who averted their eyes as they watched the enormous canine, fearing he would attack them with a snap of the witch's fingers. Haggadah was aware of the circulating rumors of her ability to cast a spell to shapeshift Barret into another animal or even a human. She grinned at the thought of possessing such an interesting capability.

She stepped onto the Royal Mile, the main street of Edinburgh Old Town. At one end of the stretch of road was Holyrood, the residence of royalty. At the opposite end was the military fortress, Edinburgh Castle. Haggadah shuddered as a chill came over her body, for Castle Hill is where many of the men and women accused of witchcraft were burned alive.

The old witch ignored the curious stares of those on the street as she walked to Saint Cuthbert and paused outside the open gate. She scanned the kirkyard. It was crowded with people visiting their loved ones.

Haggadah lifted her chin as she bravely stepped onto the hallowed ground with Barret equaling her pace. She walked along the stone wall, keeping her distance from the other visitors, and hoped to remain unnoticed as she headed toward the vacant plot where her goddaughter once laid.

People stared, aghast the haggard witch dared to set foot within the kirkyard. Did they expect her to turn to ash and blow away in the wind?

Haggadah ignored them, reached down, and petted Barret's head while leaning on her cane and resting a moment. She looked at the corner of the kirkyard to see several people huddled around the unmarked grave. They were engaged in whispered gossip and pointed at the hole and abandon shovels.

The old witch approached the curious onlookers. They scurried away like scared rats. Haggadah stared down at the open tomb that once encased Anna. She assumed the abandoned shovels and the pile of dirt remained as the resurrectionists had left them.

Haggadah looked up to see the inquisitive stares of the strangers. Their unanswered questions would become today's gossip that they would spread throughout their pathetic circle of friends. Turning, she looked up at the tower and assumed the guard who worked the graveyard shift was inside sleeping. "Barret, I believe there is someone who may have the answers we seek. Shall we pay Angus a visit?" She walked to the base of the watchtower and opened the door without knocking.

The canine darted into the watchtower. Haggadah turned and sat on a nearby stone bench, placing both hands on her cane as she centered it on the ground before her knees. Within moments, she heard a man shouting in fear, or was he possibly in pain? Barret's toenails clicked on the stone steps as he spiraled downward, encouraging the guard to precede him, or perhaps dragging him by his arm. The man's pleading ceased as the dog emerged through the doorway, released the guard's wrist, and took his place sitting next to the old witch.

"Ah, Angus, it's good of you to join me." Haggadah smiled as she petted her dog. "Please excuse Barret. He was only following my orders. As you can see, my old body is incapable of climbing that many stairs." She motioned with her cane toward the stone tower.

The nightwatchman stood before her in his bare feet and nightshirt. He rubbed his wrist and examined it for puncture wounds.

Haggadah continued. "I see there is a disturbed grave, the one where Anna Stewart was buried. I assume you were on watch last night. Tell me what you saw." She encouraged, tilting her head to one side.

"Nothing, I saw nothing." The man sneered, offended by the crude awakening.

The old witch looked at her dog, all the while watching for the guard's reaction. "Barret." The canine stood. He took a step toward the man, baring his teeth.

The guard's eyes widened, and he held the palms of his hands toward the dog as if trying to push the canine away. "All right. Call your dog off, and I will tell you."

Haggadah snapped her fingers, and the dog sat in place.

The guard sighed. "I was paid to look the other way while two men dug up the body."

The old witch's eyebrows drew together. "Who paid you?"

"A man, who dressed in black and kept the brim of his hat over his face. I don't know who he was. I've learned long ago not to ask questions. The less I know, the better, if you know what I mean."

Haggadah was aware of the punishment for those who were caught body snatching. She agreed with the guard's logic. His ignorance would make it more difficult to implicate him in the crime. She remained silent, causing the guard to squirm.

"I don't know anything else about him." He babbled.

"Your job is to watch all that goes on in the kirkyard during the night. What, in detail, did you see?" She leaned forward on her cane.

"Once the two resurrectionists got the body out of the ground, the woman sneezed and sat upright. When she came back to life, they ran, probably fearing for their lives. They left their lantern and shovels behind."

Haggadah recalled Anna carrying the lantern when she met her in the street. At least that much of his story was true.

"I assume neither of the resurrectionists paid you to look the other way." The old witch thought out loud.

"The man who paid me was nicely dressed, a gentleman. The resurrectionists looked like they all do, wearing dirty, ragged clothes. I assume they are homeless."

"I doubt it was either of the resurrectionists. They usually don't have any money to spare." Haggadah stood. "Do you know how the young lass died?"

"No, nor do I know who may have tried to kill her." He sighed. "Young or old, death doesn't discriminate."

"It's unfortunate and true." The old witch took a deep breath and exhaled. "If you can think of anything else or overhear any gossip, send word."

He nodded once.

"Thank you, Angus." Satisfied with his answers, Haggadah glanced at the mound of dirt in the distance, the only marker of the vacant grave.

She had additional questions that needed answers. Resurrectionists were known to quench their thirst after digging up a corpse. So, even though it was just past midday, the old witch would stop at the local pub and make an inquiry or two.

~

Anna stood with her arms crossed over her chest and scanned the room. She was unaccustomed to doing the work of a maid but proud of what she had managed to accomplish thus far. The dishes were washed, the cauldron refilled with water, the chickens were fed, and Anna added logs to the fire to ensure it remained lit. She scanned the room and noted the countless cobwebs dangling from the beamed ceiling, the dusty rag rug, and the floor that needed a good sweeping. Unfolding her arms, she wondered. "Where would Haggadah keep her broom?"

Anna began by searching every peg on the walls and the corners of the room. She smirked. "Every witch has a broom." Perplexed, she went to Haggadah's bed and flipped up the tattered quilt to peer under it, partially covering Nero's curled body.

The sleepy feline raised his head and watched as Anna disappeared from his site. His ears perked with curiosity as she popped up into view once again as if playing peek-a-boo, uncovered his body, and vanish as she passed through the windowless door. He covered his face beneath his front paw and returned to sleep.

Anna opened the outside door to illuminate the dark room. She scanned the four walls and saw the broom propped in the corner.

Returning inside, Anna lit a candle and climbed the ladder to the loft. She swept and dusted the small room and collected the cobwebs from the ceiling with the bristled end of the broom. Satisfied with a job well done, she blew out the candle, returned below, and cleaned the cobwebs from the corners and ceiling of the room. Anna removed the items on the mantel and brushed away the dust before replacing them, hoping Haggadah would approve if she should mistakenly rearrange them. She moved the table and chairs aside, rolled the rug, and carried it to the back yard.

The clothesline hung loosely between a pair of wooden posts. There were several notched poles to prop the thin rope skyward when burdened with wet clothing. Anna unrolled the rug and flung half of it over the line, causing it to dip to the ground. After propping the clothesline with several poles, she beat the broom against the floorcovering, releasing a cloud of dust in the air. She turned away, coughing, and blinking her eyes to clear them of the scratchy particles. Once the air cleared, she continued to beat the rug until it no longer spewed dust.

Anna swept the entire room thoroughly while allowing the rug to air out on the line. Returning the rag rug, table, and chairs to their proper places, she sat on the bench, quite pleased with her accomplishment. Wondering how long Haggadah would be away, she looked at the apothecary cupboard from the corner of her eye, curious of the treasures that lie within it.

Risking her godmother's trust, Anna went to the front window and peeked under the curtain to see if Haggadah was in sight. Satisfied the pathway and street were vacant, she stood before the large cabinet, reached toward the knob on each door, and paused. A pang of guilt pierced her heart. She was breaching the privacy of her godmother, but then the justification dawned on her. "Have I not been encouraged to learn about healing?" She opened the apothecary doors. Her mouth fell agape as she scanned the contents and realized the immense knowledge Haggadah possessed.

Eager to familiarize herself with each herb and spice, Anna began reading the labels. She knew some of the medicinal properties, while others were foreign, and she wondered how Haggadah had come by them. On the top shelf to the right, she noticed several labels with skulls and crossbones drawn on them. "Nightshade, arsenic, hemlock, foxglove...they must be deadly." She peeked in several drawers to discover crystals, stones, small bottles, and short bundles of herbs tied with string for smudging. One drawer held a fan made of feathers.

The scratching of Barret's toenails on the front door announced Haggadah's return. Anna shut the cabinet's double doors and peeked out the window to see her godmother closing the gate. She lifted the latch for the eager canine and chuckled as Barret bound into the house with his tail wagging.

The old witch, carrying a small wheel of cheese in the crook of her arm, handed it to her goddaughter as she passed over the threshold. "I stopped at the market on the way home. Put this in the cellar, please."

Anna reluctantly went to the back door. "You've been gone for a while," she stated before entering the tiny room. Lifting the trapdoor, Anna descended the stairs into the darkness of the cool chamber, placed the cheese on an empty shelf, and raced up the stairs.

Haggadah took off her overcoat and hung it on a peg. She petted Nero on the head before sitting next to the warm fire and looked at Anna as she entered the room. "I visited your grave."

"And?" Anna leaned forward on the bench.

"It has remained untouched since the night the resurrectionists dug you up." Haggadah began as Barret curled at her feet. "There were people gathered around your grave in whispered conversations. Many wondered if your body was snatched or if you had cast a spell on the shovels to free you from your underground prison." The old witched grinned at the farfetched idea. "As I assumed, they would. The watchman, who was on duty during the graveyard shift, said he was paid by a man to ignore the resurrectionists. He assumed the two men were planning to sell your body to the college for dissection."

"Aye, I caught a glimpse of them before they ran out of the kirkyard." Anna reiterated. "And they drove a flatbed wagon at a wicked speed as they left."

Haggadah laughed. "You must have given them a good scare, coming back to life as you did." She shook her head, composing herself. "The guard didn't know how you died nor of anyone rumored to be guilty of your attempted murder. I also visited a pub but did not overhear any conversations where digging up your body was discussed."

A knock sounded on the door. Both women looked at the portal as Barret stood.

Haggadah sighed. "Did anyone visit during my absence?"

"No."

"Then, they may have followed me home." The old witch rose from the stool. "Hide yourself beside the apothecary." She tapped her cane on the floor as she walked to the door and opened it.

Concealed on the side of the cabinet, Anna listened to the visitor's summary of ailments. Haggadah told the person to wait while she concocted a remedy, closed the door, and peeked around the edge of the cabinet. "Come, learn. This man says his wife suffers from unintentionally hurting herself, sleeplessness, and is expecting a child."

Anna crept out from hiding and watched as Haggadah opened the apothecary doors.

The old witch pulled on two adjacent knobs to reveal a desktop. She took a mortar and pestle from its proper place, placed it on the working area and grabbed several jars, opened them, and added bits of their contents to the mortar. "Raspberry leaf to encourage the delivery of her child, lavender to help her sleep, and mugwort and feverfew for protection." With a fluid motion of the pestle, she turned the dry herbs into a fine powder. Opening a drawer, Haggadah withdrew a small bottle and uncorked it. In another drawer, she took out a funnel and dumped the finely ground herbs inside the vessel. Lifting a glass bottle from a large drawer, she added a generous portion of spirits.

Anna's eyebrows raised. "You're prescribing alcohol?"

"Aye," the old witch confirmed as she returned the spirits to the drawer and corked the remedy. "The alcohol pulls the nutrients from the herbs, thus forming a tincture. Stay out of sight now." Haggadah tilted the bottle back and forth several times to mix the remedy.

Anna hid around the side of the cabinet as Haggadah opened the door, gave the man the tincture, and accepted his payment. When she heard the door close, Anna peeked around the edge of the apothecary to see Haggadah staring at her with a wheel of cheese in her arm.

"I hope you like cheese." Haggadah grinned.

Chapter 7

"She's what!"

Martin cringed as he scanned the crowded pub. Even though the trio sat in a darkened corner, it did not protect them from the inquisitive stares and sideways glances. The resurrectionist leaned forward in his chair, nearly to the center of the table, and whispered. "It's not our fault she's alive." He sat back and stared at the brim of the black hat, which hid the man's face.

John clasped the glass before him. "We did as you asked and dug her up. No one can accuse us of killing her, especially now that she is walking the earth once again." He drank his dram of whisky in one gulp, set the glass on the table, and leaned toward Martin. "I told you she was a witch."

With his rigid back facing curious onlookers, the man stared down into his empty glass. "But she was pronounced dead."

John nodded. "Exactly. All I know is Martin and I worked hard to get her body out of the ground, and we got nothing to show for it. No pay from the Doc, and no pay from you."

The man rose, reached into his pocket, and flipped a coin toward each resurrectionist. "I'll pay for your drinks. That's payment enough." He turned to walk away, then stopped and looked back at the pair. "Knox is expecting a body. Find one, and soon." He walked to a wooden door at the rear of the pub and knocked. A small panel slid to the side, and a pair of eyes peeked out before it snapped shut. The protected portal creaked open, allowing the man to enter, and closed quickly to ensure the privacy of those behind it.

~

With the pleasant autumn weather continuing into the afternoon, Haggadah insisted her goddaughter join her in the garden to harvest herbs. Anna carried a basket containing a pair of snipping shears as she followed the old witch down the pathway with Nero and Barret trailing behind. The old witch explained the healing properties of sweet wormwood and how to harvest it.

Barret found a nice sunny place to lay and observe. Nero wove between the stems of plants, pausing often and staring at the ground, listening intently.

Anna dropped a cutting into the basket, took a step, and winced as she reached up to untangle her hair from a low branch of the apple tree.

The old witch watched Anna struggle to free herself. It was obvious from her goddaughter's reaction that her head was still tender from the blow. She dropped a cutting in the basket. "Whoever tried to kill you must have hit you hard enough to put you into a deep sleep, yet not enough to kill you. A miscalculation on their part."

Once free, Anna gently rubbed the tender spot on her head. "Thankfully." She snipped another sprig and laid it in the basket with the others.

Haggadah pulled a wayward weed and dropped it in the pathway to wither and die in the warm autumn sun. She looked at the gathered herbs. "I think we have enough to make several nice bundles." The old witch whistled. "Barret, inside. Nero?" She scanned the garden, but the feline was nowhere in sight. "He must be hunting."

Barret's ears perked. He scampered to the back door with his tail wagging, turned, and waited for Haggadah to open the door and let him pass.

Anna picked up the basket, followed them into the small room, and hung the pruning shears on the hook where she had found them.

Haggadah grabbed a small basket from the shelf. It contained various lengths of binding from wrapped packages she received for her remedies. Passing through the windowless door, she leaned her cane against the edge of the table and sat in a chair. Anna sat opposite her, placing the basket of cuttings between them.

The women gathered small amounts of sweet wormwood, put the cut ends together, and wrapped them with a piece of repurposed cording. Once tied securely, Anna hung each bundle from a nail on a beam in the ceiling. She stood on the chair and inhaled the aroma of the green herb, finding it as pleasant as many colorful flowers.

As the last bundle was placed on a nail, Haggadah sighed. "I noticed the feverfew jar was nearly empty while making the last tincture. While you're on the chair, can you bring down the bundle?" She pointed her crooked index finger toward an herb to Anna's right. The old witch rose from her chair. With her cane in hand, she went to the apothecary, opened the double doors, and removed the herb's jar. She pulled out the make-shift desktop, set the container on it, and lifted the glass lid. Anna handed the witch the dried herb and watched as she crumbled it into the jar.

"What do you know about this herb, Anna?" Haggadah quizzed as she continued to fill the jar.

Anna thought of the many times her mother used the herb for her family's ailments. "Headaches, to ease muscle pain and the swelling of joints. I recall my mother adding it to my father's bath."

"Yes, those are some of its uses, but it also may be used to help prevent accidents, break curses, and worn as a amulet around one's neck or carried in a pocket. We as healers must consider remedies for the mind and soul as well as the body." Haggadah unbound the remaining stems of the bundle, set the twine to one side, and crumbled the herb into the glass bottle. She replaced the top and returned it to its rightful spot in the cabinet. "I need you to close your eyes."

Anna scowled before doing as her godmother asked.

Haggadah took a jar from the cabinet, removed the lid, and held it below her goddaughter's nose. "Inhale and tell me what you smell?"

Anna inhaled. "Mmmm. . ." She inhaled again to ensure she was correct. "I believe I smell mint."

"Peppermint, to be exact. Inhale its fragrance once again and then open your eyes." Haggadah waited as Anna did so. "Now tell me its properties to heal the body, mind, and soul."

Anna was familiar with mint. She often added the herb to a pitcher of water for a cool refreshing drink on a warm summer day. It often settled her upset stomach and relieved her headache. "It settles a sour stomach, relieves a headache." She chuckled as she recalled her mother making her father eat the leaves to freshen his breath. "Freshens bad breath and relieves the cramping of a woman's courses." She paused in thought, realizing she did not know how the herb healed the mind and soul.

"Very good. It's also good for renewing energy, improving sleep, and it helps to heal an inflamed wound." She set the lid on top and returned it to its proper place. "For the mind and soul, peppermint can purify the soul and bring a feeling of good luck and prosperity." She smiled. "It gives one hope."

Haggadah spent the next hour quizzing her goddaughter on various herbs.

Anna sighed. "I don't know how you can remember everything about so many plants." Anna watched as the old witch replaced the lid on a jar.

"It comes with practice and a good memory." She returned the herb to its proper place as a knock sounded upon the door.

~

Dr. Knox paused with the scalpel in his hand as he caught sight of a shadowed figure peering around the edge of the anatomy theater doorway. He looked up at his medical students sitting in the rows of tiered seats. They were attentive, staring down at him, anticipating his next cut on the cadaver. He placed the scalpel on the table, rose from his stool, and watched as his visitor disappeared behind the frame of the door.

He looked up at his students. "Excuse me. I'll be just a moment." Knox stepped into the hallway and stared at the beaver top hat shadowing the man's face. "Your delivery did not arrive last night."

"I did as you instructed. I used the back of a shovel to lay a blow to her head. She collapsed, was pronounced dead, and buried within a day. The resurrectionists said she came back to life once they took her out of the grave." He paused. "It's true then. She's a cursed witch."

Being a man of science, Knox assumed the blow to her head was too gentle. His warning to not crush her skull had saved the woman's life.

The demand for cadavers had increased as students continued to enroll in the college's renowned medical program. His usual supply of criminals hung for their crime had come to an end. The punishment was now deemed inhumane and discontinued except by a magistrate's ruling for the most heinous of crimes. Knox needed at least 90 bodies a year. He was desperate, currently down to his last cadaver. Resurrectionists knew he would pay a higher price for the young and freshly dead, less for the old and decomposing. The doctor looked down at the floor, shook his head, and placed his fisted hands on his hips.

Knox looked up as his visitor turned to leave. "Do you know where she is now?" He waited as the man turned back toward him, peering from beneath the brim of his hat. Unable to keep his students waiting any longer, the doctor signaled for the gentleman to follow him into the theater. He glanced at his students as he went to the table, picked up the scalpel, and circled to the opposite side of the cadaver. He looked at the man, who hesitantly approached the table. Knox continued to dissect the body.

The man kept his voice at a whisper. "No, like a ghost, she disappeared into the night." He stared at the dead man on the table, whose eyes were open, staring heavenward.

"Too bad," Knox said as he lifted the heart from the body. Blood trickled down the doctor's arm as he turned it in his hand to observe its intricacies and placed it in a glass bowl, "she would have been a prime one to dissect, free of age and disease."

The man stared at the heart swimming in a small pool of blood. He covered his mouth with the palm of his hand to camouflage his gag reflex, and quickly left the room.

Chapter 8

Douglas lay still, unwilling to move his aching body. He continued to shiver even though he was fully dressed and covered with multiple blankets.

"I'm never going to drink whisky again." It was a promise he knew he would break, especially when the ship's crew pressured him to join them at a local pub after a successful trip.

He had experienced a hangover before, but this was something more. His eyes hurt when he rotated them in the direction of the window to estimate the time of day. Mid-afternoon, maybe later? A knock sounded upon the door.

"What?" He was in no mood for company.

Fiona entered his room and presented a folded note. "A man stopped by and left this message. He expressed it as 'utterly important' so, I thought you may need to read it right away."

Douglas sat up in bed, reached for the note, and read it. It was signed by Mr. Townsend.

The maid noted Douglas's pale face. "Sir, if you don't mind me saying, you don't look very well. Do you need me to get a physician?"

He crumbled the note that was nothing more than an update from the harbor. An unexpected delay would keep his ships in port longer than he planned. He looked at the maid. "No. I have an aversion to physicians. Seems as if they think bloodletting is the solution for every ailment. I don't see where weakening the body can help it to heal." He recalled watching helplessly as a few of his crew succumbed to the wicked remedy and vowed he would never agree to the treatment.

Fiona went on to explain another option. "We have an excellent healer in the city. Many say she is a witch, but none complain of her successful remedies. I can give you the directions to her house, and when you are up to it, you can walk there. It isn't far." The woman took a pen, ink, and paper from the drawer of the table. "I don't read or write, so would you like to write them down?"

"When the time comes, I'll ask for the directions."

"Oh, silly me. Just ask the coachman. Everyone knows where Haggadah Blyth lives."

"Haggadah?"

"Aye, she is old and wise, renowned for her natural healing." Fiona returned the writing items to their proper place.

"What does she charge for her services?"

"She demands no specific fee, but you may pay her whatever you feel is appropriate for her remedy. I heard she receives a lot of chickens." Fiona smiled and went to the door. "Is there anything else you need, sir?"

"No, thank you." Douglas watched as the maid nodded and closed the door behind her as she left.

~

Anna wiped the crumbled leaves and wayward seeds of the sweet wormwood from the table with a damp cloth, picked up both baskets, and returned them to the shelf before shaking out the rag in the garden. She wondered if any of the seeds, tiny and resembling dust, would germinate.

Nero rose from where he had been sleeping and came toward her in a slight trot. "Well, sleepyhead, are you ready to resume your nap on Haggadah's bed?" She reached down to stroke the cat's silky fur, and noticed it speckled with dirt and dried leaves. "Did you roll on the ground?" Anna did her best to removed as much of the dirt from Nero's fur before allowing him to enter the cottage.

Returning inside with Nero leading the way, she placed the rag on the edge of the washtub and glanced down at her dress to see bits of the herb clinging to it. Anna returned outside, brushed her skirt with the palms of her hands, and tried to remove the dirt. She sighed.

The garment had been tossed onto the kirkyard ground, twisted while she slept through the night, and soiled as she worked in the garden. It was a sorry sight to behold. Anna dropped her hands to her sides, surrendered any further attempt to improve its appearance, and returned inside. "It's a good thing Mum can't see the condition I'm in. I would receive a proper reprimand, indeed." She lifted the skirt of her dress for her godmother to see.

Haggadah, busily inspecting the supply of each herb in the apothecary, looked over her shoulder at her dejected goddaughter. "I'll go to your house and request a donation of your clothes for the poor. For now, search the trunk in the loft for something to wear. Wash your garments in the washtub with the bar of soap, it's in the dish beside it. Wash yourself too." She closed the cabinet doors. "I better hurry, ye ken, so I can return by supper. Is there anything you need while I'm out?"

Anna looked down at her hands as she wrung them together. "I'm quite worried about Mum. Since Dad's death, she has not been the same. I fear my absence may compound her distress."

"If I'm allowed to talk to her, I'll offer my help. In truth, no remedy can ever heal the pain from the loss of a loved one. Grieving takes time."

The old witch put on her overcoat and pulled an old carpetbag out from beneath her bed. With her cane in hand and Barret by her side, she left the house.

Anna picked up a lit candle from the mantel and climbed the ladder to the loft. She knelt before the chest, lifted the unlocked lid, and sat back on her heels as a dried raven's foot appeared to be reaching for her. She gasped, placing her free hand on her chest to catch her breath. "Goodness." Peering into the chest, she lifted the dried foot by a talon, rotated it, and then returned it to its spot.

Anna saw a group of feathers bound together with a thin strand of black leather with various crystals dangling from the binding. She lifted it from the drawer and admired the colors dancing in the candlelight. "What is this used for? A gala ball?" Returning it, she saw a transparent glass sphere balancing on three branch nubs of a piece of driftwood. "A crystal ball? Oooo, can it tell the future?" Anna wiggled her fingers in the air as if casting a spell and smiled.

Examining the tray's contents further, she saw a small bundle of dried herbs and several candles of various colors tied with a ribbon. Empty tiny glass bottles clattered together as she searched the divided compartment. A single piece of willow lay against one side of the box. "No clothes here."

Placing the candle on the floor, Anna took the tray out of the chest and set it beside her. Peering inside, she saw an article of clothing. "Ah, much better." She removed the first item, let it unfold, and held the dress against her body, pulling it to her waist. "Seems to be my size. A nice shade of green too." There were three other dresses and hosiery too.

Anna lifted a statue of three women standing together beneath a tree. The first woman was young, the second woman was heavy with child, and the third woman was an old crone. "Interesting." She set it aside before reaching in to discover a lovely tartan folded neatly near the bottom. It was made of soft wool and woven in a plaid of light blue, pale green, and black, with pinstripes of red and yellow. "Haggadah's clan?" The last item in the chest was a lovely black hooded wool cloak. Its clasp at the neck was in the shape of a triskelion. She traced her finger over the three interlocking Archimedean spirals before setting it aside with the clothing.

Lifting the candle, she verified the chest was empty and spied a hole in the bottom left corner. "Probably a mouse." She looked at the exterior of the chest to see if the candlelight projected through the hole, but it did not. Curious, she tapped the bottom of the chest with her finger. "Sounds hollow." Poking her finger into the hole, she lifted upward, removing the faux bottom to reveal a hidden compartment.

Setting the wooden bottom aside, she looked in the chest and saw coins reflecting in the candlelight, too numerous to count. Anna touched the pointed tip of a large quartz crystal, which appeared transparent as glass. There was a book with an intricate brass clasp in the same design as the one on the cloak. Placing the candle on the floor, she reached into the chest and took out the book. Its leatherbound cover was exquisite, and the clasp seemed to glow in the candlelight. Whispered voices emanated from the corners of the loft. Anna glanced about, only to find shadowed darkness. Looking back at the book, she opened the cover, and a gust of air blew the strands of her loose hair away from her face. She inhaled an unfamiliar fragrance. Sandalwood? No, sage? Or did it smell like lilac? Perhaps it was all three. She inhaled the lovely scent again.

Anna tilted the book toward the candlelight and read the name beautifully scripted on the inside cover. "Margaret Aitken." Several other names were listed below it, all women. Again, the women were unfamiliar to her except for the last one – Haggadah Blyth. She turned the yellowed page, not entirely sure if it was aged paper or parchment. The entries were handwritten and contained the fazes of the moon, pagan holidays and rituals, illustrations and properties of herbs and spices, remedies for ailments, diagrams of runes, spells, amulet patterns, and curses. Anna compared the signatures to many of the entries. She realized each page was created by the women listed on the inside cover. The illustrations were picturesque with watercolor enhancements. Some of it was in Latin. There were blank pages at the end of the book, she assumed, for additional entries.

"A journal, handed down from one woman to another?" Uncertain when Haggadah would return from her errand, Anna set the book on her cot, hoping to read more of it when she retired for the evening. She needed to get her clothes washed and take a sponge bath as well. Biting her bottom lip, Anna stared at the book, hoping her discovery was not an invasion of Haggadah's privacy. Returning the false bottom and other items to the chest, she gathered the clothing and cloak, blew out the candle, and descended the ladder with the extinguished candle in hand. She set the clothing on the table, chose the green dress, and shook it free of dust before putting it on. Anna hung the cloak on a peg near the door and stoked the fire to heat the water for her laundry.

~

Haggadah climbed the three steps to the house, lifted the knocker on the door, and let it fall twice. Barret sat obediently at the base of the stairs and waited.

Helen answered the door but stood several steps away from the threshold. "May I help you?"

The old witch remembered the maid from years past. Now, in her forties, the loyal servant had managed to retain her employment. How she tolerated Evelyn's endless demands was a credit to her character. "Is Mrs. Stewart in?"

"Aye. A moment please."

The door closed, leaving Haggadah to stand upon the stoop. She turned to her escort. "Not very hospitable, is she, Barret. She could have at least escorted me inside to sit and wait."

The canine's ears perked as he tilted his head to the side and looked at her.

Haggadah saw a curtain in a window across the street move aside and a woman staring at her. A passerby looked at her as he walked into the street to avoid Barret.

The door of the Stewart house opened.

"Haggadah. I'm surprised to see you." Evelyn closed the door partially, shielding herself from the witch.

The old witch turned to look at the woman's red and swollen eyes. The tip of Evelyn's nose was equally as rosy.

"I'm certain word has reached you of Anna's death." Evelyn began. "I do apologize for not personally sending you the news."

"Aye, well, no apology necessary. I'm sorry for your loss."

"Thank you."

Haggadah was growing weary of the polite small talk. "I'm here on another matter. I'm collecting clothing for the poor. I thought you may like to donate some of Anna's clothes. I would appreciate anything you wish to give, and so would the children." Haggadah lifted the carpetbag toward the doorway.

Hesitant to accept the dusty old bag, Evelyn outstretched her hand to clasp the handle and quickly passed it to the maid standing behind her. "Aye, indeed. Let me gather what I can. I'll return shortly." She shut the door, leaving the old witch to stand and wait once again.

"At least it isn't raining," Haggadah muttered to herself. She looked down at her dog. "Evelyn could have offered us tea and a biscuit or two." The old witch sighed. "No matter." Haggadah inhaled the morning air and looked up and down the residential street. The people living on the road were well-to-do in society.

She recalled Oliver, a handsome and astute businessman, the owner of a thriving mercantile shipping business that ensured his family's placement high in society. Foreseeing his imminent fate, Haggadah appeared in his office and convinced Oliver to join her and Barret for a stroll along the waterfront. It was then that she highly recommended he name not only Evelyn and Lachlan as beneficiaries of the company but Anna too. He thought it was unusual for a daughter to be included but listened to the old witch as she explained that Anna may never marry because of her curse. If included in the will as an equal owner, it would ensure she would live comfortably as a spinster.

Even though Haggadah was saddened by his passing, she was pleased to hear he had taken her advice. Unfortunately, Evelyn and Lachlan were not as delighted.

Haggadah watched a woman and her child cross the street to the opposite side to avoid her.

The door opened. Evelyn placed the overstuffed carpetbag at Haggadah's feet. "I was able to fit what I could in the bag."

Haggadah knew the maid had performed the task under the watchful eye of Evelyn. She nodded and smiled in appreciation. "Thank you. If you need anything, especially something to help you sleep, do not hesitate to send word to me. Again, my condolence."

Evelyn glanced over her shoulder, knowing the maid was behind her. She wished to speak more but knew anything she said would be repeated to the cook. "Thank you, Haggadah." She shut the door without another word.

The old witch reached down and stuffed a wayward sleeve into the bag before lifting it from the stoop and placing it on the crook of her arm. It was heavier than she expected. She turned to descend the steps. "Between you and me, Barret, we are going to have to get Anna's clothes back to the house." She joined her dog, placed the bag on Barret's back, and they began to walk home.

~

Anna hung the last washed garment on the clothesline to dry. She dumped the washtub of dirty water into the garden, refilled the cauldron with water, and sat

92

on the stool stoking the fire as the front door opened, and Haggadah stepped in.

The witch released the handle of the carpetbag and allowed it to fall off Barret's back onto the floor. She patted her dog on the head in appreciation for his help. In his usual place on Haggadah's bed, Nero lifted his head to see who had disturbed his never-ending nap. Once he was assured all was well, the feline lowered his head to his paw and returned to sleep.

Anna stopped finger-combing her freshly washed hair and stared at the overstuffed carpetbag. She assumed every item of her wardrobe was inside. Was it so easy for her mother to rid herself of any remembrance of her only surviving daughter's existence?

Haggadah inhaled deeply and looked at Anna. "Ah, you discovered the Book of Shadows. I had forgotten where I placed it."

Anna inhaled the delightful fragrance. There was no point in telling a falsehood. "Aye, it was under the false bottom in the chest. I hope you aren't mad. I didn't mean to pry."

"Pry? No, my dear, you are next in line to receive it. It has been waiting for you for a long time."

Questions swirled in Anna's mind. Book of Shadows? Who was Margaret Aitken and the other women? Why was she next in line to get the book?

Haggadah waited patiently as her goddaughter stood dumbfounded. She sighed. "You might as well come out with it, Anna. There is much for you to learn, and the book is a good place to start. Go and retrieve it, and we can begin now. There should be a bundle of candles of various colors too. Bring them with you as well." The old witch went to the apothecary and retrieved her handmade fan of feathers with several crystals tied with a leather strap at its base, an abalone shell, and a small bundle of dried white sage.

Eager to explore the book, Anna looked at the carpetbag, pleased the chore of unpacking it could wait. She raced up the ladder, retrieved the mysterious book from where she had placed it on her cot, the candles from the chest, and returned to see Haggadah lighting a sage smudging stick. Once it was lit, the old witch blew out the flame, held the shell beneath the sage to catch the ash, and used the feathers to fan the smoke in every corner of the room before seating herself at the table. She placed the smudging stick within the shell and feather fan on the table.

"Before we begin, I think tea is in order. After all, there is much to learn within the pages of this old book."

Anna set the items from the chest on the table before she made tea and retrieved the tin of biscuits from the cupboard.

Haggadah ran her aged hand over the cover of the book, cherishing the detailed journal. She looked at the open tin of biscuits set before her and watched as her goddaughter gently placed the filled teacups on the table.

Once seated across from the old witch, Anna settled in for a lengthy explanation and was determined to keep an open mind, no matter how strange the education became.

"Before beginning, we must light a candle," Haggadah explained. "Each one has a purpose based on its color." She pulled the yellow candle from the bundle. "This one is used for intelligence, focus, memory, and a few other qualities."

Anna sat back in her chair and looked at the remaining candles in the bundle. "My goodness. How am I supposed to remember the purpose for each one?"

"With practice." The old witch winked her eye. "If I recall correctly, the book contains a page explaining each candle, so you have a reference to turn to when you forget." She smiled. "We must light this one before we begin." She held up the yellow candle.

Anna retrieved a lit candle from the mantel and placed it on the table. She watched as Haggadah lit the yellow candle from its flame before blowing it out, removing the taper from the candlestick, and inserted the lit candle in its place.

"Open the cover." Haggadah dunked a biscuit into the cup of steaming tea.

Anna cautiously did as she was told. The aromatic sweet fragrance was released into the air, accompanied by a gentle breeze. The flame of the yellow candle flickered but remained lit. "Does that happen every time the book is opened?" She looked at the old witch.

"Only for those who the book is intended." Haggadah bit the soggy bisque before sipping her tea. "As you can see from the signatures inside the cover, this book has belonged to many women, including me. So, the first thing you must do is add your name to the bottom of the list. There is a pen and a bottle of ink in one of the apothecary drawers. It's labeled."

A knock sounded on the door, interrupting the lecture. Anna and Haggadah looked toward it, knowing the person on the other side needed help. Barret rose from where he was sleeping near the fireplace, went to the door, and barked to announce the guest's arrival.

"Take the book with you and hide on the side of the apothecary while I answer the door." Haggadah stood and pointed her gnarled index finger toward her goddaughter. "Always remember, the Book of Shadows is for your eyes only."

Chapter 9

Evelyn looked up from the book she was attempting to read as she heard the front door shut. She had chosen her favorite book from the library, hoping to distract her thoughts, but after trying to read the same paragraph for the third time, she was thankful for the interruption. "Lachlan, I'm glad you're home from the office, dear. I've been holding dinner for you. I thought we could eat together tonight."

Lachlan took off his beaver top hat and overcoat and handed them to Helen. He looked heavenward and sighed, keeping his patience in check. His mother smiled at him as he entered the study. He leaned toward her and placed a kiss on the top of her head.

Evelyn put a ribbon in the book to save her place and closed it with a snap. "How was your meeting with Mr. Heywood?" She detested the smell of the ocean and insisted he go alone to review the ledger and inspect the merchandise imported on their ships. She was fully aware of her son's dislike for the sea, the office on the harbor, and managing the family business.

"You know . . . business." His reply failed to hide his disdain for the responsibility. He looked at his mother's swollen eyes and rosy nose. "You've been crying again." He would instruct Helen to have the family physician prescribed laudanum to ensure she rested peacefully for the night and ask for a nurse to be posted by her bedside.

She ignored her son's comment with a dismissive wave of her hand. "The strangest thing happened today. Haggadah came to call."

Lachlan scowled. "The old witch? What did she want?" He went to a side table, lifted the decanter of his favorite beverage, and removed the crystal stopper.

"She was aware of Anna's passing," Evelyn paused to keep her emotions in check, "and said she was collecting clothes for the poor."

He poured himself a generous glass of whisky.

"Lachlan, it's too early to have a drink. After dinner, dear." Evelyn reprimanded before continuing. "I donated most of your sister's clothing to the charity." His mother confessed. "I could not part with one of her dresses though, to remember her by."

"Now, Mum, you know she was a cursed child. So, it may have been better to give it away as well."

"Even though she was cursed from birth, she was my daughter, nevertheless."

Lachlan tipped his glass toward the ceiling as he drank the amber liquid, draining it dry, and poured a refill. "At least I don't have to look at her god-awful red hair anymore. You would think she was the daughter of the devil himself." A sentiment he had expressed multiple times before. He set the decanter on the table, crossed himself in a crucifix pattern, and emptied his glass a second time.

"You shouldn't speak that way about your sister. It's most unkind. You know perfectly well who her father was." Evelyn's eyes welled with tears.

Lachlan glanced at his mother as he placed his empty glass next to the decanter. He clenched his teeth as his patience reached its end and walked out of the room. "I'm not hungry."

Evelyn glared at her retreating son as he disappeared through the doorway.

He instructed Helen as she handed him his hat and coat to go straight to the physician and purchase a bottle of laudanum. He hoped to keep his mother sedated until her grieving ceased.

As the front door slam shut, a tear trickled down Evelyn's cheek. Just as the wound of her grief was closing a smidgeon, Lachlan had ripped it open once again.

~

Anna held the Book of Shadows close to her chest and watched Haggadah concoct a remedy for the woman's ailments. The old witch waved her hand, urging her goddaughter to hide beside the apothecary once again. Haggadah opened the door, gave verbal instructions, and sent the needy visitor on her way.

The old witch retrieved the pen and ink from a drawer in the apothecary. "My dear, it is time to make the Book of Shadows officially yours." She grinned at Anna as they returned to the table and sat.

Anna reverently placed the aged book on the table and opened the cover. Dipping the pen in the inkwell, she added her name to the bottom of the list and looked at the old woman, who nodded approvingly. "How old is this book?" She set the quill down on the table and blew on the wet ink to dry it.

"Hundreds of years old."

"Who is, or was Margaret Aitken?"

"She was known as one of the greatest witches in Scotland and, as you can see, this book was originally hers. Those who are listed beneath her name have passed down the legacy and legend of her life." Haggadah pointed her gnarled finger at the first name on the list. "She began the book as a journal of sorts, adding information when she thought it was important or perhaps so she wouldn't forget it. This book is her way of passing her knowledge onto those who follow in her footsteps."

"So, she was a witch?"

Haggadah sighed. "Fear is a weapon used to control, manipulate, and conform a society. Many years ago, a woman was blamed for casting a spell to create a storm at sea and preventing King James's wife from Holland from joining him. He hired 'witch prickers' to track down the woman. Others have hired them as well. Their means of obtaining a confession was underhanded, and women who were subjected to their cruelty suffered greatly. Those convicted were burned alive on the castle's esplanade."

"Margaret and the others weren't really witches," Anna concluded.

"No, not in a sorcery way. They were convicted and killed for silly reasons; being old or odd-looking, pregnant with the laird's illegitimate child, or simply being blessed as a gifted healer."

"That's terrible." Not wanting to hear any more of the gruesome tale, Anna turned the page.

"Ah, the moon." Haggadah pointed to the illustration of the waxing, full, and waning moon as she explained the cycle. Her gnarled finger reverently touched each face in the watercolor illustration of the triple goddess.

Anna recalled seeing the women's faces. "Oh, this statue is in the chest."

"Aye, I forgot it was in there. It was passed down to me when I received the Book of Shadows."

"Did it belong to Margaret?"

"I'm not certain of its age. It could have belonged to her or any of the other women. Go and get the triple goddess. We will honor her by placing the statue on the mantel." Haggadah read the script on the page to verify she had explained the moon cycle fully.

Anna quickly retrieved the statue, pushed aside a few candlesticks, and placed the three goddesses on the mantel. She took a step backward to ensure it was centered. "It's lovely."

Haggadah looked at the statue as Anna returned to the table and sat in her chair. "Aye." The old witch sighed.

"It's a nice representation of the phases of the moon; waxing is the maiden, full is the mother heavy with child, and waning is the crone." Anna admired each of the women's kind faces.

"Many believe in the moon's mystical power. They restore their crystals' energy under its light when it is full, cast spells, and celebrate life's blessings. Some even make moon water."

"Crystal energy? Moon water?" Anna rested her elbows on the table and rested her head on the fingertips of both hands, overwhelmed by the unknown she had yet to understand and learn.

"With the enormous amount of knowledge these women possessed, can you see why they were feared?" Haggadah turned the page. Together they read about the sabbaths, traditions, offerings, spells, crystal grids, altars, and rituals.

"I believe some of the items for making altars and other rituals are in the chest," Haggadah recalled. "It has been so long since I have gone through it. What else did you find inside?"

Anna tried to recall the items in the chest. "Other than clothes, a crow's shriveled foot, bound feathers, a crystal ball, empty bottles, a large crystal, and a lot of coins. Oh, there is a lovely tartan too. Did it belong to any of the women who owned this book?"

Haggadah gazed at a spot on the wall, seeing it yet not seeing it. Pensive, she searched her mind for the answer before smiling as if someone had whispered a reply in her ear. She looked at her goddaughter. "I believe it belongs to you and someone in your future."

Anna's eyebrows raised. "My future? How is that possible?"

"Possible? My dear, it's highly probable, ye ken." The old witch reached across the table and patted Anna's hand. "Just believe and listen to your heart."

Anna sighed, perplexed by Haggadah's reply. She turned the page and began to read the text for additional words of wisdom from those who were resting peacefully within the unseen world.

The old witch sensed the spirits of the former owners of the book. They approved of Anna and looked forward to guiding her in their teachings. She smiled as she stared at her goddaughter before looking at the page Anna was studying. "I think stew sounds like a good meal for tonight." She rose as Anna began to close the book. "Keep reading, dear. I'll make dinner."

~

John and Martin sat in the corner of the crowded pub.

Martin enviously watched the gentry donned with their beaver top hats and expensive overcoats go to the door and knock upon it. The small panel would open, and a pair of eyes appear and disappear before the portal allowed them entry. He recognized Mr. Stewart and several others as they went to the doorway. Martin assumed the room contained a gambling table with high stakes, nothing he could afford. He was content to sip the ale in his mug and sit near the warmth of the fireplace.

John leaned over the small table for two. "I heard of an old man who died a few days ago. He may be bloated and blue but should get us the minimum from Knox."

"Maybe Angus knows of another, ye ken. We can ask him before we dig up the old guy." Martin finished his ale and wiped his mouth on his sleeve.

John rubbed his aching right shoulder, an old injury. "I think it'll rain tonight."

Chapter 10

Sensing the change in the weather, Haggadah looked across the table at Anna. "Rain is on its way." She ate the last spoonful of stew from her bowl and sopped any remaining juice with her slice of buttered bread.

Anna looked at the witch with a spoonful of stew paused before her mouth. "Oh, my laundry is still on the line. We were so busy going through the Book of Shadows that I completely forgot about it."

"Finish eating. I'll tidy up while you retrieve your clothes." Haggadah popped the last bite of bread in her mouth before rising from the table.

Quickly scraping her spoon along the bottom of her bowl to eat the last bite of stew, Anna stuffed the remaining bite of bread into her mouth before carrying her dish to the washtub and hurrying to the backyard. She gathered the garments in her arms as lightning flashed across the night sky. A resounding thunder followed.

Stepping inside the warmth of the cottage, she saw Barret's tail tucked beneath his hindquarters as he lay under Haggadah's bed. "Why is Barret under your bed?" She turned to see Haggadah place a clean bowl in the cupboard.

The old witch looked toward her bed and smiled. "You would think a large dog like him wouldn't be afraid of storms, but he is."

Anna chuckled. She laid her dried clothing over the back of a chair and hung any damp garments on a peg to finish drying. Assuming her wardrobe would be stored in the chest, she folded them carefully to keep the wrinkles to a minimum.

The pattering of rain sounded on the rooftop. Anna looked at the beams above her head, uncertain of the roof's age or condition, but hoped it would not leak. A flash of lightning illuminated the room. She squinted her eyes shut, shielding them from the brightness.

Dragging the carpetbag to the table, Anna withdrew the garments. She was pleased to find several of her dresses, undergarments, stockings, and several shoes.

Nero went to the front door, scratched his paw on it, and looked over his shoulder at Haggadah to ensure he had her attention.

"Of all nights, Nero, you insist on going out to hunt in the rain?" The old witch shook her head, unable to fathom the logic of the feline.

Anna stared at the cat, questioning his sanity. Why would Nero want to leave the shelter of the cottage on such a wicked stormy night? She watched Haggadah walk to the door. "Are you going to let him outside in this storm?"

The old witch glanced at Anna as she opened the portal, and Nero scooted out into the darkness. "He isn't daft, ye ken, and knows where to travel to stay dry." She closed the door. "It's safer for him at night. There are no horses to trample him or carriage wheels to run him over." She spotted the Book of Shadows still on the table. "When you retire for the night, take the candles and the Book of Shadows with you. Keep it safely hidden, for its protection as well as yours."

Anna nodded and glanced at the aged journal as she continued to fold her clothes and place them into neat piles.

~

"I told you it was going to rain," John complained. The hole they had dug to retrieve the body was filling with water and turning to mud. "We should have waited until tomorrow night to dig this old man up."

"Just keep digging. The sooner we can get him out, the sooner we can get out of the rain." Martin encouraged as he held the lantern above the hole, caring little if the light was seen by anyone. He was confident the unpleasant weather would keep the constable and anyone else away from their misdoing.

John's shovel hit something solid and made a muffled sound through the water. He looked up to his partner and smiled. "Ha!" He continued to shovel around the end of the casket, broke it open, and pulled the corpse out. "Oh, this one has a bit of stink to it."

"Nothing we can do about it. We'll just take it to Knox. He wanted a body. He will get a body, stink and all."

The men tossed the corpse aside and filled the hole.

"I got his feet. Grab him under his arms." Martin laid his shovel on the body and waited for John to do the same.

"Why do I always get the smellier, heavier end?" John complained as he put his shovel on the body, wrinkled his nose, and grasped the corpse under his arms as Martin clasped the dead man's ankles. They carried the body to the kirkyard fence, tossed it onto the street, and climbed over the barricade after it.

"Leave the shovels next to the fence. We'll come back for them." Martin instructed as he grasped the dead man's ankles once again.

John tossed the shovels aside and picked up his end of the body. "I wish we had a horse and wagon."

Keeping to the shadows, they began walking to the college with the body suspended between them. Their actual destination was the house next door to the anatomy theater. The cellar was intentionally left unbolted to allow access to a tunnel between the house and college.

"Can't you just put this guy over your shoulder and carry him?" John tried to wipe his face with the sides of his sleeves to clear the rain from his eyes.

"He's stiff as a board. I can't balance him on my shoulder." Martin justified.

"My end is getting heavy. I always get the heavy end." John turned his head away from the emanating stench.

Tired of his partner's whining, Martin dropped his end of the body and wiped the droplets of rain away from his eyes. "Fine, you take this end." He caught the body as John removed his grip. "Auch, this end is a bit more rancid," he admitted.

John grabbed the ankles and lifted.

They carried the corpse through the gate in the stone wall and went to the backyard. John lifted the cellar door with the edge of his foot and kicked it aside. The men descended the wooden stairs into the darkness and entered the short tunnel.

"There's a light at the other end," John reported, easing his mind that the tunnel was somewhat illuminated. "Doc must be in. We'll get paid tonight."

"Keep moving." Martin stared at the light over John's head.

Knox looked at the men as they stepped into the basement room. "Lay the body on a table."

John and Martin remained silent as they laid the body down and stepped aside for the doctor to inspect the corpse.

"Not exactly a fresh one." He looked at the dead man's face. "An older one too, thin. At least I won't have layers of fat to cut through." Knox sighed. "Poor quality, so you won't get more than £8."

"Quite understandable, Doc," Martin readily agreed, distracted by the preserved organs in jars as he scanned the shelves in the room. A shiver ran up his spine. He was eager to get paid and leave the gruesome environment.

John looked to his left and stepped back with a jolt as a pair of blue eyes in a jar appeared to be staring at him. A small table covered with a white cloth displayed dissection instruments. One was a wicked saw. He imagined the rasping sound of the tool as it cut through a bone. He averted his eyes.

The doctor reached into his pocket, withdrew some money, and placed the bounty in Martin's outstretched palm. "Be on your way."

The men scurried back through the tunnel, out of the cellar, and headed straight to the pub. They anticipated warming themselves by the fireplace, ridding their bodies of the night's dampness, and enjoying a dram or two of whisky.

Chapter 11

His teeth chattered, and gooseflesh prickled his skin. Douglas assumed he was running a fever. After tossing and turning throughout the night, he reluctantly rose from the bed and changed into clean clothes. His head and body ached, and he was unable to breathe through his nose.

After two quick knocks on the door, Douglas opened it for the all-too-cheery maid.

"Good morning, sir." Fiona set his breakfast on the table. She turned to see his face, still quite pale. Suspecting he was in no mood for her advice, she walked to the door. "I'll return as soon as I deliver the last breakfast."

Douglas simply nodded as he closed the door and went to the table. Unable to detect the aroma of the food, he poured himself a cup of coffee, cupped his hands around it, and sipped it caring little if he burned his tongue. He stared out the window and watched the organized chaos of the city below.

A knock sounded on his door.

"Come in." He continued to stare out the window.

Fiona entered. "I'll tidy your room now for you, sir."

"Very well."

"I've news." She pulled the covers of the bed toward the headboard. "The owner of a boardinghouse and his neighbor in the Tanner Close have been arrested. Mr. Hare and Mr. Burke have been charged with murdering several people and selling their bodies to the college for the past nine months. It's such a scandal. The entire city is gossiping about it."

Douglas turned toward the maid. His eyebrows drew together in thought. "No one reported the missing people to the authorities after they simply disappeared?"

"I don't rightly know, sir. Mr. Hare, the boardinghouse owner, well, many of the victims were once his guests. They may have been people with no connections, possibly women of the night, or boarders from out of town. Word is their wives turned them in. Maybe they could no longer withstand their husbands' wrongdoings." She fluffed the pillows and set them in place. "Did you rest peacefully, sir?" She noticed his untouched breakfast.

"Not as well as I would have liked." He turned and looked out the window once again.

"Still feeling ill?"

"Quite." He admitted.

"I can call a physician for you, or you can visit Haggadah, ye ken." Cringing after reiterating his options, she waited for his reply.

Douglas turned toward the maid and lowered his half-empty cup to the table. "This Haggadah, you indicated she is a healer, not a physician?"

"Aye, not a physician." Fiona shook her head. "I've used several of her remedies myself. She can fix what is ailing you."

Douglas took his watch from his pocket and checked the time. It was quite early in the morning. He would finish his coffee before calling on the acclaimed witch. "Very well. Thank you for your advice, Fiona."

"You're welcome, sir." The maid nodded as she left the room.

~

Anna stoked the fire and ensured the cauldron contained enough water. Haggadah had gone into the garden with Barret. She assumed her godmother was gathering herbs or maybe using the privy.

Scratching at the front door drew Anna's attention. She looked at Haggadah's bed, expecting to see Nero, but he was not there. "It's nearly midmorning. Nero, are you finally returning from your night of prowling for mice?"

She opened the door to see the ebony feline facing away from her. Nero's back was arched, and his tail was bushy. The cat darted off before she saw the polished black shoes standing before the door. Anna traced the pantlegs upward until her eyes met the hazel orbs staring at her. The man was stylishly dressed in a tailored black overcoat and top hat. He nodded his head. His fisted hand remained poised as if he were about to knock on the door.

Anna's heartbeat quickened, fearing the man may recognize her, yet she did not recognize him. He was tall, at least a head taller than she, if not more.

She had learned a lot about the medicinal and spiritual properties of herbs, spices, and crystals so far. Many of the visitor's complaints were minor, and their remedies similar in nature. Confident she could create a cure for whatever ailment the gentleman may have, she lifted her chin and assumed the professional role as Haggadah's apprentice.

"May I help you?" She waited for his reply.

Douglas lowered his hand as he stared at the woman's red hair, her porcelain skin looked as soft as a rose petal, and her deep green eyes reminded him of emeralds.

Anna grew uncomfortable under his stare. She scanned his expensive black coat with tails and a beaver top hat with ebony curls peeking from beneath its brim. Was he injured? His mesmerizing hazel yet bloodshot eyes finally blinked. He took a step backward and scanned the old building.

Douglas assumed the driver had taken him to the wrong location. He reached his hand up to hold his hat in place as a gust of wind threatened to send it toppling from his head.

"Sir?" Anna noticed the lack of color in the man's face. His lips were cracked and dry. His eyes were red and puffy, with dark circles beneath them. It was apparent the man was unwell.

Douglas shook his head slightly, bringing himself back to reality. He opened his mouth to speak but was dumbfounded. He snapped it shut, gathered his thoughts, and tried once again. "I was told that an elderly witch resides here. Unless you have transformed yourself into the most beautiful woman I have ever seen, you are clearly not her." He took another step backward and scanned the exterior of the house again. "Do I have the correct residence? Is this where Haggadah lives?"

Anna blushed, and assumed the gentleman was delirious. "She does but is currently unavailable. I'm her apprentice. How may I help you?"

A wave of dizziness caused Douglas to blink his eyes as he tried to clear the blackness from his vision. He swayed as he walked forward and leaned against the frame of the door for support.

Barret charged through the front door and sniffed the visitor.

"Anna, let the man enter."

Anna looked behind her to see Haggadah motioning toward a chair. She hoped the old witch would not be angry with her for answering the door.

"But Haggadah, you said . . ."

"Never mind. This man needs to sit." Haggadah's voice was stern, insistent.

Anna stepped aside. "Please, sir, come inside."

Douglas nodded his head as he passed Anna. "Thank you." He looked at the old woman, who fit the description given by the maid. "Haggadah?"

The old witch smiled. "Yes, please sit and let me have a look at you."

Anna closed the door and stood silently by the apothecary, waiting for instructions. Barret pranced to

Douglas with his tail wagging. The canine took an instant liking to the visitor.

Douglas removed his hat, placed it in his lap, and looked at the witch's wrinkled face as she lifted his chin with her gnarled index finger and put her hand on his forehead.

"Ah, fever, a good sign." She placed the palms of her hands on each side of his face and looked at his eyes. "Bloodshot eyes and cracked lips." She put her hands on each side of his neck and applied pressure. "Open your mouth and stick out your tongue."

Douglas complied.

"Ah." She stood upright, took her cane from where it leaned against the table, and placed both of her hands on its handle. "Your name, sir."

"Douglas, Douglas MacEwan." His reply was a raspy whisper.

Haggadah glanced toward the loft. An all-knowing smile briefly appeared on her face. She turned to Anna. "And what brings you to Edinburgh, Mr. MacEwan?"

"Business."

"Aye, your 'business' is taking longer than you wish."

"Aye, it usually does, but I'm a patient man."

Haggadah grinned. "Anna, make some tea for Mr. MacEwan. He is quite parched."

Douglas noted the young woman's name as he watched her cross the room to retrieve a teacup and tin. He listened as she went to the fireplace behind him to prepare the tea.

"How long have you been ill, Mr. MacEwan?" Haggadah knew the answer but preferred to hear if his reply was honest.

"A day, going on two." He admitted.

She leaned close to his face, stared into his eyes, and shook her gnarled index finger at him. "Perhaps a little less drinking with the men late at night is in order."

He raised his eyebrows, surprised by her intuition, and watched as the old witch went to a cupboard and opened both doors.

Barret protectively lay at Douglas's feet.

Anna stirred the tea, placed the spoon on the saucer, and presented it to the patient.

"Thank you." His fingertips grazed the back of her hand as he accepted the beverage.

Anna ignored the contact and went to Haggadah's side. "What about your strict rule? She whispered."

"What rule would that be?" Haggadah knew perfectly well what her goddaughter referred to as she took two glass bottles from a drawer – one clear and one brown.

"A patient is not allowed in the house." She no longer kept her voice quiet.

"And what about the rule for you not to open the door when someone knocks?" Haggadah countered mockingly.

"He didn't knock. I was letting Nero inside, and Mr. MacEwan was standing on the stoop."

"Anna is correct. I didn't knock."

Anna and Haggadah both turned and looked at Douglas.

He shrugged his shoulder, signaling his innocence. "I apologize for eavesdropping, but then again, you weren't exactly whispering." His eyelids drooped, heavy with sleep.

Haggadah motioned toward the patient, looked at her goddaughter, and continued. "We couldn't allow him to pass out at our front door. How in heaven's name would the two of us get him inside? In truth, I doubt we would be capable of doing so." She handed Anna a small clear glass vessel containing herbs. "Find a cork to fit each bottle." She pointed to the drawer. "Can you think of the scandal if we were seen dragging him inside? We would have a constable knocking on the door within minutes. You and I both know you would be discovered, and you must stay hidden, at least for now."

Anna had to agree. She looked over her shoulder as Douglas finished the tea and set the empty cup on the table. He looked as if he was ready to fall asleep. She opened the drawer and examined several corks before finding the proper size for each bottle.

The old witch filled a brown glass bottle with several herbs and spirits to make a tincture. She accepted the cork from her goddaughter and inserted it securely. Anna gave her the clear bottle. Haggadah held both bottles before her. "These should work well."

Douglas watched as Anna removed the teacup from the table and walked away as Haggadah stood before him.

"Mr. MacEwan, the contents in this bottle," Haggadah held the clear glass bottle before him, "must be put into a hot cup of tea. You must drink it while the water is hot. It'll help you sleep, so drink the tea before retiring for the evening. The brown bottle," she held it up for him to see, "is a remedy. Take a spoonful three times a day. If you are still sick after three days, please return." She placed the bottles in his hand.

"Thank you, both." Douglas rose from the chair, placed the bottles into his overcoat pocket, put on his hat, and stepped over Barret.

Anna went to the door and opened it. She remained silent as Douglas tipped his hat.

"Anna." He exited the cottage as Nero scooted through the open portal and hopped onto Haggadah's bed.

Anna stared at the cat as she shut the door and placed her fisted hands on her hips. "I should skin you alive, scaredy-cat." It was an idle threat but made her feel better once she said it.

Nero looked at her, blinked his eyes, and began licking his dirty paws.

~

Douglas climbed inside the awaiting coach. With a slap of the reins on the horse's rump, it rolled forward and headed to the boardinghouse. The rhythmic sound of the horse's hooves and the slight rocking of the coach encouraged his eyelids to close. He removed his hat and leaned his head back against the interior of the coach. Two thoughts crept into his mind – the need for sleep and Anna.

The coach came to a halt, and the driver opened the door. "Sir?"

Douglas lifted his head and put on his hat before exiting. "Thank you." He dropped the appropriate amount of money into the awaiting palm of the driver and entered the boardinghouse.

"Mr. MacEwan?" The owner, a short, stout man with a bald head, shuffled toward his guest.

Douglas desired nothing more than to go directly to his room, take the prescribed remedy, climb into bed, and sleep until the illness ravishing his body disappeared. He looked down at the man's round face and sighed. "Aye."

"Fiona mentioned that you're ill. Is there anything I can get you?" His brown eyes conveyed concern, and his voice was sincere.

"Upon your maid's recommendation, I've visited your city's renowned healer." He recalled Haggadah's instructions. "I'll need hot water, a teacup, and a spoon."

"Very well, sir. I'll send it up with her shortly."

"Thank you." Douglas climbed the stairs to his room. He took off his hat, overcoat, and jacket and hung them on a chair. Retrieving the two bottles from his coat pocket, he set them on the table and turned toward the door as a knock sounded. "Come in."

"Mr. MacEwan, I'm so pleased to hear you went to see Haggadah. I know her remedy will have you feeling better in no time." She set the tray of items on the table. "As requested, sir." She picked up the tray of uneaten breakfast food. "Will you want your evening meal?"

"No, thank you. If Haggadah's remedy works as well as you say it does, I hope to sleep the remainder of today and through the night."

"Excellent, sir. I'll bring your breakfast in the morning and pray you are fully recovered by then."

"Thank you, Fiona." Douglas heard the door click shut as he poured the hot water into the teacup. He added whatever was in the clear bottle to the hot water, allowed time for it to steep, and drank the entire cup. He ate a spoonful of the concoction from the brown bottle, pulled the drapes shut on the window to darken the room, undressed, and climbed into bed, hoping not to open his eyes until morning's light.

Chapter 12

A knock sounded upon the door pulling Douglas from his sleep. "Come in," he stated with his eyes closed.

"Good morning, sir." Fiona entered carrying a tray containing his breakfast, set it on the table, and opened the drapes on the window to reveal an overcast sky. She glanced at the guest's face as he sat up in bed and looked at her. "The bags under your eyes have disappeared. I assume you're well-rested."

Douglas inhaled, taking an inventory of his body. No longer did he feel feverish. His aches were nonexistent, and he could breathe easily. "Aye, I'm feeling like my old self again."

Fiona smiled, pleased to see the remedy had helped him overcome his illness. "Whenever you revisit Edinburgh, you can rely on Haggadah's remedies to set your health straight."

He looked at the teacup on the table and the brown bottle beside the teaspoon. He had taken the dosage as instructed. "Aye, it worked wonders. Thank you for the recommendation."

"You're welcome, sir. Is there anything else you need before I leave?" She set the bottles aside and lifted the tray from the previous day.

"Have there been any messages for me?"

"No, sir. I always inquire before bringing your breakfast."

"Thank you, Fiona, that's all."

"Excellent, sir. I'll return later to tidy your room." Fiona closed the door behind her as she left.

Douglas got out of bed, went to the table, and sat. Uncorking the tincture, he poured another dose in the teaspoon, winced at its bitter taste as he swallowed, and chased it down with a quickly poured cup of strong coffee. He exhaled, appreciating the brew's flavor as he thought of no better way to begin his day. As was his habit, he went to the window and looked down at the main street. Coaches traveled opposite ways as people darted around them. Douglas wondered how much longer he would have to remain in the city. He was eager for his ships to be loaded to capacity and begin his return trip to Virginia.

Even though Douglas was in his early twenties, he had accumulated a vast amount of wealth through investments and intelligent decisions. His shipping business was the pinnacle of his achievements thus far. It allowed him to do as he had always wished – travel the world.

Selecting an over-buttered slice of toast from the plate, Douglas absentmindedly bit into the homemade bread and paused in chewing as he thought of Anna. He assumed she was too young to be the old witch's daughter. In fact, they did not appear to be related at all.

Douglas looked at the bottles, thankful for the remedy's effectiveness, but groaned inwardly as he realized he had failed to pay the witch for her service. Always a fair man, his first order of business was to correct his oversight.

After rejuvenating his body's strength with the healthy breakfast, he donned his overcoat and hat and left the hotel. His hazel eyes scanned the city's old architecture as he opted to walk to Haggadah's cottage. His commanding long strides, handsome face, and fine clothing caught the attention of those on the street, especially the poor.

~

Anna lay on her cot, staring at the beamed ceiling. She listened, but only heard silence. Assuming the day had begun, she climbed down from the loft and scanned the inside of the cottage. The embers in the fireplace were ashen white. Other than Nero sleeping on the bed, she was alone in the room. Making a necessary trip to the privy, she discovered Haggadah was absent from the garden too. Anna assumed Barret was with the old witch, wherever she was. Returning inside, she changed out of her nightdress and into a pale pink muslin with a rose-colored ribbon tied beneath her bustline.

Passing by the table, Anna spotted a scribbled note anchored under the edge of the lamp. It was in Haggadah's handwriting and indicated she had been called away to help deliver a baby. She shrugged her shoulder, a bit disappointed. It was not unusual for Haggadah to assist an expected mother during a difficult delivery. In her opinion, to witness an infant take its first breath would be the greatest of experiences. She wished she could have accompanied her godmother on the call, but it would be most unwise at the present time.

Anna stirred the dying embers in the fireplace with the poker and added several logs to rekindle it. While she waited for the water to heat, Anna made a simple breakfast of bread and butter. Once the water boiled and her tea was made, she retrieved the Book of Shadows and the yellow candle from the loft. As instructed, she lit the candle before opening the book. Anna sipped her tea while she read, enjoying the solitude of the morning.

A knock sounded upon the door as she turned a page. Anna kept reading, ignoring the plea for help, but the insistent knock sounded again. She rose and peeked out from beneath the curtain of the window to see Mr. MacEwan standing before the front door. "Is he still ill?" She mumbled to herself. "Since he has already seen me, it can do no harm to answer the door." Placing her hand on the latch, she glanced at the table where the Book of Shadows lay open. Anna rushed to the table, blew out the candle, closed the book, and hid it beneath Haggadah's pillow on her bed. She inhaled deeply to calm her racing heart, brushed the palms of her hands on her skirt, and opened the door. "Mr. MacEwan, how may I help you?"

"Ah, Anna, good morning." He nodded and smiled.

Anna noticed his enthusiastic reply. Obviously, the tincture and herbs had improved his health overnight.

Douglas continued. "I came to apologize for my oversight. May I?" He motioned toward the interior of the house.

Anna hesitated. It was inappropriate for her to be alone with him, but her only alternative was to rudely deny him entry. She took a step backward, motioned for him to come inside, and followed him to the center of the room. "Please, sit." She gestured toward a chair at the table.

He removed his hat, pulled out a chair, and sat.

"You look as if you are feeling much better." She began as she sat across from him.

"Yes, the remedies worked well. Thank you. I wanted to thank Haggadah as well. Is she here?"

"No, she was called away to help an expected mother through a difficult delivery."

"I see." His eyebrows drew together. "You did not go with her?"

Anna simply shook her head. "Perhaps another time."

"Ah, well, as I stated, I came to apologize. I failed to pay the two of you for your services yesterday."

Anna grinned. "No need to apologize. In your condition, it was quite understandable."

"Aye."

"But you must understand, Haggadah and I do not require a payment for our services. Many who appear at our door cannot afford to see a physician. They express their gratitude through various gifts as payment."

"Such as?" He leaned forward, staring into her green eyes, which reflected the dancing firelight. Her wavey scarlet hair tied away from her face complimented her dainty jawline.

"Many things, chickens, cheese, bottles of wine, and other food items. Some share their talents and make crafts such as that bench." Anna pointed to the item before the fireplace.

Douglas turned toward it and examined its craftmanship. "Impressive, quite impressive."

"Aye, Haggadah must have performed a miracle to receive such a generous payment. I admired it upon my arrival a few days ago as well."

Douglas was puzzled by her choice of words. "A few days ago? With your vast knowledge of remedies, I assumed you have lived with Haggadah for some time."

She teetered on the precipice of a lie yet was compelled to tell the truth. "We are strangers even though we have been connected in a small way all of my life. As far as my knowledge, I still have much to learn."

He sat back in his chair. "Anna, you are a mystery, a puzzle in which I'm determined to fit the pieces together."

Her mother had often reprimanded her for being outspoken. Fearing she may have revealed too much, Anna clasped her hands together in her lap and gathered her thoughts. "I'm not a mystery nor a puzzle. I'm her goddaughter and her apprentice." She lifted her chin to convey the truth.

The front door opened. Barret trotted ahead of Haggadah through the portal. Anna and Douglas stood as if they had been caught doing something inappropriate.

Anna went to the door to greet her godmother and explain. "Haggadah, Mr. MacEwan has stopped by to pay us for his remedy. As you can see, he is feeling much better." She took the carpetbag from the old witch's hand.

Haggadah was tired, too tired to show any concern over the matter. She had been up most of the night and successfully delivered a healthy baby girl. "Mr. MacEwan, you are looking much better." She slipped off her overcoat and handed it to Anna to hang on a peg. "Sit, let me have a look at you."

Douglas complied and looked toward Anna as she stood behind her godmother.

Haggadah placed her palm on his forehead, neck, inspected his eyes, and took a step backward. "Excellent. You responded well."

He smiled. "I feel as good as new. Thank you." Douglas glanced at Anna before he continued. "I stopped by to apologize. I forgot to pay you for your services." He stood and pulled his money from his inside coat pocket. Uncertain of the appropriate amount, he presented double the fee he last paid a physician.

Haggadah looked at the generous sum. Anna's eyes nearly popped out of her head.

"That is exceedingly kind of you, but what I would like is a smoked ham." The old witch admitted.

Anna stared at her godmother's boldness.

Haggadah's back ached, and her feet hurt from standing most of the night. "Do you think it would be possible for you to purchase one for us?" She went to Anna's vacant chair and sat.

Douglas was taken back by her request. He looked at Anna, her mouth agape, and back to the old witch. "I would be more than happy to do so." He returned the money to his inside coat pocket. "On two conditions." He negotiated.

The old witch grinned. "Name them."

"Since I'm not familiar with the city. I don't know where to purchase a ham. My first condition is that Anna accompanies me."

Anna inhaled and looked at Haggadah for her reaction. There was none.

"And my second is that I join you for dinner. I've stayed alone at the boardinghouse for several days now and wish to spend the evening in the company of others. Allow me to dine with the two of you tonight."

"Haggadah?" Anna's tone conveyed a warning.

The old witch refused to be influenced by her goddaughter. "I agree, as long as you travel by coach and take Barret with you."

~

As the noon hour chimed on the grandfather clock, his mother's incessant crying woke Lachlan much earlier than he wished to rise. His head throbbed with each beat of his heart. He squinted his eyes, shielding them from the daylight streaming through his bedroom windows. Vague images of the previous evening flashed within his mind. He remembered staggering home after consuming far more whisky than he should, and falling into bed. Rolling onto his side, the piece of paper containing a list of IOUs from lost poker games crinkled in his pants pocket. His level of intoxication, an obvious hindrance to making sound decisions during each poker hand, would now cost him dearly.

Lachlan tried to return to sleep, but he could no longer withstand his mother's sobbing. He rose and left his room, nearly bumping into the maid in the hallway.

"Pardon me, sir." Helen apologized.

Grabbing her arm to emphasize his desperation, he nearly growled his request. "Stop my mother's crying now."

"I've tried my best, sir."

He burst into his mother's room to find her a hysterical, blubbering mess.

"She's dead." Evelyn waled.

"Who's dead?" He scowled impatiently.

She continued to cry.

He grabbed his mother by her shoulders, forcing her to stand still. "Mum, who's dead?" He shook her, trying to bring her out of her hysteria.

"Anna, Anna is dead."

"Aye, she died. You must come to terms with her loss, Mum." He scooped her into his arms, carried her to her bed, and pulled the blankets over her body. He turned toward the maid standing behind him. "Did you get the laudanum from the physician as I asked?"

"Yes, sir."

"Retrieve it and bring a spoon too." Lachlan watched his mother wither with grief, curling her body as she turned away from him. Placing his fisted hands on his hips, he waited, unsure what else he could do. Hearing footsteps behind him, he turned to see the maid appear in the doorway and hand him the items.

Helen stood beside Lachlan, willing to offer her assistance.

"How much should I give her?" He opened the bottle.

"Half of a spoonful." Her eyes widened as she watched Lachlan pour the liquid into the spoon until it nearly overflowed.

"Mum, I have something to help you sleep." Lachlan waited, but his mother was too overcome with grief to hear her son. He looked at the maid and barked an order. "Help her sit up."

Helen went to the other side of the bed, placed a knee on the mattress, and managed to get the sobbing woman to sit upright.

"Mum, open your mouth," Lachlan ordered. As she did so, he pushed the spoon into her mouth and withdrew it as she swallowed the dose.

Evelyn sank down into the warmth of the covers pulling the blankets over her shoulder.

Lachlan handed the items to the maid. "I hope to employ a nurse to watch over her. Stay here until she falls asleep."

"Aye, sir."

Lachlan left the room, closing the door behind him. He sighed as he ran his hand through his hair, pulling it back over his head. "This has to end, and soon." He muttered to himself, dropping his hand to his side. The list crinkled, reminding him of his obligation. Lachlan returned to his room, changed his clothes, scribbled a request on a piece of paper, and left for the company office. He needed to pay off his gambling debts and knew where he would find the money.

Chapter 13

Lachlan walked along the waterfront. He reached into his overcoat, retrieving the note that requested a nurse from the family physician, and handed it to a boy.

"Deliver this at once." He reached into his pocket and dropped a coin into the lad's outstretched palm.

"Thank you, sir." The boy ran off.

The cries of seagulls hovering in the chilly autumn breeze drew Lachlan's attention. He placed his hand upon his hat and looked skyward, hoping the scavengers were far enough away so as not to drop excrement on him. Several fishermen were cleaning their catch at tables on the edge of the waterfront. They dropped the entrails back into the sea, where several gulls gobbled them up before they could sink. Feral cats patiently sat near each table, waiting for a morsel from the generous fishermen to be tossed their way.

Lachlan stopped before his father's ship and inhaled the salty air, clearing the alcohol-induced fog from his mind. Even though he despised the chaos of the shipping business, it was a welcomed escape from his mother's incessant crying. He pulled his overcoat closer to his neck and watched as the second of his father's ships was brought parallel to the dock and tied off. Heavy in the water, he assumed it was loaded to its compacity with cargo.

The Stewart Mercantile Shipping Company sign squeaked as it swayed from its rusted brackets above the door.

Lachlan shivered before stepping into the office and closing the door behind him.

Mr. Heywood sat behind his desk, scribbling an entry into a ledger.

The accountant reminded Lachlan of his father, ebony hair sprinkled with gray at his temples and wire-rimmed glasses resting on the bridge of his nose. "Good morning, Corbin. I swear I will never adjust to the dampness of the docks."

Corbin closed the ledger before him. He opened a desk drawer and withdrew a second ledger, exchanging it for the one in his hand. "Aye, some never adjust." He placed the account book on the desk and opened it to the next blank entry.

Lachlan removed his overcoat and hat and hung them on the freestanding coat rack, added another log in the small fireplace, and stood before the window rubbing his hands together to warm them. He read the name on the ship's bow and checked the chalk schedule on the wall as he crossed the small office. "Ah, she's a few days late. Must have run into bad weather."

"Aye, more than likely, sir." Corbin dipped his pen in the bottle of ink and wrote the date on the page. His russet eyes looked over the rim of his glasses at Lachlan, who had sat at his father's desk, uncharacteristically pensive and quiet. "You seem a bit off. Something on your mind?"

Lachlan pursed his lips as he looked at his accountant and sighed. "Mum seems to be getting worse. Even though it hasn't been very long since my sister's death, I thought with time her grieving would wane, but it has only increased."

"No disrespect, but she did appear quite distraught and reflexive when I last saw her. Perhaps she needs professional help." Corbin returned the pen to the inkwell.

Leaning forward in the wooden office chair, Lachlan steepled his index fingers as he clasped his hands and leaned his elbows on his knees. "What are you suggesting?"

"I'm no expert in the matter, ye ken, but putting her in an asylum may be best, for her sake. That way the doctors can monitor her condition, and with time, nurse her back to health."

"Isn't that quite expensive?"

"I imagine you would like your mum nearby." Corbin paused, testing to see if Lachlan wished the same. He went on to explain. "So, you can visit her often." No reaction from the young man, not even a twitch of his eye. Corbin sighed. "The Edinburgh Lunatic Asylum is closest. I believe it is a private facility that charges a monthly fee either paid by the patient or their family." The accountant refrained from smiling at the young owner, whose facial expression indicated his displeasure. He was uncertain if Evelyn's possible proximity or the asylum cost was the cause of his distress.

Averting the accountant's inquisitive stare, Lachlan sat upright and looked out the window. He focused on a ship docked at the waterfront. He weighed the options. A monthly fee? Would the asylum be more expensive than a private nurse? If admitted to the facility, at least his mother would be out of the house. He looked at the accountant. "Nevertheless, I want to be prepared. Make an entry for a withdrawal of fifty pounds." Lachlan lied as he went to the corner of the room, opened the company safe, and took the money. Whether he used it for the asylum, or his gambling debt would depend on his mother's state of mind when he arrived home.

"Very well." Corbin took the pen in hand, held it to the edge of the inkwell to drain off the excess ink, and made the entry in the ledger.

~

"Haggadah, this is not a good idea." Anna stood with the black cloak over her arm. Within minutes she knew Douglas would return with the hired coach, and she was trying her best to convince her godmother that she should not leave the cottage.

"Nonsense. Mr. MacEwan is a good soul. I trust he will keep you safe." The old witch continued to advise as she handed Anna a white ribbon. "Tie your hair back."

Anna set the cloak on the back of the chair as she pulled her scarlet locks behind her head and tied them in place.

Haggadah selected a hairpin from the palm of her hand. "Pin your wayward hair." She handed her several others as needed. "The hood should be able to conceal your hair nicely. Avoid eye contact. Above all, don't draw attention to yourself."

Anna pinned the last loose strand away from her face. "Aye." She donned the black cloak and fastened the triskelion clasp in place.

"It's windy, so hold the hood firmly to keep your head covered and stay in the coach. Mr. MacEwan can go into the shop and purchase the ham." She pulled the hood over Anna's head, ensuring it would conceal her goddaughter's hair and shadow her face.

"But what if someone should see me?" Anna gathered her cloak around her. She turned and looked at the door as she heard a coach stopping before the cottage. Her heart seemed to jump within her chest. She inhaled, trying to calm herself, and looked at her godmother for reassurance.

"My dear, I've every confidence you'll remain safe." Haggadah patted her arm. "While you're away, I'll make scones and cook vegetables for our dinner."

A knock sounded upon the door.

"Haggadah?" Anna's apprehension rolled like a somersault in her stomach.

The old witch sighed. "Anna, trust Mr. MacEwan as I do." She went to the door and opened it. "Mr. MacEwan, Anna, and Barret are looking forward to riding in the coach."

Hearing his name, Barret rose from his spot and pranced toward Douglas, who patted the dog on his shoulder.

Douglas looked at Anna. He smiled. "Good. Shall we be on our way?"

Anna sighed. She glanced at her godmother before looking at Douglas and returning his grin. "Aye." She placed her hand on the top of her hood to hold it in place and exited the cottage.

Haggadah looked at her faithful dog. "Barret, go." He followed Anna out the door.

"We'll return shortly." Douglas assured as he turned to leave the cottage.

Haggadah reached for his arm, halting his exit. "Please, for Anna's safety, keep her within the confines of the coach with Barret."

Douglas tilted his head to the side, puzzled by the old witch's concern. "As you wish." He nodded in acknowledgment before joining his traveling companions in the coach. Seating himself across from Anna, questions for her safety arose in his mind. He hoped to have the answers before returning to the cottage.

~

"I'll wait here." Martin stood near the entrance of a close. He watched a man climb a ladder and light a streetlight as the darkness of nightfall would announce the end of another day soon. He reached into his pants pocket and withdrew a few coins. "Here, get what you can with this." Martin dropped the coins into his partner's hand, leaned his shoulder against the stone wall, and sighed as he stuffed his hands into his pockets for warmth. His stomach grumbled.

John turned and counted the money as he entered the butcher shop.

~

Douglas watched Anna's fidgeting fingers in her lap. Her skirt shuddered near the floor, indicating she was shaking her foot. She stared out the window as the coach jolted forward. "You seem nervous. Are you afraid of me?"

She looked at his inquisitive hazel eyes before looking down at her hands and stilling her fingers. "No."

"But you are afraid of something, or shall I say, someone?" He waited patiently as she gathered her thoughts.

Anna looked at his kind face and wondered how he had drawn the conclusion. "Why would you think that?" She surmised the less he knew, the better.

"Even though I was quite feverish when we met, I overheard your need to remain hidden and your godmother's concern that a constable could come to the door."

Dare she trust him with the truth. Haggadah's advice replayed in her mind. She simply nodded once.

He pressed on. "Why must you stay hidden?"

She stared at him and sighed, quite convinced his line of questioning would not cease until she replied. "My life is in danger, or so Haggadah believes."

Douglas sat forward in his seat. "In danger? How? From whom?"

"If you must know the entire truth, she believes someone tried to kill me." She opened her mouth to explain more but looked out the window to avoid doing so.

"Please, go on." He encouraged, mystified by what little she had revealed.

"I was sent on an errand. It was dark when I left the house." She continued to look out the window to avoid his stare of earnest concern. "I assume from the lump on my head, someone knocked me unconscious. The next thing I knew, I woke up in the kirkyard with two men staring at me. They were resurrectionists and had dug up my body." Anna looked at Douglas and grinned. "I gave them quite a scare, ye ken, rising from the dead. They ran out of the kirkyard."

"They were probably more afraid of getting caught." Douglas justified.

"Since it was the middle of the night, I left the kirkyard and began to walk home. That is when I met Haggadah and Barret." Anna affectionately petted the dog on the head. "Haggadah was waiting for me in the street. I assumed she had a premonition that I would be there. My godmother insisted I live with her until we can discover who tried to kill me."

Douglas was no stranger to such wrongdoings. Some of his crew would disappear during the night. Were they killed? Taken hostage and smuggled onto other ships to work? With crime high in most large cities, especially those with ports, he was surprised she was not sold into servitude. He looked at Barret, her protector. "Why would anyone try to kill you?"

Anna refrained from laughing. "I believe many wish I was dead."

Douglas scoffed. "You appear as an upright citizen, pleasant, well mannered, educated, and kind. Who on earth would wish you dead?"

Anna shrugged her shoulder. "Anyone and everyone who believes I'm cursed." She sighed before continuing to explain. "I was born the seventh daughter of the seventh daughter. Many know me by the color of my hair - a trait of the devil, many say. They don't think I overhear their whispered conversations, see their heads turn and stare, their sideways glances as I pass by them, but I do. So, they suspect I'm a witch."

He huffed in disbelief. "Your birth order or the color of your hair has nothing to do with being cursed. A witch? Such a silly superstition."

"All I know is that I must remain unseen, at least until Haggadah and I can discover who tried to kill me."

"I agree." Douglas glanced out the window as the coach stopped at the main street. "Where is the butcher's shop?"

Anna peeked out the window. "It's just on the left a few blocks down."

Douglas banged against the wall of the coach behind him. "The butcher shop," he ordered.

Even though it was dusk, Anna leaned back against the seat, hoping to remain out of sight by anyone on the street.

The coach came to a halt. Anna peeked out the window to see the shop located next to a close. "You will find Mr. Bennett inside. He is the butcher and has the most delicious smoked hams."

"Very well. I'll return shortly." Douglas opened the door and stepped down to the street.

Barret raised his nose skyward and began to growl.

"Hush, Barret." Anna petted the canine, trying to calm him.

The dog continued to growl.

"Goodness, what has gotten into you."

Barret hopped from one front foot to the other, eager to chase after something.

"It's probably a cat, settle Barret." She stroked his fur. Within minutes Douglas emerged from the butcher shop with a nice size ham wrapped in brown paper.

Without warning, the dog darted forward, bursting through the coach door as Douglas unlatched the handle.

"Barret!" Anna rose from her seat and stood in the doorway. A gust of wind blew the hood from her head. She watched in disbelief as Barret clamped his massive jowls onto the wrist of a man. Her eyes widened as she recognized the stranger's face.

"Anna, please get inside." Douglas grabbed the coach door to shut it.

Her face drained of color as she looked at Douglas. "It's him. The man in the kirkyard."

He pulled her hood over her head. "Get inside."

She stood transfixed as she watched Barret twist his head back and forth while the man winced in pain and hollered.

Douglas stepped up into the coach, blocking her view. "Sit down. Here, take the ham." He placed the package in her lap before turning to see who the dog was holding. The man was tall. His clothes tattered and dirty, possibly homeless. Douglas closed the coach door and sat.

"That's one of the men. I'm certain of it." She stared out the window as Barret continued his attack.

"Did he see you?"

Anna sat back in her seat. "I don't know."

Douglas banged on the carriage wall for the driver to move on.

Anna gasped. "What about Barret?"

"He'll find his way home." Douglas assured.

"No, you have to whistle." She insisted.

"Whistle?"

"Aye, I can't whistle. Open the door and whistle for Barret to come."

The driver kept the horse at a steady pace and turned the coach at the next block. Douglas opened the door slightly and whistled. He closed the door. "Barret will most likely return to the cottage on his own."

The coach continued down the street. Douglas looked at Anna as he heard a bark. He opened the coach door, and Barret jumped inside.

~

Lachlan could hear his mother's whaling as he climbed the steps of the house. He fisted his palms and clenched his teeth. "Did the doctor send an incompetent nurse?" He paused with his hand on the doorknob, trying to decide whether he should enter the house or go to the pub. He looked up at her bedroom window. The light was on. He entered, and Helen rushed toward him.

"Did the nurse arrive?" He looked up the staircase as his mother cried out.

"No, sir." She presented the note on a silver tray.

Lachlan broke the seal, read it, and frowned. The doctor's nurse was not available. He looked at the maid, who awaited his reply. "Give her laudanum, enough to help her go to sleep."

"Aye, sir."

Unable to withstand the sorrow in his mother's cries any longer, he left, slamming the door behind him. He decided what he needed was a mass quantity of whisky and several rounds of poker to distract his mind from his troubles. If his funds held out, he would remain in the pub until the wee morning hours. Lately, however, the cards he was dealt had not been so kind. Perhaps tonight, his luck would change.

Chapter 14

Douglas paid the coachman as Anna and Barret entered the cottage.

Haggadah looked up from the vegetables she was stirring in a pot over the fire. Her smile faded as she recognized the look of panic on Anna's face. "What happened?" She stood from the stool with the wooden spoon still in her hand.

Anna lowered her hood and unclasped the cape. "Barret jumped from the coach and attacked a man. It was one of the men from the kirkyard." She hung the garment on a peg and joined her godmother at the fireplace.

"One of the resurrectionists?" The old witch patted the dog's head as Barret greeted her.

"Aye, the taller one," Anna confirmed, pacing the floor.

Haggadah watched Douglas enter, closing the door behind him. He placed the ham on the table before removing his overcoat and hat. She returned her attention to her goddaughter. "Did he see you?"

"I don't know." Anna stopped pacing and looked at Douglas for reassurance. But instead, he placed the palm of his hand on the small of her back and guided her to the carved bench, motioning for her to sit.

"When I came out of the butcher shop," he looked at Haggadah, "she was standing in the door of the coach yelling for Barret. Your dog held a man by the wrist and was growling while twisting his head from side to side."

"The wind blew the hood off my head." She removed the hairpins and untied the ribbon, letting her locks fall around her shoulders. "So many people know who I am because of the vivid color of my hair." Anna lifted a silky strand to emphasize her point before dropping it back in place.

"I believe the man was too preoccupied fending off Barret to notice her." Douglas consoled. "I ushered Anna inside the coach and instructed the driver to move on.

Barret caught up with us as the coach rounded the corner."

"Nearly everyone in the city knows the dog belongs to me." Haggadah sighed and looked at Anna, her head bowed, staring at her entwined fingers in her lap. "Let's hope people were preoccupied watching Barret and ignored you, Anna." Her goddaughter looked up at her. "If there was that much of a disruption, there may be a constable assigned to investigate the attack."

Douglas placed a chair before the fireplace and sat. He looked at the old witch, concern masking his face. "If the man is guilty of exhuming Anna's body, he probably will avoid reporting the incident." He watched the old witch resume her seat and Barret lay on the floor near her feet. "Barret is such a gentle dog. How did he know he was one of the men in the kirkyard?"

Haggadah stirred the pot, then looked at Douglas. "He's quite smart, observant, and, as you have witnessed, protective. I don't know how Barret was able to determine the man was one of the resurrectionist from the kirkyard." She saw Anna wipe a tear away from her cheek and knew a distraction would help calm her nerves. "Anna, set the table so we may enjoy that delicious ham."

~

Blood dripped from Martin's wrist. He clasped his hand tightly over the wound as he disappeared into the darkness of the close.

John appeared from a shop with a loaf of bread, cheese, and sliced ham. He stood in the opening of the close, scanning the area in search of his friend, who was not where he had left him.

Martin sat on a bench beneath a tree in the enclosed courtyard. He looked up from his arm to the street. "John!"

Hearing his name, John hurried toward his friend, slowing his gait as he stared at the injury. "What happened to you?"

"Bloody hell! Look at my arm!" Martin exposed the wound for his partner to see. "The damn witch's dog attacked me."

"What did you do, tease the beast?"

"Nothing, I did nothing. I was just standing there waiting for you when the thing showed up out of nowhere and latched onto my wrist."

"Where is it now?" John turned around scanning the close for the dog, afraid it may attack again.

Martin nodded once in the direction Barret had gone. "It ran off."

"Did the old witch sick her dog on you?"

"No, but I swear I saw the lass we dug up the other night. She was in a coach, yelling for the beast as it attacked me."

John's eyebrows raised. "You saw her? You saw the witch?""

"Maybe not. I thought I saw her devil-red hair, but I was busy trying to shake off the dog." Martin took a soiled handkerchief from his coat pocket and wrapped it around his wrist.

"Here, take these." John handed the food to his friend, sat on the bench, and tied the makeshift bandage securely. "I think we need to let him know she's still in the city."

"How are we going to find him? We don't even know who he is?" Martin opened the brown paper containing the ham.

"I guess we go to the pub. He may be there."

The resurrectionists shared the food in the quiet of the close, allowing Martin time to regain his wits from the attack. John wadded the paper into a ball and tossed it aside. They stepped onto the street and dodged several coaches as they crossed to the opposite side. With streetlights illuminating their way, they walked to the pub, and stood outside its entrance.

"Do you think he is in there?" John looked at his friend.

"Won't know until we go inside, ye ken."

"Why are we even bothering to tell him?"

Martin looked heavenward. "He may give us a reward."

It was John's turn to look heavenward.

The pub was busy with many of the seats taken. Martin scanned the smoke-filled room for their contact, elbowed John, and nodded his head toward the rear of the pub.

Men stared at the pair as they walked to the back-corner table.

The man sat with his back facing them and could hear them approaching. "Well?" He lifted the glass of whiskey, drained it dry, and refilled it from the bottle on the table.

"She's still in the city. I saw her, well I think I saw her." Martin confirmed as he plopped into a vacant chair. Only the man's chin could be seen beneath the shadow of his black top hat.

"Then she needs to be like everyone believes she is, dead." His voice tinged with revenge. He swirled the amber liquid in his glass.

Martin looked at his partner. "We're not murderers. Besides, the street was crowded. I'm certain others saw the lass too. It was quite a commotion. I was yelling in pain, and she was trying to call the witch's dog."

Martin explained as he watched the man empty another glass and fill it again. He placed both arms on the table, drawing the man's attention to his injury. "The dog attacked me."

The black hat tilted toward the crudely made bandage. "What did you do to offend Haggadah?"

"Nothing," Martin confessed. "I didn't see her there. I was just waiting for John. He was buying us something to eat from the butcher."

The man exhaled. "The lass you dug up is the old witch's goddaughter."

John's mouth dropped open. "Haggadah is after us, ye ken, revenging her goddaughter. We're cursed."

The man looked toward John. "So, you were in the butcher shop when the dog attacked?"

John nodded twice. He leaned toward Martin. "Are you sure it was the old witch's dog? Maybe the lass we dug up has a dog just like it too. After all, she's a witch. Maybe all witches have dogs like it."

The man looked heavenward while keeping the brim of his hat tilted over his face. He slammed the whiskey glass down on the table to stop the resurrectionist from babbling. "Go to Haggadah's house. You can use the excuse of Martin's injury as the reason for your visit. See if she is keeping any hidden guests." He flipped them each a coin. "Go."

Once outside the pub, John looked at Martin. "He knows Haggadah lives alone. What did he mean by hidden guests?"

"He wants us to see if the lass we dug up is being hidden there." Martin sighed as he shook his head.

"Oh." John pushed his coin into the pocket of his pants. "At least he gave you money to pay the witch for her remedy."

Martin sneered. "I would rather use my coin to buy whisky than to waste it on a remedy."

"Now, Martin, you can't let that bite fester. You might get lockjaw, ye ken."

Martin's heart skipped a beat, knowing a remedy was necessary, yet fearing a visit to the witch's cottage could mean another encounter with her vicious dog.

Chapter 15

Anna took three plates from the cupboard, turned, and nearly bumped into Douglas, who stood behind her.

"Allow me." His fingertips touched her trembling hands as he grasped the plates and stared into her emerald eyes. "Try not to worry." He whispered.

Haggadah glanced at the couple and grinned at his kind reassurance before she spooned the vegetables into a bowl.

Douglas continued. "I promise, we will resolve this matter, so you are safe once again." A thought gnawed at the back of his mind. What if he was unable to discover the person who tried to kill Anna before his ships were ready to depart? Would he remain in the city to honor his promise? If he could not stay, would she accept an offer to leave the city and come with him to Virginia where she would be safe?

Anna exhaled. Her mouth turned up at each end but quickly faded. Even though his words were soothing, they were of little comfort. She turned and retrieved the silverware.

They set the table while Haggadah placed a bowl of steaming potatoes and carrots with chives on the table. Douglas unwrapped the ham and put it on a platter while Anna retrieved the freshly baked currant scones.

"Anna, we need the butter and jam. Oh, and bring a bottle of wine too. I'll get the glasses." Haggadah pointed toward the cellar.

With a nod of her head, Anna disappeared through the door, entered the cellar, and found herself in complete darkness. She turned to climb up the stairs when a lit candle appeared before her."

"Haggadah thought you may need this." Douglas met her halfway down the stairs.

"Yes, how absentminded of me."

"Quite understandable after your scare."

Anna scanned the shelves as Douglas held the candle aloft, casting light throughout the tiny room. Finally, she spied a dusty bottle lying on its side, and pulled it from the shelf. "I think this is it." She gave the bottle to Douglas's outstretched hand before retrieving the small crocks of butter and jam.

Haggadah sat at the table and scanned the plentiful meal. Barret, hoping for his share, obediently sat next to her chair. Nero rose from the bed, arching his back as he stretched, and joined his canine friend.

Douglas and Anna placed the items on the table. He kindly held her chair while she sat, uncorked the bottle of red wine, and filled each glass.

"My, this looks like a delicious feast." Douglas complimented as he carved the ham before sitting.

The old witch looked from Anna to Douglas and smiled internally. "Douglas, I appreciate you going with Anna to get the ham." She handed him the plate of scones.

"My pleasure." He selected a scone and placed it on his plate before handing the dish to Anna. "Thank you for allowing me to dine with you both. My room at the boardinghouse is nice, but the conversation is a little one-sided when eating alone." He grinned.

"How long are you in town?" Haggadah ate a wedge of potato.

Douglas pulled his scone into two pieces and smothered each half with butter and jam. "I'm not quite sure. A week, maybe longer." He glanced across the table at Anna, who was staring at him as if interested in his reply.

Searching for a topic of conversation, Anna hoped he would not find her question offensive. "Do you mind me asking about your line of business?" She cut a large piece of carrot in half.

"I own a fleet of mercantile ships. We sailed from Virginia. As soon as the ships are loaded, we will depart for the return trip." He lifted his glass of wine from the table and took a sip. "Mmm, this is an excellent wine."

Anna opened her mouth to mention her father's business when a knock sounded on the door.

The trio turned their heads toward the noise. Barret stood on all fours, went to the door, and began to growl.

The hackles on the back of Haggadah's neck rose. She gently set her silverware on the edge of her plate and stared at her dog. "Apparently, Barret doesn't like our caller. Anna, you and Douglas need to hide on the side of the apothecary before I open the door." She rose from her seat, lifted a lit candle from the table, and waited.

Anna tilted her head to the side as she looked at her godmother, puzzled by her strange behavior, then looked at Barret, who continued to resonate his warning. Cautiously, she stood from her chair, looked at Douglas, and motioned for him to follow her.

Douglas wondered who was in more danger, Anna or Haggadah. He rose and followed Anna across the room.

Anna wedged her body into the corner, scooting as close to the cabinet and wall as possible. She hoped they would remain hidden and inhaled as Douglas joined her, protectively guarding her with his body as they nearly touched.

Sensing her distress, Douglas looked down into her green orbs and grinned to alleviate any anxiety she may feel.

Anna's cheeks filled with color before she looked away. She tried to listen for the visitor's voice but only heard the pounding of her heart.

"Barret, sit," Haggadah commanded. "Stay." She cracked the door open as Barret continued to sound his warning. Two men were standing on the stoop. "May I help you, gentlemen?"

"I injured my arm at the docks." Martin lied. "A grappling hook caught it." Removing the handkerchief, the resurrectionist held his wrist so the old witch could see his injury.

Haggadah opened the door wide enough for her to clasp the man's arm and examine his wound in the candlelight. The old witch had seen enough injuries in her time to easily distinguish the difference between a dog bite and the prongs of a grappling hook. She concluded the man was bitten by a dog, and a rather large one too. She had a good idea which dog had bit him as well.

John peeked into the house, scanning the room. The table was set for the witch's evening meal. But why were there three glasses? He thought she lived alone, or so the circulating rumors indicated.

The old witch stood erect and looked Martin in the eye. "It looks like a nasty injury. Wait while I prepare a remedy." She shut the door.

Barret had yet to move from his spot and continued his low resonant growl.

Haggadah patted the canine on the head before opening the apothecary, pulling out the desktop, and placing the candle upon it. She peeked around the side of the cabinet. "There are two men," she whispered, "one tall and one short. The tall one has a nasty dog bite."

Douglas took a step backward to see Barret staring at the closed door. He looked at Anna. "Did you recognize the man's voice?"

She shook her head. "He spoke too softly for me to hear it. I was a bit dazed when I awoke in the kirkyard, so the resurrectionists voices were like a far-off dream. I remember their height difference and what they look like, though. Apparently, Barret does too." Anna sighed. "Do you think they know I'm here?"

Douglas shrugged his shoulder. "Well, the one man is injured. Maybe they genuinely need help for the wound. Then again, they may have recognized Barret as belonging to Haggadah and came to see if you are here with her. After all, you are a witch too." He grinned.

"Hush, you two," Haggadah warned as she took a small crock from the cabinet and placed a chunk of bee's wax in it, went to the fireplace, and ladled water into the same pot she used to cook the vegetables. She placed the crock in the water to melt the wax. Returning to the cabinet, she retrieved several herbs and combined them in a wooden bowl.

Knowing the old witch was preoccupied, John stepped off the pathway and peeked in the window. Even with the curtain drawn, he could see the silhouette of Haggadah moving about the room.

"Get over here before she comes back," Martin warned, leery of the witch's wrath.

Haggadah retrieved the crock of melted wax, added the herbs and a bit of sweet oil, and stirred the mixture. She placed a square cloth over the remedy and tied it in place with a string. "I'm opening the door," she warned as the old witch grabbed a rolled bandage from a drawer.

Douglas took a step closer to Anna and heard her gasp as he placed his hand on her waist, drawing her near him. He looked down into her eyes once again, wondering when she would stop holding her breath.

Martin peered over the witch's head as she opened the door. He spied a black cat jumping onto the seat of a chair and a cauldron hanging in the fireplace. Items a witch would typically possess. Dried herbs hung from the ceiling. A chill ran up his spine as he imagined her casting wicked spells and curses. The table was set for three. He scowled, assuming other witches were joining her for dinner - a coven, perhaps.

"Did you hear what I said?" Haggadah had stated her instructions, but the man's mind, what little there was of it, was preoccupied. She extended her finger and jabbed him in the stomach.

Martin flinched as his attention was redirected. He looked at the old witch. "Sorry, what?"

"Apply this several times a day, wrap it with this clean bandage." She held both items before him. "Once the redness has gone away, and it is no longer sore to the touch, then uncover it and let the air finish healing the wound." She gave both items to Martin and waited.

Martin nudged John with his elbow. "Pay her for her kind service."

John scowled. "Me? It's your injury."

Martin quickly came up with a lame excuse. "My hands are full." He held up the crock and bandage for his friend to see and lowered the volume of his voice. "We gotta pay her, or she may curse us."

John scowled. "Fine." He reached into his pants pocket and pulled out a coin.

Haggadah outstretched her hand. "Thank you. If you need anything else, please return." She closed the door and peeked out the window. The pair argued as they passed through the gate and walked away. "It's safe for you to come out now."

Douglas looked down into Anna's eyes, reluctant to release her, but withdrew his hand and stepped aside. He escorted her back to the table as Haggadah lifted Nero from her chair and sat. The trio resumed their meal.

Barret continued to stand guard until he was confident the men were gone. Then, he returned to sit next to Haggadah's chair, expecting to be well rewarded for his effort of keeping everyone within the cottage safe.

Chapter 16

Haggadah lifted her wine glass and looked at her goddaughter. "From your description of the resurrectionists and the wound on the tall man's wrist, they may have been the same men from the kirkyard."

"I wish I could have seen their faces to verify it was them." Anna glanced at Barret as she cut a wedge of potato in half. "I'm puzzled," she stabbed the vegetable with her fork and paused with it in midair, "how did Barret know it was them?" She looked at Haggadah, ate the vegetable, and redirected her attention to Douglas, who placed his fork and knife on the edge of his plate.

"I believe dogs possess an intuition to discern when someone has bad intentions." He lifted the wine bottle and waited for Haggadah to place her glass on the table before refilling all three.

"Barret has a keen sense of smell," Haggadah added. "As I recall, he approached you on the night you were unearthed and sniffed at your feet. He may have detected their scent lingering on your clothing."

"Have you contacted the authorities?" Douglas pressed.

Anna and Haggadah looked at each other. The witch replied, "No. We aren't certain if the two men tried to kill her or were simply exhuming her body."

"With your permission, I'll talk to a constable and inform him of the situation. Then, maybe the resurrectionists can be brought in for questioning." He paused for their reaction to his suggestion, but they remained silent. "We may be able to discover if someone else was involved."

Anna glanced at Haggadah before posing a question. "I'm the only one who can positively identify the men. How am I to do so if I must remain out of sight?"

Haggadah grinned. "There is another who can identify them."

Douglas and Anna simultaneously asked, "Who?"

"Barret."

Everyone looked at the dog, who tilted his head and perked his ears as he looked at each member at the table, secretly wishing for a tidbit of ham to eat.

~

"I swear she had the table set for three. She wasn't alone." Martin spoke his mind as they stopped outside of their favorite close and dressed his wound.

"Aye, I saw three glasses too. You and I both know that no one dares to set foot inside her house. Tales have reached my ears of the few who did, and they never came out and were never seen again. Maybe she was just entertaining the spirits, celebrating a pagan holiday, ye ken. Or maybe her witch friends were invisible to our eyes." John tied the bandage securely on his partner's arm.

Martin tucked the remedy in his coat pocket. He tilted his head to the side and displayed a sarcastic expression as he looked at John. "Entertaining spirits? Invisible to our eyes? Are you daft?"

"Well then, if you think she has guests in her house, let's go back, peek in the window, and watch to see who comes out."

"Fine." Martin agreed. The pair began walking back to the witch's cottage.

John huffed. "Oh, and you owe me your coin too."

~

There was a lull in the conversation, so Haggadah stood from the table. "Anna, why don't you walk Mr. MacEwan to the door." She began gathering the dishes from the table.

Douglas took his watch from his pocket, flipped open the gold protective case, and looked at the time. He looked across the table at Anna. "My, the hour is late. I do apologize for staying so long, but your company has been most pleasant." He rose from the table and pulled Anna's chair out for her to stand. "I thank you both for the lovely meal and good company. I'll stop by tomorrow with the details of what I discuss with the authorities." He looked at the old witch. "If that's agreeable with you, Haggadah?"

"Aye." She recorked the bottle of wine and left the room to return the unused portion to the cellar.

Alone with Douglas, Anna spoke from her heart. "Even though you don't have to involve yourself, thank you for helping us try to find who is responsible for my near death. As you can see, Haggadah has difficulty walking, and it would be too dangerous for me to do this on my own." She retrieved his overcoat and hat.

"We shall see what comes of it." He slipped on his coat and placed his top hat on his head. "Until tomorrow, then. Goodnight, Anna."

She opened the door and looked skyward. The night sky was cloudless and dotted with twinkling stars. Anna crossed her arms over her chest to shield herself from the frigid evening air.

Douglas stood before her and smiled. "I have truly enjoyed spending this evening with you."

She smiled, admitting to herself she equally enjoyed his company. "Until tomorrow. Goodnight."

"Goodnight." Douglas stepped into the darkness as Anna closed the door and hurried to help Haggadah with the dishes.

~

The heals of Douglas's shoes echoed throughout the nearly vacant street. Only a few coaches, with their oil lamps lighting the way, traversed the main road. He rounded the corner and headed toward the boardinghouse. Voices echoed from the open doorway of the pub. Capping off the night with a drink or two was tempting, but after enduring his recent illness, his body needed a good night's rest. Vowing to rise early the following day, Douglas planned to go straight to the authorities and bring Anna's case to their attention.

~

Martin and John remained silent as they approached the stone wall outlining the witch's yard and paused before the gate.

"Looks quiet." John could see flickering flames piercing through the loosely woven window curtain. "There's a lamp on, or maybe a lit candle on the table."

"Let's get a look inside and then get out of here." Martin looked up and down the street to ensure they were alone.

John opened the gate. The unoiled hinges squeaked.

~

After receiving a generous portion of ham to share with Nero, Barret lay before the warm fire, sound asleep. His ears twitched at the sound of the gate opening. He darted toward the door and began to growl.

Haggadah turned from the washtub upon hearing her canine's warning. "Anna, stay clear of the window. Whoever is outside may be able to see your silhouette through the curtain. Quickly now, duck beneath the sill and go to the side of the apothecary."

Anna set the dish she was drying in the cupboard, placed the damp towel on the working table, and did as her godmother instructed. She looked at Barret as she passed in front of him. The canine continued to stare at the door and growl.

Haggadah grinned as an evil trick came to mind. She kept the volume of her voice just above a whisper. "Barret has taken a dislike to whoever is on the other side of the door. Maybe your resurrectionists are snooping about. Since they scampered out of the kirkyard like scared rats, perhaps a little exaggerated drama would deter their superstitious minds from ever returning to my cottage again. So, let's conjure some evil spirits to send them on their way, shall we?"

Anna's eyebrows drew together in a scowl, uncertain of her godmother's intention.

The old witch grabbed a wooden spoon, a cast-iron frying pan, and handed them to Anna before opening the apothecary. She selected jars of finely shaved copper, dried catmint, a smudging stick of sage, and a jar of dried dill. Haggadah continued to scan the shelves. "Where is it, where is it?"

Anna peeked her head around the cabinet door. "What are you looking for, Haggadah?"

"Brimstone, ah, here it is." Placing the jars on the table, Haggadah added wood to the fire and put the cauldron on to boil. "Hopefully, it won't stink us out of the cottage. We may have to prop open the back door." Selecting various amounts from the jars, she added them to the cauldron and threw some copper powder and the smudging stick into the fire. She ladled some of the fragrant water onto the hot embers causing bluish-green steam and smoke to go up the chimney.

"Anna," she whispered to draw her attention, "hit the pan with the spoon, slow enough for me to dance."

Hidden beside the apothecary, Anna beat the pan like a drum and watched as her godmother began to chant and stomp her feet. Haggadah occasionally added a pinch of copper and drizzled the herbal water over the raging fire. She danced around the room, passed by Anna, and winked. "This ought to convince them to stay away."

"How?"

"I'm a witch, and I'm casting a spell tonight." She smiled and waved her fingers in the air.

Her silly antics caused Anna to chuckle.

She watched as Haggadah occasionally added ingredients to create the strange, unpleasant steam.

Barret had yet to move from the door. His ears were perked, tilting his head left and then right, listening.

Anna looked at the door. Even though it was bolted shut, she questioned if the aged wood could withstand someone kicking it in. She held her breath as she watched Barret lower his head and the hair along his spine stand on end.

~

Martin and John peered through the window as the sound of a strange drum began beating. They could see Haggadah's silhouette dancing through the curtain.

John wrinkled his nose as he detected the bizarre and odorous fragrance. He looked skyward and saw the strangely colored smoke coming from the chimney. "Looks like she is casting spells tonight."

Martin looked upward. "Conjuring something, I suppose. The smoke looks like it's glowing. She's evil, pure evil."

"Have you ever noticed how people get out of her way when she walks the streets?"

"Auch, I don't blame them. I don't know which one is more intimidating, her or her dog." Martin gingerly rubbed his bandaged arm.

"She appears to be alone." John covered his nose with his sleeve. "I don't want to smell that stink. No telling what it may do to us, ye ken."

Martin coughed. "Let's go." He hurried down the pathway with John trailing.

~

Haggadah continued to move her feet rhythmically and wave her arms about until Barret returned to his favorite spot on the floor. She signaled for Anna to stop. "I don't think they will bother us anymore tonight." Haggadah sat on the stool, winded, and breathing heavily. "My goodness, that was more work than walking uphill to the castle."

Chapter 17

Sleep deprived once again; Lachlan rose early, dressed, and grabbed his overcoat and hat as he left the house, slamming the front door. "The Edinburgh Lunatic Asylum," he shouted to the driver as he inserted his arms into the coat sleeves and put on his hat.

The money he had taken from the company safe was used to pay off his gambling debts. For once, Lachlan managed to win a few hands. He believed his luck was changing for the better.

Putting his mother into the mental hospital weighed heavily on his mind. The household staff had duties to attend to and little time to watch over her day and night. Nevertheless, he convinced himself he was doing what was best for her.

Once she was committed, declared mentally unstable, and established as a permanent resident of the asylum, power of attorney and the sole proprietorship of the Stewart Mercantile Shipping Company would default to him.

His chest puffed with pride like a strutting rooster. Lachlan lifted his chin as he looked out the window of the coach. He would do what must be done to benefit them both.

~

Feeling more like himself, Douglas rose early. He read the local paper the maid had tucked under his plate while he ate his breakfast. The lead article covered the scandal of Burke and Hare.

"Were they so desperate for money that they set aside their morals, if they ever had any, or did greed corrupt their conscious?" He muttered to himself as he folded the paper and tossed it onto the table.

A commotion on the street piqued his curiosity. Douglas picked up his cup of coffee, went to the window, and looked down at the horse pulling a farmer's cart. It reared and whinnied, apparently spooked by something or someone. The owner struggled to get the animal under control.

Douglas turned away from the window as thoughts of Anna and the previous evening flashed like photographs in his mind. Her vivid emerald eyes and scarlet locks of hair were easy to picture. He sipped his coffee as he thought of her kind nature. Why had she not left the city? It was dangerous for her to stay with her godmother. What if she was discovered and word reached the assailant? Would Douglas and the authorities be able to find the person responsible for putting her deep within the kirkyard's hallowed ground?

He drained his coffee cup and returned it to the tray. Douglas put on his coat, hat, and grabbed his walking stick as he left his room.

"Going out, sir," Fiona inquired as she stepped aside to allow him to pass in the hallway. The maid held a stack of clean sheets in her arms.

"Yes, for most of the day." He hailed a coach as he exited the boardinghouse. "The law enforcement headquarters," Douglas called to the driver as he climbed inside. He mentally rehearsed the details of his plan to bring in the resurrectionists for questioning. At the very least, he would bring Anna's case to their attention and hoped his proposal was accepted.

The coach slowed to a halt. Douglas leaned forward to view the stone building out the window. He stepped out of the coach as the driver held open the door.

"Shall I wait, sir?"

He scanned the headquarters building before looking at the driver. "Yes, but I don't know how long I may be inside."

"Quite all right, sir." The driver watched as his passenger entered the building.

Douglas scanned the perimeter of the room, where several people sat in wooden chairs. He approached the front desk and politely waited for two officers to finish their conversation.

One of the officers left, disappearing down a hallway. The other looked down at Douglas from the desk elevated on a dais. "May I be of assistance?"

He took a step forward. "Aye, Good morning, Constable."

"Sergeant." The officer corrected.

"My apologies, Sergeant. I would like to report a murder, but the victim is not dead."

The sergeant scowled. "I'm not following you, sir."

Douglas glanced at the curious onlookers in the room. He leaned toward the sergeant and lowered the volume of his voice. "Would it be possible to speak to someone privately?"

A sour expression appeared on the sergeant's face. He scanned the room to see the inquisitive stares, stood, and nodded his head to the side, indicating Douglas was to pass through the door to the left of the desk.

The sergeant met him on the other side of the portal and escorted him to a small room. He opened the door and motioned for Douglas to enter. "Make yourself comfortable."

The room contained an oak table with a chair on each side. Douglas sat in the chair facing the door.

"Someone will be with you in a moment." The sergeant closed the door leaving him alone in the room.

~

Lachlan followed the short and stocky secretary down the hallway to an office. He sat in a leather-covered chair before a large mahogany desk to wait. The door clicked shut as she left to inform the physician of his arrival. Lachlan took off his hat and fidgeted with its rim as he rotated it in his lap. When hearing the door open behind him, he clasped it in his left hand, inhaled deeply, and exhaled to calm his nerves.

"Hello, I'm Doctor Esmond." He presented his outstretched hand.

Lachlan stood. As expected, the physician was dressed in a white linen overcoat. He was tall and lean with gray hair, an indication of his years of experience. "Lachlan Stewart," he introduced himself as he shook the physician's hand.

The doctor sat in the chair behind his desk. "Please, sit." He clasped his hands together, placed them on the top of the desk, and stared at Lachlan with empathetic pale-blue eyes. "How may I help you, Mr. Stewart?"

Lachlan sat forward in the chair. "My mother, Evelyn, has been overcome with grief as of lately. She has lost six daughters over the years, my father, and most recently, my sister. Her incessant crying is more than I can bear. The staff and I have tried to help her cope with the loss. We resorted to giving her laudanum to calm her hysteria. In truth, she is more than the staff and I can handle. I hope she can be admitted and receive the proper care that is needed from you and your staff until she can come to terms with her loss."

The doctor sat back in his chair. Over the years, patients were admitted to the asylum for various reasons, primarily women. Some were accused of reading too much, others had become defiant of their husbands, or the more common case of husbands simply wanting to rid themselves of their wives because they had fallen in love with someone else. Grief was a genuine excuse, one that could drive a poor soul to madness.

"When would you like to admit your mother?"

"As soon as possible." Lachlan breathed a sigh of relief.

"Bring her tomorrow for a full assessment. Then, if we find her in need of our assistance, we will admit her."

Lachlan looked down at his hat in his lap. Uncertain if he could afford the care for his mother, he needed to know the asylum's fee. He looked at the physician. "And the cost?"

"Once she is evaluated, we will determine the monthly fee." Dr. Esmond rose and extended his hand. "Until tomorrow."

Lachlan stood, shook the physician's hand. "Aye, tomorrow, thank you." He put on his hat and left the office confident his mother would be deemed mad, be well cared for in the asylum, and no longer his responsibility – that is if he could afford it.

~

"If I understand you correctly, this woman, Anna, is alive, yet she was declared dead and buried. Two men, resurrectionists, dug her up." The chief inspector sat across from Douglas with his arms crossed over his chest, summarizing the information in detail.

"Yes, that's correct." Douglas nodded his head.

"And her life may still be in danger."

"Yes."

"So, you are assuming these two men are guilty of attempted murder?"

"That has yet to be determined."

Chief Inspector Roger McLeary sighed, uncertain if he believed the man's story. "What is the young lass's full name?"

Douglas stared blankly at the officer sitting across from him. "I don't know. She never told me, and I never asked."

"What does she look like?"

"Not yet twenty years old, vibrant red hair, green eyes, quite pretty actually."

"Anna Stewart?"

Douglas shrugged his shoulders, uncertain if McLeary had guessed the name correctly. "If she was declared dead and buried recently in Saint Cuthbert's kirkyard, then, yes."

The officer had been called to the close when Anna's body was discovered. He was aware of the rumors circulating about the young witch over the years. "I received several reports from witnesses indicating her grave had been tampered with and her body possibly exhumed. Many claimed she rose from the dead on her own accord. I'll pay the guard a visit and see what information he can add to the case. Backdoor deals and payoffs are usually involved when wrongdoings are afoot. Maybe Angus can tell us who the men are."

"Do you mind if I tag along?"

It was against protocol, but McLeary could not see the harm in Douglas joining him. "Come along then."

"I have a coach waiting." Douglas rose from his seat. "If the pair of resurrectionists are captured, Anna saw their faces and can identify them. Barret, Haggadah's dog, can identify them too."

The officer nodded, not wanting to know how the old witch and her dog were involved. At least, not yet anyway. He motioned for Douglas to exit the room before him.

They left the building. Officer McLeary shouted the destination to the driver as he and Douglas boarded the awaiting coach.

"The kirkyard is not far away," McLeary explained. "I assume you aren't a resident of Edinburgh?"

"Correct, I'm here on business."

"How do you know Miss Stewart?"

"Our paths crossed by coincidence." Douglas's answer was vague. For Anna's safety, he did not want to reveal where she was hiding.

"I assume you have only known her for a short time?"

"Yes."

McLeary spied the iron gates of the kirkyard. "Ah, here we are." The driver reined the horse to a stop, halting the coach. As anticipated, the gate was open for daytime visitors. Douglas and McLeary entered the hallowed ground and went directly to the tower.

"Unless the guard has slept during his graveyard shift, it may take a bit to wake him this time of day." McLeary pounded on the wooden door.

Douglas turned and scanned the numerous headstones. Many were old, blackened with age, and covered with green moss. Some were made simple, while others were tall, intricate, and a tribute to the person who laid peacefully in the ground. Most of the elaborate grave plots were covered by iron cages, a silent guard to watch over and protect against body snatchers. Douglas was overwhelmed by the loss of lives and sorrow. He imagined the cemetery was an intimidating place for those who were superstitious, especially at night when restless spirits may wander. Douglas tried to imagine the thoughts going through Anna's mind as she awoke amongst the dead. Was she afraid to find herself confined in the kirkyard with two men staring at her? He scanned for the overturned soil of her entrapment, curious where her plot was located.

McLeary pounded his fist on the door as he grew impatient. He was poised to strike again when the door creaked open, drawing Douglas's attention.

"What in God's name is so damn...." The guard dressed in a nightshirt and unfastened pants blinked his eyes to clear the sleep and focus on the uniform standing before him.

"If you don't mind, Angus, we need to ask you a few questions." McLeary waited for his request to register within the guard's mind.

Angus, half-awake, nodded as he stepped aside and allowed the men to enter. "What can I do for you, Roger?" He looked at Douglas and back at the officer.

"Not more than a week past, a young lass was dug up by two resurrectionists."

Angus's heartbeat increased. He did not want to be implicated in any crime.

McLeary continued. "Tell me what you know of that night?"

Angus sighed. He thought it would be best to cooperate and hoped by doing so, McLeary would overlook any infraction he may have committed. "A man came early in the evening and paid me to ignore a pair of men. He said they were coming to dig up the witch's body."

"Did you recognize the man?"

"No, never saw him. The brim of his black hat covered most of his face."

Douglas tapped his foot on the stone floor, unable to remain silent. "Do you know the men who dug up Anna?"

The guard looked at Douglas. "I don't know them, but I have seen them before. One is tall, the other short. They are two of the city's poor just trying to make a living." He looked at the chief inspector. "Ever since they quit the hangings of prisoners, the college needs bodies for the anatomy theater, usually two a day. Men like that don't hurt anyone. They just dig up the dead to make a little money to survive. Even though it upsets people, it isn't a crime since the dead don't belong to anyone."

"Do you believe they killed Anna?" Douglas stared at the guard, who looked at him.

"I don't know for sure, but I doubt it. Digging up the dead is hard work. If the men killed her, they would have taken her body directly to the college and collected the fee."

"Very well, Angus. Thank you for the information." McLeary turned to leave.

"If you don't mind, Angus, can you tell us where Anna was buried?" Douglas waited for the guard's reply.

"Back in the corner." He waved his thumb in the general direction. "It's unmarked."

"Thank you." Douglas heard the door close behind him as he headed toward the back corner of the kirkyard. McLeary trailed behind him. Isolated from other graves, he found the remnants of the unmarked grave and the pair of shovels, one standing upward in the mound of dirt. He stared down into the hole in the ground and saw the opening of her casket. "Can you imagine being trapped underground, buried alive, knowing you would never see the light of day again?"

"There may have been a bell for her to ring when she woke," McLeary suggested. "It is customary to bury one with the dead."

Douglas looked at the officer. "Even for one who is cursed?"

The officer shrugged his shoulder. "Most likely, no."

They stood silent for a moment, staring at the empty grave.

"You said she could identify the men." McLeary was developing a plan.

"Yes," Douglas confirmed as the pair began walking to the front gate.

"Where is she? I would like to interview her to get her side of the story." The chief inspector pressed.

"Her location may be under watch by those responsible. But, for now, she is safe, and I plan to keep her that way." Douglas exited through the kirkyard gate, climbed into the coach, and sat.

McLeary looked about the kirkyard before joining him. "I suggest we return to my office. Maybe between the two of us we can devise a plan to bring in the resurrectionists for questioning. Perhaps they can shed some light on who is responsible."

Douglas placed both of his hands on the bulbous brass handle as he set his walking stick on the coach floor between his knees. He nodded in agreement.

McLeary shouted their destination to the coach driver.

~

Shortly after midday, Barret greeted Douglas as he entered the cottage.

"Good day, ladies." He patted the dog on the shoulder.

Anna closed the door and courteously offered to take his coat. He declined with a shake of his head. "I'm not staying long."

"You seem rather upbeat." She grinned at his infectious smile.

"I just came from a meeting with Chief Inspector Roger McLeary."

Haggadah looked up from the herbs she was crumbling into a jar.

Anna's smile faded. "You met with a chief inspector?" She stared as he began pacing.

"Yes, we must get to the bottom of this, Anna, if you are to renew a life of normalcy."

Nero lifted his head from the bed, blinked away the sleepiness from his eyes as he watched Douglas walk back and forth across the room.

"What did you find out?" Haggadah stilled her hands, waiting for his reply.

"Very little. We discovered a man in a black hat paid the guard to look the other way while the resurrectionists removed Anna's body from the ground."

"Aye, Angus told me the same." Haggadah lifted a saucepan pouring warm sweet oil into the jar to cover the herbs.

Anna huffed. "A man in a black hat? That could be anyone. Most men in society own a beaver top hat. My brother owns one." She motioned toward Douglas. "Even you own one."

"I agree. It will be difficult to find the man who paid off the guard. However, with the help of Barret and McLeary, we have devised a plan to find the resurrectionists and interrogate them." Douglas nodded with a smile, conveying his confidence. "Anna, we will need your assistance as well."

She looked at her godmother for reassurance.

Sensing her goddaughter's apprehension, Haggadah grinned and nodded to indicate all would be well.

Douglas went on to explain. "Since the men were spotted close to the evening hour, McLeary suggested we may be able to find them about the same time and near the same location. I'll return later with a coach for you and Barret." He grinned. "Until then."

Chapter 18

Haggadah set another tincture on a shelf in the apothecary as the clip-clop of horse's hooves sounded from the street. She closed the cupboard doors, moved aside the curtain, and peeked out the front window to verify the coach had come to a halt outside of her cottage. A second coach pulled up behind it.

Douglas looked out the coach window at the graying sky. It would be dark soon. The driver opened the door. "I'll be just a moment, gentlemen."

"Aye," McLeary replied as he patiently waited with two other officers.

Haggadah opened the cottage door a mere crack and watched as Douglas stepped onto the pathway. "He's here, and it looks as if a half-dozen officers are with him too."

Anna clasped the cloak about her shoulders and raised the hood to cover her hair.

The old witch stroked Barret's head, placed her hand beneath his jaw, and tilted it, so his eyes stared into her aged orbs. "You know who they are, don't you? Find them and stay close to Anna once you do." She patted his head. "Good boy." She looked at Douglas as he stepped over the threshold. "Keep her safe."

"I promise I will." He looked at Anna. "Shall we be off?"

Her stomach fluttered as if there were butterflies inside it. Anna sighed and nodded her head before looking at her godmother for reassurance.

With the officers, Barret, and Douglas to keep her goddaughter safe, the risk was minimal and a necessary step toward capturing her murderer. "All will be well, my dear." Haggadah placed her hand on the small of Anna's back as a silent encouragement.

Douglas motioned for Anna to pass through the door before him.

Haggadah looked at Barret, who was still sitting next to her. "Barret, you too. Off you go." The obedient canine trotted out the door and entered the coach after

Douglas. "Do take care, all of you," the old witch whispered to herself before closing the door.

~

The three officers stared at Anna as she stepped into the coach. She kept her head bowed. The hood protectively shadowed her face.

"Sit next to the window. I'll stand unless you would like to sit on my lap." Douglas instructed as he stood outside the coach and waited.

Anna turned and looked at him to see if he was joking. He displayed a devilish grin on his face and winked. She looked heavenward, smirked, and shook her head slightly before sitting in the vacant seat.

"Here, sir, you may have my seat." The officer stood from his place next to Anna and crouched between the seats. He placed his hands on the edge of each bench to help keep his balance while traveling.

"Thank you." He sat next to Anna and across from McLeary, who stared at Barret as the canine jumped into the coach and sat protectively at the young woman's feet.

Douglas leaned toward Anna and whispered, "I do apologize for the crowded coach. McLeary wanted to ensure he had enough men to capture the suspects."

Anna nodded once and looked out the window as the coach jerked forward.

"I have directed the driver to take us to the butcher shop first; from there, we will travel up and down the Royal Mile," McLeary informed.

"Very well. We assume the men are homeless. Scanning each close would be in our favor as well." Douglas looked at McLeary, who nodded once.

The coach slowed as it approached the butcher shop. Anna looked at Barret, who gave no indication of danger. The pair of coaches traveled the main street in one direction and then the other. There was no sign of the men.

"Perhaps they have taken refuge for the night?" Douglas suggested.

"I doubt they can afford a room. Maybe the men are in a pub, having a pint or two?" The officer across from Anna suggested as he glanced out the window to determine their location and distance to the next pub.

Anna noticed a man climbing a ladder to light a streetlamp. "Do you think they are digging up another body in a kirkyard?"

"Too early. The men would be seen and reported to the authorities." McLeary reasoned.

"Unless the guard was paid off," Douglas added before looking at the chief inspector. He looked out the coach window. Nearly dark. "The gates to most kirkyards should be locked by now."

McLeary pounded the palm of his hand on the coach to get the driver's attention. "Saint Cuthbert's Kirkyard." The coach turned down a side street to circle the block and head in the opposite direction.

Anna stared at her house as they passed by it. She assumed her mother was doing what she always did this time of day - reading a book or playing the piano.

"Something of interest?" Douglas leaned forward and looked out the window to see a brass knocker on a doorway. He assumed the building was a residence.

Anna looked at him. "My house. Mum doesn't appear to be in her bedroom. I wonder how she is doing without me."

The driver reined the horse through several turns as it wove through the streets and stopped before the entrance of the kirkyard. Douglas and McLeary went to the gate. It was unlocked.

"Looks as if Angus is expecting visitors." The chief inspector opened the gate and entered. He turned to Douglas as he joined him. "Maybe the resurrectionists are returning."

Douglas scanned the headstones amongst the darkness. His ears were met with eerie silence.

McLeary pounded his fist on the wooden door of the tower. He could hear the muffled footsteps descending the stone stairway.

Angus opened the door and held up a lantern to illuminate his visitor's faces. "Roger, what can I do for you?" He glanced at Douglas.

"Are you expecting company tonight?"

"Resurrectionists? No."

"Why is the gate open?" McLeary pressed.

"An old man was visiting his wife's grave past dark. I was just on my way to lock the gate." Angus lifted the keyring and jingled the keys. "I'll walk you out."

The lock of the gate clicked behind McLeary and Douglas as they returned to the coach.

Douglas shook his head as he saw Anna's inquisitive stare. He leaned toward her after resuming his seat. "The guard isn't aware of any 'expected' visitors tonight."

"Do you think, as the officer suggested, they may be in a pub?"

"I doubt they would have the money to buy whisky. The men are probably bedded down in a close for the night." He admitted.

"Maybe if an officer took Barret into each close, he would find them." She petted the dog on his head.

Douglas looked at the dog sitting obediently at her feet. Barret alertly stared out the window of the door. "I have a feeling he won't leave your side, and it's too dangerous for you to leave the coach."

"Perhaps we should try another night?" She scanned the men who stared at her suggestion.

Barret rose on all fours. A growl, deep within him resonated a warning as the coach passed by a close. Everyone's attention was drawn to Barret.

McLeary pounded his fist on the side of the coach. "Halt!" He looked at the constable nearest to the door. "Let him out and get ready to follow."

The young officer stared at Barret's curled lips and white fangs. He hesitantly extended his hand to the door handle and rotated it. Barret charged forward, leaping out of the coach, and raced away. The officers filed out of both coaches and blocked the entrance of the close like a well-rehearsed military drill.

~

"Auch, I've had enough." John held the grease-stained paper before his friend containing a single wedge of potato. They had purchased the fish dinner with the last of their money. Sitting at the base of a tree in a close, they sighed with satisfaction at the end of their meal.

Martin belched before forcing the last chip into his mouth.

People parted to avoid the vicious beast. Their screams echoed from the entrance of the close.

Martin's eyes widened as he saw the familiar canine racing toward him. His heart hammered in his chest as he scrambled to his feet. "Oh, God, run!"

Unfortunately, there was nowhere to run in the dead-end close. Martin looked left, then right, then up. He scaled the limbs of the tree.

John wondered what had frightened his friend. "Martin?" He looked at the entrance and saw the dog bounding toward him. He tossed the greasy paper aside, shimmied up the trunk, and grasped the lowest branch.

Barret became air born as he leapt upward and clamped down onto John's ankle, sinking his teeth into the tender, sensitive skin of the resurrectionists.

"Ah! He's got me! Martin, he's got me!" John's grip on the branch gave way as he was pulled from the tree and landed on the ground with a thud.

Several of the officers ran into the close, with McLeary following.

"Get the dog off of him!" The chief inspector ordered. Two of the officers grabbed Barret's collar and patted his shoulder for a job well done.

John scrambled to his feet. "Keep that dog away from me!" He limped behind an officer to shield himself.

Barret barked as he tried to charge toward the tree, paws flailing in the air. The officers' arms nearly jerked from their shoulders as they held the canine at bay.

McLeary spotted the second man amongst the branches. "Come on down."

"Not until that demon animal is out of my sight." Martin insisted.

McLeary ordered the pair of officers to take Barret to the coach, another to apprehend John. With the dog removed from the close, Martin climbed down and was arrested.

"The two of you will be spending the night in custody." McLeary began.

"On what charges?" Martin spat.

"Body snatching."

"You'll have to prove it, ye ken."

McLeary nodded with a smirk and ordered his officers to take the suspects to the awaiting coach. His men performed their job well. He was pleased the resurrectionists were apprehended and followed them out of the close at a leisurely pace. McLeary stopped before the first coach and looked in the window to see Douglas clasping the dog's collar. The chief inspector opened the door. "My officers are going to make sure the alleged resurrectionists have a nice cozy jail cell to sleep in tonight. I expect to see the two of you in the morning, and hopefully, Miss Stewart, you can make a positive identification of these men as being the same you saw in the kirkyard."

Douglas leaned forward in his seat. "Can we drop you at headquarters?"

McLeary inhaled, patting his chest with the palms of his hands. "It's a nice night. I think I'll walk. Goodnight." He closed the coach door and told the driver to return them to the cottage.

Anna looked at Douglas. "Don't you think we should identify them tonight? What if Barret has the wrong men?"

"I saw a bandage on the wrist of one and the other was limping. They seemed out of breath too, as if they tried to run away."

Anna laughed. "Wouldn't you run if you saw Barret racing toward you?"

Douglas chuckled as he reached forward and petted the dog, whose tongue hung out one side of his mouth, and he seemed to be smiling.

Chapter 19

Douglas exited the boardinghouse. He looked at the cloudless sky, an unusual sight for an autumn morning in Edinburgh. Giving his desired destination to the driver, he stepped up into the awaiting coach. Once he was seated, the driver slapped the reins of the horse's rump, and it rolled forward.

~

Haggadah unlatched the front door as she heard the coach come to a stop. Barret wedged his nose into the slit of daylight near the doorframe, squeezed through the opening, trotted down the walkway, and wagged his tail as he greeted the frequent visitor.

Hello, Barret." Douglas patted the canine on the shoulder. He entered through the open doorway to see Anna put on her hooded cloak.

Anna exhaled. "I must admit, I'm feeling a little jittery. I've never had a reason to interact with our city's law enforcement before." Her hands quivered as she pulled the hood over her head and looked at Douglas and Haggadah for reassurance.

"Nonsense," the old witch began, "you did nothing wrong. You're the victim, and the law is on your side." She looked at the handsome gentleman for confirmation.

"Haggadah's right. Don't worry. I'll remain by your side at all times." He smiled and presented his bent arm.

Anna threaded her arm through his offered guidance and looked up into his hazel eyes staring down at her. She could not help but return his smile.

"Remember, I want to hear every detail." Haggadah walked the couple to the door. Barret stepped onto the pathway, tilted his head to one side, and watched them board the coach. "She'll be safe without you, Barret. Come." The obedient canine joined the old witch as she closed the door.

Anna watched as the cottage door closed. She looked at Douglas as he sat across from her, and spoke the burning question haunting her mind. "Do you think either of the men tried to kill me?"

Douglas stared into her green orbs, tinged with fear. He glanced down at her fidgeting fingers in her lap, leaned forward, and placed his hand upon hers, causing them to still. His voice was confident, reassuring. "They're resurrectionists, nothing more. They worked hard to dig you up, thankfully." He grinned. "Once you woke in the kirkyard, they could have killed you then, but instead, they ran. Perhaps they believe you are cursed, especially after rising from the dead." He smiled as he sat back in his seat, hoping he had calmed her anxiety.

Anna sighed as she scanned the handsome features of his face. She grinned, agreeing with his logic. She looked out the window as the coach turned onto the main street.

~

The constable turned the large iron key in the lock until the portal swung free. "Martin, John, let's go."

The pair sat on the cold stone floor. John elbowed his sleeping partner as he looked at the three officers in the hallway. "Are we being set free?" He rose to his feet and took a moment to stretch the kink in his neck, his aching back and legs. He limped forward.

"No, just being questioned." The constable swung the iron door open for them to pass.

Martin blinked his eyes several times, inhaled deeply, and scowled. He looked about the crowded cell, realized where he was, stood, and stared at the nearly overflowing bucket of odious excrement and urine. The pungent smell helped revive his senses. He watched as John walked out of the cell and followed.

The constable grabbed Martin's arm, pulled him through the door before slamming it shut, and turned the key to secure the remaining offenders inside.

The trio of officers escorted the resurrectionists to a small room and instructed them to sit in the chairs behind a narrow table. All three guards stood behind the suspect's chairs. John looked at Martin, his eyebrows raised in question, as not a word was spoken by anyone.

The door swung open, and a nicely dressed gentleman entered the room, followed by a woman in a black cloak and Chief Inspector McLeary. The woman turned toward the table and lowered her hood displaying her vibrant scarlet hair delicately pinned away from her face.

John's eyes widened as he stared into the emerald orbs of the woman. "Jesus, Mary, Joseph above, pray for us." He muttered as he rose from his seat and crossed himself with the sign of the crucifix. "The witch," he whispered to himself. An officer pushed him back down into his chair.

"Ah, you recognize me." Anna stepped forward. She placed the palms of her hands on the table. McLeary had advised her to play the part of a revengeful, evil woman. Anna squinted her eyes, remained unsmiling, and stared at the pair who had saved her life. "That's good. What I need from you, gentlemen, is information. Are you going to give it to me willingly, or do I have to revert to a spell that will loosen your tongue until it falls off?" She stared at each man, ensuring she had captured their full attention. "Why did you dig me up from the grave?"

John looked at Martin, who nodded once. "To sell your body to the college. The doc needs bodies to cut up, ye ken, and was going to pay us quite handsomely."

Anna raised her eyebrows as she stood erect. "To sell my body." She placed her fisted hands upon her hips.

Douglas rolled his lips inward to stop from smiling. He was impressed by her dramatic change in character. He watched Anna began to pace, embellishing the role she was playing to perfection.

"Well, dissecting a witch will invoke the vapors of Hell to curse those involved." She turned toward them quickly, her cape flailing.

Startled, John jerked, pulling away from the table to the back of his chair. Martin averted his eyes to avoid the witch's piercing evil orbs that seemed to glow with anger.

Anna continued. "My spirit separated from my body and watched as it was lowered into the ground. I wandered the kirkyard wishing to be rejoined with my body. Unfortunately, I was not given a bell. So, if I entered my body to resume my life, I would have been forever trapped beneath the ground to die a slow and agonizing death."

John leaned toward his partner. "There wasn't a bell, was there?"

Martin shook his head, confirming.

Anna leaned on the table once again. "What I want to know is, which one of you killed me?"

Martin looked the young witch dead in the eye. "We didn't kill you."

John motioned toward Anna. "Well, she's not dead."

He turned to his partner. "I can see that." He looked at Anna and continued. "We're resurrectionists, not murderers."

"If you didn't do it, then who did? I want to ensure they get their comeuppance, ye ken." She displayed her teeth in a silent growl and squinted her eyes.

The suspects glanced at each other. John divulged the truth. "A man in a black hat told us of your death. He wanted to make sure you wouldn't rise from the grave, so he told us to go and dig you up and sell your body to Knox."

"Who was he?" Anna pressed.

"Don't know," Martin added. "Couldn't see his face. It was shadowed by his hat."

"How do you know him?"

"He's a stranger, who sat at our table at the pub." Martin explained. "He wanted us to dig up your body, sell it, and tell him when the deed was done. He said he would pay us for doing the job but wasn't too pleased when we told him you came back to life."

"All that work for nothing," John added. "He paid for our drinks, though. That was nice of him." He nodded with a grin, displaying his missing front tooth.

Martin looked heavenward. "But we dug her up and got nothing for our work."

"Oh, aye. That wasn't fair." John scowled.

"Can you describe the man?" Anna persisted.

"Average height." Martin began.

"Well, taller than me," John added.

Martin shook his head. "Everyone is taller than you."

"Not children." John jutted out his chin.

Martin scowled at his friend, then continued. "We think he comes from money. After telling him the bad news, he disappeared through the door at the back of the pub. Never been back there. Heard there's gambling, though."

Their endless bantering had yet to reveal any pertinent information. Anna sighed. "Enough, so you don't know who he was, and you were cheated out of being paid."

"Aye, that's right," John confirmed, crossing his arms over his chest.

Anna turned toward McLeary, who took over the inquisition.

"We know at least one thing, gentlemen, you're guilty of body snatching. Back to the cell with you both then." He ordered as he opened the door to leave the small room.

John looked at his partner. "How can we be guilty if she's alive, Martin. There's no body, ye ken."

Anna began to follow McLeary but stopped in the doorway and looked back at the accused. "I'm grateful to you both, for exhuming my body from its underground prison. Thank you." She stepped into the hallway with Douglas closely behind her.

McLeary led the couple to another small room and closed the door. "Well, it's clear they recognized you, Miss Stewart."

"Aye, they were the men in the kirkyard."

"We still don't know who tried to kill you." Douglas removed his hat and ran his hand through his ebony curls, pulling them back away from his face.

McLeary sighed. "Miss Stewart, do you have any idea who may have wanted you dead?"

Anna chuckled. "Anyone. Everyone. I'm known as the cursed witch."

"Anyone with a smitten of intelligence would not believe so." Douglas placed the palm of his hand on the small of Anna's back as he went to her side. He looked at the detective. "The men did reveal a few clues."

"Aye, the man they met at the pub had on a black hat." McLeary glanced at Douglas's hat on the top of his head.

"I assume there are several pubs in Edinburgh." Douglas surmised.

"Aye, over a half-dozen."

"Then perhaps they can tell us which pub. The mysterious man may return to it for a few hands of poker," Douglas suggested.

With a nod, McLeary left the room to obtain the needed information from Martin and John.

Douglas smirked as he looked at Anna. "I must admit, you were quite intimidating. Are you certain you aren't a witch?" He smiled, raising his eyebrows up and down teasingly.

Anna chuckled as she held out her hand before her, still quivering. "I was shaking the entire time."

"Well, your performance was believable. You had me convinced. Well done."

"Thank you."

He sighed. "I've a feeling the man guilty of your attempted murder may be a frequent visitor at the pub. Since I'm unbeknownst in the city, I'll pay it a visit tonight and see what I can learn." Douglas looked into Anna's eyes, conveying his determination to solve her murder once and for all.

Chapter 20

Douglas escorted Anna to the cottage while the driver waited with the coach door open.

"Do be careful." She warned as she opened the front door. Barret pranced around the couple, demanding their attention.

"No need to worry." Douglas reached down and patted the dog's shoulder. "I'm only on a seek and find mission. If I win a few hands in poker, then I'll treat you to a fine meal in an establishment of your choice," he winked, "most likely in another city, Glasgow; perhaps."

Haggadah appeared in the doorway and looked at Douglas. "Not staying for a visit?"

"As much as I would enjoy being in the company of you lovely ladies for the day, I need to go to the harbor."

"Was your meeting a success?" Haggadah looked from Douglas to Anna for a reply.

"Anna can fill you in on the details. I must be on my way." Douglas touched the tip of his index finger to the brim of his hat bidding them a good day. He returned to the coach, sat, and raised his hand at the two women who waved from their doorway. With a slap of the reins on the horse's rump, the coach moved forward.

Douglas relaxed as he sat back in the seat. Between his illness and spending time with Anna and Haggadah, he had neglected to monitor the progress of his business. Mr. Townsend, his assistant, would have sent a message if he had encountered a problem that he could not handle. Since Douglas had not received any additional notes at the boardinghouse, he assumed all was well.

The coach rounded the corner and headed toward the waterfront. Douglas inhaled the salty air as his thoughts drifted to Anna. Even though he had known her for only a short time, he had become quite fond of her. It was a strange and new feeling, caring so deeply for someone. Maybe Anna was a witch after all, for she had unknowingly captured and possessed a piece of his heart.

Douglas needed to know his ships timeline before setting sail. He looked out the window at the ships' masts pointing upward like needles piercing the gray sky. The efficient crew of each vessel tended to its maintenance and loaded and unloaded cargo.

The coach rolled to a stop. Douglas dropped the fee into the driver's open palm, thanked him, and walked along the waterfront. Scanning the crowded harbor filled with men, women, and children, he muttered to himself. "Black hat." He watched them move up and down like bobbers on a fishing line. They were too numerous to count.

Douglas nearly bumped into a man, who crossed his pathway and entered a small office. Glancing above the door, he read 'Stewart Mercantile Shipping Company' on the sign. He thought it a coincidence that Anna had the same name.

Strolling along the waterfront, Douglas spotted his ships, three in all, and lifted his chin with pride. With a spring in his step, he scanned the deck for the captain as he made his way up the gangplank.

Captain Williams turned away from a crewman and saw Douglas. "Welcome aboard, Mr. MacEwan." The captain extended his hand toward the young entrepreneur. His gray eyes still had a sparkle to them even though his weathered face from years at sea was tanned and wrinkled like a raisin. His brown hair, dusted with gray, peeked out from beneath his hat. Clean-shaven, his uniform with its brass buttons looked neatly pressed, a reflection of the tight ship he ran under his command.

Clasping the captain's hand, Douglas gave it a good squeeze. "Good afternoon, Captain Williams. Is she close to shoving off?"

"Mr. Townsend says she's fully loaded, sir. Upon your order, we can leave port to open the slip for an awaiting ship and wait in the bay for the other two to finish loading."

"Captain Williams is correct."

Douglas turned to see Mr. Townsend standing behind him. Old enough to be his father, the gray-haired assistant with his leather ledger in hand looked up at Douglas with kind blue eyes as if awaiting his instructions.

"Mr. Townsend, how are you on this fine afternoon?" Douglas leaned on his walking stick and smiled.

The assistant tilted his head, mystified by Douglas's cheeriness and the twinkle in his eyes. "I can only surmise your good mood is the result of a special woman who has finally melted the icy exterior of your heart." He jested.

Douglas laughed, tilting his face skyward. "Perceptive as usual, Mr. Townsend." He wished to divulge nothing more on the subject. "Captain Williams tells me this ship is loaded."

"It is, with the remaining two ships scheduled to be fully loaded with in the next three days at most."

"Very well. If necessary, you know where to reach me."

"Aye, I do." Mr. Townsend nodded before turning away and walking down the gangplank.

Douglas turned back to the captain. "If there is another ship waiting to pull into a slip, then take her into the bay. Otherwise, have her remain in place until all three ships are ready to sail."

"Aye, sir."

Douglas spent the remainder of the day reviewing paperwork with Mr. Townsend and visiting with the captains of the remaining two ships. As the sun set below the horizon, he strolled along the waterfront and climbed into an awaiting coach.

His stomach grumbled as he checked the time on his pocket watch. Douglas touched his overcoat to ensure his wallet was in the inside pocket of his jacket. A meal and dram of whisky while observing the establishment's clientele would set him up nicely before pushing in on a few hands of poker.

The driver pulled the reins, stopping the coach before the White Hart Inn.

Douglas scanned the exterior of the building. The silhouettes of patrons sitting at tables with a single candle illuminating their faces resembled ghostly figures through the paned windows. Douglas exited the coach and paid the driver. He inhaled deeply to calm his nerves and stared at the elaborate entrance. The front door was embellished with thistle carvings on each side of its frame. He glanced overhead at the white stag staring down at him with its gilded golden eyes that seemed to glow. Stepping through the doorway, he stood a moment to allow his eyes to adjust to the dark interior. Every table was occupied. Spying an empty stool at the bar, Douglas sat.

"Sir, what will you have tonight?" The burly bartender wiped the polished oak counter with a damp rag as he stared at the unfamiliar face.

"Whisky and the evening meal."

"Haggis, neeps, tatties, and a side of bread with butter." The bartender raised his eyebrows, confirming the menu agreed with his patron.

"Aye, thank you." Douglas looked over his shoulder to see a mixed crowd of gentlemen of wealth and those without. The wealthy were easy to spot. They proudly donned black beaver top hats. He heard something slide the length of the counter, turned, and picked up the glass of whisky. Sipping the amber liquid, he turned in his seat, leaned his elbow on the bar, and observed the patrons. A few disappeared through a doorway at the rear of the room.

He signaled the bartender for another drink. When the half-full glass was placed before him, he ventured a question. "Can anyone join the card game?" He tilted his head toward the door and nodded once.

The bartender scrutinized Douglas's gentleman attire and assumed he possessed enough wealth for several hands of poker. "As long as you pay me for your drinks and meal before you leave your seat."

A woman brought the plate of food from the kitchen and placed it before Douglas. She handed him a cloth napkin and silverware. He nodded his appreciation, spread the napkin on his lap, and cut into the haggis.

Douglas found the meal well prepared and surprisingly flavorful. He kept a watchful eye on the comings and goings of the poker room.

A man to his left lit a cigar and blew a plume of smoke into the air. "Not from around here, are you?"

Douglas preferred not to socialize. "No." He placed his fork and knife on his empty plate and ate the last bite of bread. He turned his back to the nosy stranger and watched as two men passed through the door to join the card game.

"Do you need another dram?" The bartender waited for a reply.

Douglas took the napkin from his lap, wiped his mouth, and set it on the plate. He emptied the last of the whisky from his glass. "Yes, then I believe I'll try my luck."

The bartender removed his plate and empty glass and set another dram of whisky before him.

Douglas read the white price list on the slate hanging on the wall, withdrew his money, and placed the correct amount on the bar. Taking his drink with him, he went to the door and knocked. The small panel opened. The pair of eyes looked at the bartender. Douglas turned to see the burly man behind the counter nod once before the window closed and the door opened, allowing him entry.

As expected, several scantily dressed women of the night roamed the smoke-filled room. There were two vacant chairs at a round table where several men were playing a game of poker. He removed his overcoat and hat. A young woman came forward and hung them amongst the many others on the wall. Douglas stood and watched the current hand be played out. One of the women caressed his bicep and leaned toward him.

"Can I get you anything?" She pressed her nearly exposed breasts against his arm. "Anything at all?"

Douglas glanced down at the round mounds exposed above her bodice. He lifted his glass to his mouth and took a sip. "I'll let you know." She smiled and winked before moving onto another gentleman.

He sat in one of the empty chairs as the game finished. Several of the men nodded a silent greeting. The dealer clenched his cigar between his teeth and announced the amount of the ante and game.

~

Lachlan knocked on the door at the rear of the pub and waited. The panel slid open and closed quickly as the pair of eyes recognized the regular gambler and allowed him entry.

Kenzie anticipated the somewhat foolish young man's arrival. Lachlan liked to impress the others by being quite generous with his money. He spent it without a care. She was more than happy to receive whatever he was willing to give her.

Kenzie ran her hand up Lachlan's chest and snaked it around his neck as she snuggled against him. Her brown eyes, outlined with charcoal, stared at his face as she removed his hat from his head. She leaned toward his ear and whispered. "I'm glad you are here. Let me take your coat too." Kenzie helped him disrobe and hung both items up as he sat in the last available seat at the table.

The cards were shuffled for the next hand. Lachlan put his ante on the pile of money in the center of the table and sat in the vacant chair.

Anticipating her favorite customer's need, Kenzie placed a glass of his usual drink before him while pressing her nearly bare breast against his shoulder. Lachlan drank the whisky in one gulp and raised his glass in her direction, signaling for another.

Lachlan ignored the loose woman and focused on the cards in his hand. He was determined to have a profitable night.

Douglas estimated the newcomer was quite young and from a wealthy family. He observed each man as they bet. Some were conservative, others thoughtful in weighing the odds of the cards in their hands, and others simply careless. The young man grew increasingly intoxicated and took unreasonable risks as the evening progressed. Douglas, often distracted from the game, eavesdropped on as many conversations as possible, hoping to determine if 'the man in the black hat' was present. Unfortunately, nothing came of his effort except a few lost hands.

Douglas yawned. The hour was late. Only three men remained at the table. He was ready to retire for the evening and it was his turn to deal. "This is the last hand for me, gentlemen. Shall we go all in and call it a night?"

The elderly man nodded his consent. Lachlan looked down at his meager pile of money before him and then at the stacks across the table. "If I lose, the only way I can match the winning hand is to pay you afterward."

The elderly man nodded once.

Douglas pursed his lips. "Very well." He shuffled the cards and offered the deck to Lachlan to cut. Instead, the young man simply tapped his knuckles on the top card.

Five cards were dealt to each player. Lachlan requested three and discarded the trio of unwanted cards. The other player asked for one card.

Douglas discarded two from his hand and took their replacements from the top of the deck before setting the remaining cards on the table. He fanned out the cards in his hand and rearranged them in ascending order. "Call."

Lachlan sighed as he laid down his hand. "Ace high."

The elderly man threw his cards on the table, face down. "Got me beat." He stood and watched Douglas lay his hand down, face up.

"Three queens."

"Shite!" Lachlan stared at the winning hand, wondering how luck had evaded him once again. He tilted his glass up, drinking the last drop of whisky before slamming the vessel to the table. "Let's hope there's a coach. Otherwise, it's going to be a long walk to get what I owe you." He pushed away from the table, stood, and teetered to the side. Kenzie pushed against his shoulder to keep Lachlan upright.

Douglas put on his overcoat and hat before retrieving the remaining garments from a hook on the wall. He handed them to Kenzie, who helped Lachlan dress, turn him around, and guided him through the open door.

As the pair exited the pub, Douglas saw a nicely dressed couple emerge from a coach across the street. He assumed they were returning from a late dinner party. Douglas waved his hand, drawing the driver's attention as he led Lachlan to the coach and pushed him inside.

"The waterfront," Lachlan mumbled. Douglas told the driver their desired destination.

"The waterfront?" Douglas sat across from Lachlan, who looked at him with his eyelids nearly closed and his hat askew on his head. The coach jerked forward.

"Aye, my family or I should say, I own a mercantile company." Lachlan admitted.

"I'm in the mercantile business as well. What is the name of your company? Perhaps I'm familiar with it." Douglas encouraged.

"The Stewart Mercantile Shipping Company." Lachlan proudly stated as he sat up from his slouched position on the seat and puffed up his chest like a strutting rooster. "Lachlan Stewart, sole proprietor."

Douglas stared at the young man. "I saw your office on the waterfront. You say you are the sole proprietor?"

Lachlan stared at the floor of the coach. "I am now. Father died a few years ago, leaving the responsibility of the company in our hands. The three of us had equal shares."

"The three of you?"

"Aye, my sister, my mum, and me." He sighed, blinking his eyes lethargically. "It's been only a week, maybe two, since my sister passed away. The grief was too much for Mum." He spoke as if talking to himself. "I had to place her in an asylum. She gave me no other choice." His bloodshot eyes stared at Douglas. "Once she was committed, I obtained the power of attorney and full control of the company."

"I'm sorry to hear of the tragedy your family has endured."

Lachlan's eyebrows drew together, nearly becoming one as anger crept into his slurred words. "More like a curse. Many believed my sister was a witch." He sneered, curling his upper lip.

Douglas's full attention was on the drunk man, who may have revealed more than his sober conscious would have. "If you don't mind me asking, what was your sister's name?"

Lachlan expelled his breath. "Anna." He looked away, averting his blurred vision to the stone buildings as they passed by the coach window like moving photographs.

Douglas stared at the profile of Anna's brother. "Do you believe she was a witch?"

Lachlan looked back at Douglas. "Our family has experienced more than its fair share of bad luck. I see no other reasonable explanation other than she brought it upon us."

The coach came to a stop. Lachlan impatiently opened the door. The driver caught him as he nearly tumbled onto the cobblestone street and set him upright. He walked away without a word of thanks and grabbed an oil lamp from the front of the coach as he passed by it.

Douglas stepped down and looked at the driver. "Wait for us. We should only be a few moments."

"Aye, sir."

The ocean waves rhythmically lapped against the seawall. Oil lampposts dotted the length of the waterfront, helping to light their way.

Douglas pulled the lapels of his overcoat closer to his neck to protect it from the dampness of the brisk evening air. He followed Lachlan, who seemed unaffected, or perhaps he was too intoxicated to notice the chill. Douglas watched as Anna's brother stumbled on an uneven cobble and sidestepped until he was able to regain his balance. He took the lamp from Lachlan's hand as they walked along the waterfront.

Lachlan stopped and tilted his head back to look at the swaying sign overhead. "Here we are." He reached into his pocket and withdrew a keyring with several keys.

Douglas held the lantern aloft to illuminate the keyhole. He listened to the scratching of metal against metal as Lachlan struggled to insert the key into the lock. Wanting to get the matter settled quickly and be on his way to the boardinghouse, Douglas impatiently reached for Lachlan's hand. "Here, let me try."

Lachlan handed him the key, leaned against the door for support, and waited. His heavy eyelids closed.

Douglas inserted the key. It rotated easily and clicked. He turned the doorknob and watched as the weight of Lachlan's body forced the door to swing open. Anna's brother fell into the small office landing with a thud on the wooden floor. Sighing in frustration, Douglas stepped into the office and looked at the man groaning and withering in pain. He placed the lamp on the desk. "Here, let's get you upright." Douglas reached to help Lachlan, but his hands were pushed away.

"I can do it myself." Lachlan crawled to his father's desk. He grasped the chair and used it to pull himself up and stand. "Let me get your money so we can get out of here. I hate everything to do with this place." He went to the safe. "Light. I need to see what I'm doing."

Douglas held the lamp near Lachlan as he fidgeted with the combination on the safe. Much to his surprise, the drunkard was able to open it on his first attempt. "You must have done this a few times before."

"Nearly every day," Lachlan admitted as he reached into the safe. He walked his fingers over its interior, took the lamp from Douglas, and shined the light within the darkness of the iron cube. "Where's the money?"

Curious, Douglas's eyebrows raised. He bent over the squatted man's shoulders and peered inside the safe. It was indeed empty.

"I don't understand. We just got a shipment in. There should be cash in the safe." He stood and looked at Douglas. "Corbin, the accountant told me the business was doing poorly. I guess he was right."

"Your accountant? Where are the account books?"

Lachlan pointed to the accountant's desk as he leaned against the wall, sunk to the floor, and passed out.

Douglas retrieved the lamp from the floor, went to the accountant's desk, and opened several drawers until he discovered the ledger. Lifting it from the drawer, he noticed a second ledger. Uncertain which ledger had the most recent entries, he retrieved it as well. He placed both account books side by side on the desk, opened them to the most current entry, and brought the lamp near the pages. The balance in one ledger indicated the shipping company was operating with a nearly negative balance. An entry had been made showing a payment to the Edinburgh Lunatic Asylum. The second ledger showed the identical payment was made to the asylum, but there was a substantial capital balance in the account. He looked at Anna's brother, pathetic and crumbled on the floor. Douglas assumed Lachlan was unaware of the two account books. Had the 'sole proprietor' ever reviewed the financial status of the company with his accountant? Was the accountant skimming funds from the company? Was he protectively stopping Lachlan from spending all the company funds?

Douglas returned the ledgers as he found them, closed the safe, and decided it would be best for Anna's brother to remain in the office for the night. He stirred the ashen embers in the small fireplace, added a few logs to keep him warm, and looked at the pitiful young man on the floor before closing the door, locking it, and returning to the coach with the lamp and office keys in hand.

"Is the other gentleman coming?" The driver opened the door of the coach and accepted the lamp from Douglas.

"No, he has decided to remain in the office." Douglas entered and sat. He asked the driver to take him to the boardinghouse. Had he obtained a clearer perspective on Anna's predicament? Was she aware of the two ledgers? He would share his discovery with her and Haggadah in the morning. Maybe between the three of them, they could come up with a reasonable explanation.

Chapter 21

Lachlan's body shook, pulling him from his drunken slumber. He refused to open his eyes.

"Sir, what are you doing here?"

The accountant's voice rang in Lachlan's ears like a church bell calling its parishioners to service. He ignored the disturbance and tried to return to sleep. Unfortunately, the amplified sound of the rain falling on the roof resonated like the beating of drums of a Highland military band. He cringed. Lachlan was cold, thirsty, and extremely hung over.

His body shook again, forcing him to open one eye a mere crack and look at the accountant's face within inches of his. "What?" He pulled his body up from its slouched position against the wall, and rubbed his arms, warming them from the chill in the room.

Corbin wrinkled his nose as he caught a whiff of Lachlan's whisky breath. He stood and looked down at the pitiful young man. "Good god, another one of your wild evenings of drinking and gambling. How much did you lose this time?" He waved his hand across his face trying to dissipate the retched smell.

Lachlan scanned the room. "How the hell did I get here?"

Corbin went to the fireplace and added several logs. "I imagine you walked or took a coach." There was little emotion in the tone of his voice as he turned to watch Lachlan struggle to his feet and lower his body in his chair. Corbin sat at his desk, took out the ledger from the drawer, and turned his chair to stare at Lachlan. "If you don't mind me saying, your drinking and gambling is getting out of hand. If that is your priority in life, why don't you sell the shipping company to someone who will care for it more than you do."

"You told me it isn't worth anything?"

"The company has assets, ye ken. There are several ships, this office."

"Sell each ship one by one?"

"No, it would be better to sell the company as a whole." Corbin sighed. "The repetitive withdrawals to cover your 'entertainment' has drained the coffers dry."

Lachlan stared out the window at a ship, and assumed it was one he owned. His accountant was right. His gambling debts were beginning to accumulate. The vague memory of a gentleman sitting across the table from him last night came to mind. Did he owe him money too? He checked his pockets for a written IOU but found none. Who was the man? His name? He shrugged his shoulder, relieved he had no way of tracking the man down to pay his debt, whatever it may be. Corbin's garbled comment interrupted his foggy thoughts. "What?"

"I said you must also pay for the care for your mum in the asylum too. You signed a letter of commitment stating payments would be made weekly. This week's payment is due."

~

Douglas shielded his face from the rain as he hurried up the flagstone walkway to Haggadah's cottage. As expected, the old witch opened the door.

"Mr. MacEwan, it is good to see you this morning. Please, come inside and sit by the fire to take the chill away from your bones."

Barret lay in his usual spot on the floor and wagged his tail.

"Barret, you aren't going to come and greet me?" Douglas removed his hat and coat.

"It's raining. He won't move from his spot unless there is a clap of thunder, and then he will dive under my bed." Haggadah explained as she grinned.

"Oh, poor dog. You're afraid of storms." Douglas consoled as he placed his damp clothing in the old witch's outstretched hands. "Thank you, Haggadah." He went to Barret and gave the canine a good pat down along his neck and body and seated himself on the bench before the fire. "Good morning, Anna."

Anna stirred a skillet of eggs and flipped slices of ham in another before looking at the handsome gentleman. "Good morning. Haggadah assumed you would be joining us for breakfast."

Douglas left his room before Fiona arrived with his morning meal. He scowled at the table set for three and wondered how the old witch knew he had not eaten. "Only if you have enough." He inhaled. "It smells delicious."

Haggadah retrieve a cutting board, bread, butter, and a sharp knife.

"Here," Douglas stood, "allow me." He relieved her of the items and placed them on the table.

Once the meal was served and everyone seated, Douglas could no longer contain the news he wished to share. "I met Lachlan last night."

Anna ate a forkful of egg, stopped chewing, and stared at him from across the table. Once she regained her wits, she picked up the slice of bread from her plate and smothered it with a generous portion of butter. "Where?"

"At the pub where the resurrectionists said I may find their contact. I joined the gambling table in the back room. Lachlan arrived shortly afterward. He lost a substantial amount on the last hand and insisted on paying his debt promptly. We took a coach to the Stewart Mercantile Shipping Company where he tried to withdraw the funds from the safe, but it was empty."

Anna scowled. "Empty? Father's business has always done well." She looked at Haggadah, who remained silent.

"Your brother was confused as well. He said the accountant told him the company has been doing very poorly lately. After discovering the empty safe, Lachlan told me to take the ledger from the accountant's drawer. Unfortunately, he passed out before he could examine it. In his condition, I doubt he could have read the entries." He paused as he looked at Haggadah. "When I removed the ledger, there was a second beneath it. Uncertain which one was the most recent, I examined both. One had a sizable cash balance while the other had the opposite, justifying the empty safe. Also, there was a payment to the Edinburgh Lunatic Asylum."

"The lunatic asylum? I don't understand." Anna looked at Haggadah and back at Douglas.

"Lachlan said he admitted your mum to the asylum because she was too overcome with grief from the loss of your father, your sisters, and you."

Anna's mouth fell agape. "Mum? My mum is in the lunatic asylum? Overcome with grief?"

Haggadah finally spoke. "Perhaps I should pay Evelyn a visit."

Anna and Douglas looked at the old witch.

She cut a small piece of ham and fed it to Barret and Nero, seated at the base of her chair. "Anna can't go. She's dead. Mr. MacEwan, why would you, a stranger, be concerned about someone you don't know. It's only logical that I'm the one to inquire about her mental health."

Anna sighed as she stared at Haggadah.

Douglas agreed with a nod of his head. "I'll employ a coach to take you there." He looked at the dog. "And Barret too." He picked up the teapot. "More tea, anyone?"

~

Much of the previous evening remained an enigma. Lachlan's throbbing headache was amplified by the rhythmic horse's hooves as the coach traveled to his house. He had to borrow money from Corbin to pay the driver. Lachlan treaded lightly on each step as he ascended the stairs to the front door. Pausing before the doorway, he reached into his pocket for his keys, but they were not there. "Shite!" He knocked, placed his hand on the doorframe for support, and waited for Helen to answer.

The maid opened the door and froze, unaware Lachlan had not come home during the night. "Mr. Stewart, good morning." Helen curtsied quickly, so as not to appear impertinent.

"If you say so." He took off his coat and hat, shoved them at the maid, and promptly climbed the stairs to retreat to the solitude of his bedroom.

~

Corbin jotted down a note, sealed it with wax, and tucked it in the inside pocket of his overcoat. He knew a ship was scheduled to arrive later in the afternoon, so he locked the office door and flagged down a coach.

~

"Are you certain you don't want either of us to go with you?" Anna handed Haggadah her cane.

"Dinna fash. I'll be fine." She pursed her lips and whistled. Barret rose and went to her side.

Douglas presented his bent arm as Anna opened the front door.

Haggadah took advantage of his kind gesture and threaded her arm within his as they stepped into the misting rain that was so fine it resembled fog. Douglas helped the old witch into the awaiting coach. Barret climbed inside and sat on the floor at her feet as the driver shut the door.

"Take her to the Edinburgh Lunatic Asylum, walk her to and from the door, and return once she has completed her visit." Douglas ordered the driver as he gave him the money to cover the cost of the round trip.

"Thank you, sir." With a slap of the reins on the horse's rump, the coach's wheels rolled forward.

Douglas looked at Anna's askance face as he entered the cottage and closed the door.

"Do you think the asylum will allow Haggadah to see my mum?"

"With Haggadah's reputation and Barret by her side, I dare them not to," Douglas smirked.

~

Haggadah examined the interior of the coach. She tried to recall the last time she had ridden in one. The old witch assumed it was many years ago.

The driver took her directly to the asylum, a facility that opened a few years ago. The coach turned into the main entrance. As it rounded the bend in the driveway, Haggadah stared at the intimidating three-story stone building. A cold chill ran up her spine as she perceived the patients' emotions housed within its walls. Many were mentally unstable, depressed, and waiting at death's door with no option of ever being released. It was a medical prison. However, she was confident Evelyn was receiving the best care, probably at a high cost to Lachlan.

The coach pulled up to the entrance and stopped before the stairs. Haggadah accepted the driver's hand, assisting her out of the coach, with Barret following closely behind. They paused at the base of a half-dozen stairs leading to the front double doors.

"I'll guide you up," the driver insisted.

Haggadah looked at the climb and sighed. "I would be most grateful. Thank you."

They ascended the steps one at a time, with Haggadah momentarily resting on her cane at each elevation. The driver held open the door for the old witch to enter the facility.

Haggadah stepped into the main entrance of the building and paused, uncertain which direction she should go. The scent of sterile disinfectant lingered in the air. The old witch wrinkled her nose. She watched several nurses walk past her. They were dressed in light blue blouses with white collars covering most of their neck. Their ankle-length overdresses resembled white aprons with a pair of pockets, and their hair neatly pinned and topped with a white hat resembling a doily. One of the nurses sidestepped to keep her distance from Barret. A nurse walking in the opposite direction carried a small tray with several medicine bottles on it. She nodded politely as she passed.

"May I help you?" A rather stout woman stood in a doorway across from Haggadah.

"Yes, I'm here to visit a patient, Mrs. Evelyn Stewart."

The woman with a pruned mouth looked down at Barret. "Dogs aren't allowed in this facility."

Haggadah looked at her canine companion. "Did you hear that, Barret? She said you aren't supposed to be in here."

Barret growled, displaying his sharp white teeth, and lowered his head as he stared at the woman. The canine took a step forward.

The woman retreated a step, quickly realizing who the old woman and her canine companion were.

Haggadah posed an idle threat. "If you try to have Barret removed from my side, he will swiftly yank your right arm from your shoulder. Since you are holding a pen in your right hand, it would be most unfortunate to have to write with your left the remainder of your life, ye ken. I promise you, Barret will remain by my side at all times, that is, unless I'm threatened." Haggadah petted the dog's head as he calmed.

The woman ignored the comment. "Who are you here to see?"

"Mrs. Evelyn Stewart."

"The doctors will never allow you to enter the room she is in, especially not with the dog."

"That's quite all right. I would just like to observe Mrs. Stewart for a few moments." Haggadah smiled, displaying her crooked teeth.

"Let me verify which room she's in. One moment." The woman disappeared into the office as the shouting of obscenities echoed from down the hallway. The patient, whoever she was, cursed like a sailor.

Haggadah looked in the direction of the echoed scream. "Poor tortured soul. May she find peace." She watched the receptionist step behind her desk, turn the pages in a book, trace her finger down one, and return to the hallway.

The woman lifted her nose in the air. "Follow me."

They walked through several hallways, twisting left and right like a snake. Benches were sparsely placed along the walls for roaming patients to sit and rest. Haggadah and Barret were led to a set of double wooden doors with a square glass window used to observe the patients.

"You may watch your friend from here." She looked down at Barret. "No matter the consequence, you will be immediately escorted from the building if you enter the room."

Haggadah stared at the woman's back as she turned and disappeared around the corner. She shook her head. "My, my, my, Barret. So rude."

The glass window was nearly a half-head above Haggadah's line of vision. More than likely, it was an accommodation made for the tall male doctors. She searched the hallway but thought it impossible to stand on a chair or bench to observe Evelyn.

"Do you need something?"

Haggadah turned to see a nurse paused in the doorway as she exited the room.

"I'm here to observe a friend of mine, but I'm too crippled with age to see through the window, ye ken."

The nurse grinned. "I have just the thing." She disappeared back into the room and moments later reappeared carrying a rectangular wooden box. "We have a doctor who is rather short in stature. I don't think he will mind if you borrow this." She placed it on the floor before the door. "Which patient are you here to observe?"

"Mrs. Evelyn Stewart."

"Ah, aye. A pleasant lady. She is on the left, third bed back."

"Thank you. You have been most kind."

The nurse nodded before disappearing down the hall.

With the aid of her cane, Haggadah stepped onto the box. Peering through the window, the large room contained two rows of beds along opposite walls. In the center of the room was a beautiful display of flowers on a table. "They must have a conservatory on the property to have flowers this time of year." Several nurses were attending patients. She saw two doctors dressed in their white attire. Some of the patients were sleeping. Others rocked back and forth against their headboards. The room was bright and airy, with several windows along the walls adding natural light.

Haggadah looked at the row of beds on the left and counted back three. Evelyn was sitting up, propped by several pillows, with a book in her lap, and appeared to have a visitor. Haggadah did not know the gentleman who was talking to Evelyn.

Something seemed amiss. Haggadah perceived Evelyn's calmness, complacent in the environment. It was most unexpected. Where was her grief? Her crying? Her shouting or muttering to herself? Was she sedated?

"What is the meaning of this?"

Haggadah looked over her shoulder before carefully turning around to see a man standing at the end of the hallway. He was tall with glasses on the bridge of his nose and a thick mustache. Since he was wearing a white jacket over his dress shirt and black belted pants, she assumed he was a doctor. "I'm here to observe a dear friend," Haggadah stated as he approached her.

"Is that so. Well, we don't allow dogs in the facility."

"Barret is my protector and remains by my side. If you touch me, he will attack you."

"Then I suggest you leave on your own accord, ye ken. Immediately."

"Not until I ensure my friend's health is improving and she is well cared for."

The doctor approached Haggadah. Barret curled his upper lip and began to growl, forcing the physician to take a step backward. "I'm not allowed to give you that information. I must respect our policy of patient confidentiality."

"I'm not leaving until I'm assured my friend is well." Haggadah tilted her head to the side.

The doctor sighed. "Who is your friend?"

"Mrs. Evelyn Stewart."

"She came in quite upset, but since then has been doing well."

"I was able to watch her a few minutes through the window. She appears quite calm. Is she being given any medication?"

"No, there is no need. Perhaps Mrs. Stewart just needed to rest."

"Do you know when she will be released from your care?"

"Release? Mrs. Stewart is under no obligation to stay. She may leave anytime she wishes. We have given her a clean bill of health."

Haggadah stepped down from the wooden box. "Thank you, Doctor, for your time and information. I can see my friend is in good hands. I appreciate your patience. Good day." She turned and walked away, hoping to find her way through the maze of corridors to the exit and her awaiting coach.

Chapter 22

While Haggadah was away, Anna prepared a lovely tea with biscuits as midday drew near. Douglas brought up several topics throughout their conversation, wanting to learn more about her past, but much of what she divulged he already knew. They speculated on what Haggadah would discover at the asylum.

Nero jumped onto the table and sat. He listened to the chatter of their voices and turned his head back and forth as he watched them bite into their biscuits.

They looked at the front door as the sound of an approaching coach's wheels became silent.

Anna placed the partially eaten biscuit on her saucer next to her teacup and stood from her chair. She pulled the curtain aside and peered out the window to see the driver help Haggadah down from the coach. "She's back."

Nero stretched his paw toward the morsel on Anna's saucer, extended his claws to embed them in the treat, and pulled it toward him. He pushed it toward the edge of the table until it toppled over onto the floor and jumped down to devour his treat.

Douglas stood as he heard Barret scratch his toenails on the door. He opened the portal to allow the canine inside and looked at the driver as Haggadah entered. "Thank you for walking her to the door and taking great care of her."

As Douglas closed the door, Anna looked at Haggadah, eager to hear of her mother's condition. She helped her godmother removed her coat and hang it up. "Did you see Mum?"

"Let me catch my breath, child." The old witch went to the table and sat.

Anna retrieved another teacup and saucer, filled it with tea, and placed it before her godmother. She and Douglas sat, leaned forward, and waited for the old witch to begin her story.

Haggadah cupped her aged hands around the teacup and sipped the warm liquid as she gathered her thoughts. "The facility is quite nice. However, those within it, in my opinion, are either lunatics or committed under duress. I was not allowed to talk to Evelyn, especially since Barret was with me, but I watched her from a distance. The room she was in was spacious, with many patients lying in their assigned beds. Several doctors and at least a half-dozen nurses were in the room. Evelyn was sitting up in her bed, propped by several pillows, and a book in her lap. She had a visitor, a man I did not know. She appeared calm, quite at ease."

Anna looked from Haggadah to Douglas and back again. Her eyebrows raised in question as she picked up her teacup. "A visitor?" She sipped her tea. "I wonder who it was." She looked at her saucer, expecting to see her half-eaten biscuit, but it was gone. Feeling a tug on her skirt, she glanced at the floor and saw Nero extract his claws from her garment. The feline looked at her as he licked his lips and sat. Crumbs were scattered near his feet. "I see you have helped yourself to the remainder of my biscuit. Clever boy."

Haggadah continued. "Dogs aren't allowed in the facility, so I told the receptionist Barret would attack her if she tried to remove him from my side. He understood my cue and began to growl. Once she escorted me to the room where Evelyn was resting, I was confronted by a doctor. He took one look at Barret and explained the asylum's policy to me again. I told him I wasn't leaving until I could assure my friend was well. He went against the facility's patient confidentiality policy and told me your mother was distraught when she first arrived but quickly settled down and has been resting ever since. I asked when she could be released from the facility. He indicated she is well and is free to leave whenever she wishes.

"Mum appeared mentally stable?" Anna sat back in her chair.

"According to what the doctor revealed and what I witnessed with my own eyes, aye." Haggadah helped herself to two biscuits and placed one on her saucer as she bit into the second.

"Is she medicated?" Douglas helped himself to another biscuit.

Haggadah sipped her tea. "I assume they gave her something when she first arrived. The doctor didn't mention any medication. I perceived a feeling of safeness or perhaps security within her as if she is hiding from society."

Anna looked at Douglas. "Since Dad's death, she has become a recluse of sorts. Those who were her friends quit calling, except for Mr. Heywood. He is the accountant she employed, but he only visits to give an update on the status of the business."

"Friends support their friends. If they quit calling, then they were never truly her friends." Haggadah sighed before taking a sip of her tea. "Maybe Lachlan, with his drinking and gambling lifestyle, no longer wanted the responsibility of her grieving condition and put her in the asylum to get her out of his way."

"He did mention having power of attorney now that Anna is dead, and his mum is in the asylum." Douglas redirected the conversation. "Well, for now, she is safe and well cared for by the doctors and nurses." He sipped his tea. "Martin and John said they met with a man, the one who told them of your death." He looked across the table at Anna. "He was not pleased to hear you are still alive. Unfortunately, they did not see the man's face, but since he spoke to them, they could probably recognize his voice."

Haggadah paused in chewing. "Mr. MacEwan, what are you scheming?"

Anna sat forward in her chair.

"I could speak with McLeary and try to make arrangements for the resurrectionists to accompany me when I visit your brother," Douglas smirked.

"To get the money he owes you?" Anna added.

"Aye, and to return these?" Douglas held up the keys and jingled them. "But I think tonight, Anna, you and I should go to the office and get a good look at the two ledgers."

"Break into the office?" Anna scowled.

"My dear, you are part owner, and besides, we have the key." He smiled before wiping his mouth on a cloth napkin. "Until then, I'll go and talk with McLeary, propose my idea, and see if he is in agreement." He stood from the table. "Haggadah, your mission to the asylum was a success. Anna, thank you for the tea and the good company. I'll return later tonight for our spy mission." He raised his eyebrows up and down and displayed a silly grin on his face.

Anna chuckled and walked him to the door.

~

The resurrectionists were escorted into an empty courtroom by three constables and McLeary leading the way. They stopped before the magistrate's elevated bench.

The elderly judge, dressed in a white horsehair wig and black robe, stared down at the criminals with a sour expression on his face. He scowled over his wire-rimmed glasses, which sat low on the bridge of his nose. "Gentlemen, you are being brought up on charges of body snatching. How do you plead?"

Martin looked at the judge. "Not guilty."

The magistrate looked at John. "And you?"

"Not guilty."

"Have the witness brought into the room, please."

The resurrectionists heard footsteps behind them. They turned to see Douglas and sighed inwardly.

"Martin, John." Douglas acknowledged. "It's good to see both of you again. Chief Inspector McLeary, the magistrate, and I have been discussing your case. Thanks to the two of you, Anna Stewart is very much alive."

John leaned toward Martin. "That should be in our favor, shouldn't it?"

Martin looked at the ceiling wishing John had kept his mouth shut.

The magistrate continued to stare over the rim of his glasses at the criminals. "Who here has seen Anna Stewart alive recently?"

The three constables, Douglas, McLeary, and John, raised their hands. Martin scowled at his partner before raising his hand.

The magistrate tilted his head to the side, a look of disdain in his eyes. "Do you wish to change your plea?"

"It would be foolish for us not to do so, your honor," Martin admitted.

"Now, do the two of you want to explain why you were digging up Miss Stewart?" He looked at one man, then the other impatiently waiting for a reply.

"A man promised to pay us money after taking her body to the college." John began. "You see, your honor, the lass, is said to be cursed. The flaming-red color of her hair is the mark of the devil, some say. She was born the seventh daughter of the seventh daughter. The man wanted to make sure she never came back to life." He became quite animated, his voice increasing in volume. "But then she did. She sneezed after we threw her body on the ground. We turned around and watched her sit up. She turned her head, her eyes wide as saucers, and looked at us. We ran from the kirkyard before she could put a curse on us."

"Were you paid to dig her up?"

John inhaled to reply.

Martin held up his hand, signaling his partner to remain quiet. "No, sir, your honor. We didn't get paid because we didn't deliver the body to the anatomy college." Martin explained.

"Ironically, by exhuming her body, you saved her life." The magistrate sighed. He placed his elbow on the bench and rested his chin on the palm of his hand. He had heard many tales in his time, but this one would be a story he would long remember. "Aye. The lass was buried without a bell, trapped beneath the earth to die a slow death." Martin confirmed.

The magistrate thought for a moment. Two doctors at the college were known to purchase corpses for dissection – Dr. Knox and Dr. Tertius. He assumed there were others as well. Moreover, he was aware of the increase in the enrollment of medical students, thus the demand for cadavers. He drummed the fingertips of his hand on the bench and sighed before clasping both hands, threading his fingers. "Robbing a grave is a serious crime."

"Oh, we didn't rob her, your honor. Just dug her up." John explained.

The magistrate scowled at the simplified interruption. He picked up the piece of paper before him. "One of the constables obtained a signed affidavit from the guard of the kirkyard swearing a man bribed him to ignore your misdoings. Is that true?"

Martin nodded his head. "Aye, the man with the black hat told us the guard would turn a blind eye at what we were doing. So, we assume he had given the guard a bribe."

"Were you responsible for causing injury to Miss Stewart, sending her to her grave?"

John's eyes widened. He shook his head. "No, your honor. We may have dug her up, but we are not guilty of putting her in the ground."

Martin nodded his head in agreement. "We'll admit to being resurrectionists, but we are not murderers, ye ken."

"So, an unbeknownst man asked you to dig up the supposedly cursed lass, he bribed the kirkyard guard to look the other way while you dug up the body, and then you planned to deliver her body to the college for dissection where you were to be paid by the doctor and the man. Is that correct?"

The men looked at each other, shrugged their shoulders, and nodded.

"Aye, your honor, that sums it up nicely," John confirmed.

The magistrate glanced at Douglas before speaking. "Mr. MacEwan." He urged Douglas to step forward as he continued to explain the sentence to the resurrectionists. "Since the two of you have admitted to digging up Miss Stewart, the punishment for the crime is to have you aboard the seafaring vessel, the Georgiana, by the 24th of November, where she will take you to Van Diemen's Land. I believe you will be in the company of nearly 170 other convicts. You shall remain there to live out the rest of your lives."

Martin's mouth fell agape. "Australia?"

John leaned toward Martin. "At least we won't be hung."

The magistrate looked heavenward before continuing. "However, I have met with Mr. MacEwan, and he indicates there are a few loose ends to this case in which you may be of assistance."

Martin and John looked at Douglas as he approached the bench.

"Mr. MacEwan, would you be willing to accept the custody of these two men, to work with them to reveal who is responsible for the attempted murder of Miss Anna Stewart?"

"Your honor, if the men give me their word to do their best to resolve this crime, I will see that they are taken care of for the remainder of their lives." Douglas turned and looked at the men.

John stared at the magistrate. "I don't know how we can help him. We never saw the man's face?"

Martin backhanded John in the chest. "We'll do our best, your honor."

The magistrate sighed. "Against my better judgment, I'm placing the two of you in the custody of Mr. MacEwan." He looked at Martin and John. "Mr. MacEwan, if these two should ever give you any trouble, please contact me, and we will ensure they receive a worse punishment than being banished from Edinburgh."

John's eyebrows rose as he imagined his body hanging from a noose on the main street before an audience.

"Aye, your honor, and thank you." Douglas nodded in appreciation.

"Don't thank me just yet. It may not turn out the way you have planned." The magistrate rose from the bench, descended the stairs, and withdrew to his chamber.

"Follow me, gentlemen." Douglas put on his top hat and led the men out of the courtroom. He winked at McLeary as he passed by him with the resurrectionists in tow.

Chapter 23

"Thank you, Mr. MacEwan. We are indebted to you."
Martin followed Douglas out of the courthouse. He
inhaled, filling his lungs with clean air, thankful to no
longer be in the retched jail or on a ship headed to
Australia.

"Aye, sir, we truly appreciate it," John added as he
quickened his steps to keep astride with the taller men.

Douglas stopped short, turned around, and braced
himself as Martin nearly crashed into him. John plowed
into Martin, bounced off his backside, and fell to the
ground. "I'll admit, I have an ulterior motive for having
both of you released into my custody. I require your
service," Douglas explained.

"You need us to dig up a body?" John brushed himself off as he stood.

"No. Since the two of you are capable of recognizing the voice of the man who, let's say, encouraged you to dig up Miss Stewart's body, I need you to identify his voice when you hear it again. Until I come to retrieve you for the task, you will live on my ship and earn a decent wage as part of the crew."

"But Martin gets seasick." John scrunched his face at the thought of his friend upchucking over the side of the boat the last time they were aboard one.

"Then he will have to find his sea legs, and quickly." Douglas allowed the men to enter the awaiting coach before him. "The harbor." He ordered the driver and climbed inside.

~

"Your dinner is ready, sir. Shall I have the cook dish it up?" Helen watched Lachlan descend the staircase. His hair was messed, and his clothes were wrinkled.

"Aye."

She curtsied and left to notify the cook.

Lachlan went to the study and poured himself a drink from the decanter of whisky. He checked his pants pockets once again, ensuring he had not overlooked his set of keys.

"Sir."

Lachlan turned to see Helen in the doorway. "Aye."

"Your dinner has been served in the dining room."

"Thank you."

"Will you be going out tonight?"

"Is there another set of keys I may use? Mum's perhaps?"

"I'm sorry, sir. I don't know where Mrs. Stewart's key is. Perhaps she took it with her. Would you like to borrow my key? I can have the locksmith make another one for you in the morning."

"No, that's quite all right. I'm planning to remain home tonight." He drank the contents of his glass in one gulp, refilled it, and headed toward the dining room.

"Very well, sir." The maid curtsied as she watched him disappear through the doorway.

~

The evening sky filled with heavy clouds, and an ache settled into Haggadah's bones. The damp, colder temperatures of the late fall toyed with her arthritis as of lately. She rubbed her throbbing fingers. "Anna, can you retrieve the turmeric. I wish to add some to my tea. Oh, and the wintergreen oil too."

Barret stood from his cozy place before the fire, went to the door, and wagged his tail. Anna smirked. She knew the dog had taken a liking to Douglas and assumed he was approaching the front door. As she retrieved the requested spice and oil from the apothecary, a knock sounded.

"Who's there, Barret?" She teased the canine, who pranced in place. Anna opened the door. Barret seemed to dance toward Douglas, as he twisted his body side to side while staring up at him.

"And how are you lovely ladies this evening?" Douglas bent down and patted Barret on his shoulder. The canine seemed to smile.

"We're both doing well." Anna closed the door and offered to take Douglas's hat and coat.

"No, thank you." He held up the palm of his hand and shook his head. "The office should be empty at this late hour. We should go and examine the account books. Maybe between the two of us, we can figure out why there are two ledgers."

Anna set the bottles on the table before Haggadah.

The old witch looked up at her goddaughter and offered her opinion. "I think Mr. MacEwan's suggestion is wise."

Anna nodded. "Would you like me to add more water to the teapot before I go?"

"There is enough for another cup. Take Barret with you." Other than Douglas keeping her goddaughter safe, it was the only protection Haggadah could offer if, by chance, the outing took a turn for the worse.

"We won't be too long," Douglas reassured as he helped Anna with her cloak.

Anna pulled her hood over her head and tucked her wayward strands inside.

The trio disappeared into the darkness of the night and boarded the awaiting coach. The interior was illuminated by a small lantern attached to the wall. The golden glow allowed Douglas the privilege of appreciating Anna's beauty as she sat across from him. In his opinion, if she was cursed, she was cursed with elegance, intelligence, and an angelic face - all amiable qualities.

Anna grew uncomfortable under his stare. "What are you thinking?"

"Pardon me?" Douglas glanced out the window before looking into her emerald eyes once again. "If I may be honest?"

"Please."

"I was admiring your beauty." His unsmiling face conveyed his sincerity.

"Beauty?" She scoffed with a single chuckle. "Truly, I've received nothing but criticism for as long as I can remember, all because of my birth order." She lifted an escaped strand peeking out from her hood. "They have painted me a monster, a witch because of the color of my hair, accusing me of being the spawn of the devil, my green eyes filled with evil, and...."

"Because others cannot begin to compare, they degrade you with the hope of boosting their own esteem. Yet, from what I see, they are pathetically unsuccessful."

She looked away from his passionate eyes, both flattered and embarrassed, and petted Barret's head. "Such kind words..."

Douglas interrupted. "All true and spoken from my heart."

She looked at his face and grinned.

The driver reined the horse to a stop, opened the coach door, and assisted Anna as she stepped down to the street. Barret jumped down and waited beside her.

"Please wait." Douglas instructed the driver. "We will return shortly." He placed his hand on the small of Anna's back before offering his bent elbow to escort her into the foggy darkness, with Barret following.

Douglas searched for the business sign overhead, withdrew Lachlan's set of keys from his pocket, and unlocked the office door. Once everyone was inside, he turned the lock to ensure they were not disturbed.

"There should be an oil lamp on Mr. Heywood's desk." Anna scanned the desk with what little light filtered through the window from the street. "Ah, here it is." She removed the hurricane glass chimney. Anna retrieved a splinter of wood from the stack by the door, set it aflame from the remaining glowing embers in the fireplace, and lit the lamp. She replaced the chimney to protect the flame and adjusted the light as Douglas went behind the desk and withdrew the two ledgers. Anna peered down at the closed ledgers.

"From what I could gather, your brother is unaware that both ledgers exist." Douglas opened a ledger to the last entry and pointed his finger at the balance. "This one indicates your shipping company is low on cash." He opened the second ledger and pointed to the balance. "While this one indicates it is extremely profitable."

Anna examined the entries. "This is Mr. Heywood's handwriting." She traced her fingertip down the page, looked at the nearly negative balance, and flipped to the front of the ledger. The date of the first entry was after her father's passing. She reached for the second ledger and froze as Barret began to growl.

Douglas turned down the lamp's wick, diffusing the room into darkness, and whispered. "Anna, get behind the desk." He grasped Barret's collar, encouraging him forward as they ducked down out of sight. The trio listened as the doorknob jiggled.

"Sssshhhhh..." Anna petted the dog's head to keep him calm. She looked up as a light danced upon the walls and assumed the illumination was from a lamp used by the watchman. Footsteps faded as the office became blanketed in darkness once again. Anna expelled a sigh of relief as she stood next to Douglas, who held onto the dog's collar until he was confident the watchman was a good distance from the office.

Douglas inched the wick upward, casting a golden glow in the office once again.

Anna paged through the second book and stopped when she recognized the handwriting. "These are Dad's entries." The last entry was dated a week before his death, after which the writing changed. "Mr. Heywood began making entries here." She let her fingertip rest on the first entry made by the accountant.

"Why are there two sets of ledgers?" Douglas traced his finger down an identical page in both ledgers, comparing their entries. "Interesting, this ledger has the entries as income while the other has it as an expense, a subtle difference with opposite outcomes. However, cash withdrawals have been recorded the same in both."

Anna looked at her father's last entry, wishing he were still alive to help sort out the mystery. She reverently closed the account book. "There is little reason for Mr. Heywood to begin a second ledger when there were blank pages for him to continue after Dad's last entry."

"I can think of a few reasons for doing so, but I have no proof for the justification of each." Douglas closed the second ledger, returned both account books to the drawer, extinguished the lamp, and guided Anna to the door. He unlocked it, opened the door wide enough for him to glance up and down the walkway. With no one in sight, Douglas stepped out of the office and waited for Anna and Barret to join him. He locked the door and twisted the knob to ensure it was secure before clasping Anna's hand and guided her to the street.

The driver opened the coach door as the trio approached. Once his passengers were safely inside, he returned to his seat, slapped the reins on the horse's rump, and headed toward the witch's cottage.

Anna petted Barret's head as he sat at her feet. She looked at Douglas, her curiosity piqued. "If you are willing to share them, I would like to hear your assumptions as to why there are two ledgers?"

Douglas inhaled, pleased she valued his opinion, yet wrestled in his mind which assumption was most valid. "Two sets of ledgers are useful when stealing money. The accountant presents one as the truth, while the other may or may not be the truth, depending on the motive."

Anna scowled. "How so?"

Douglas leaned forward in his seat. "The accountant could report to the owner the less profitable ledger while pocketing money for himself."

"But then why keep the ledger showing the profitable balance?"

"Yes, quite intriguing." He paused as he leaned. "Let's say an owner wants to sell his business for a high price. He would present the ledger showing the significant profit to justify his high asking price. Conversely, if the lower price is desired, the less profitable ledger would be presented." Douglas watched Anna's face as she comprehended and understood his logic. "Last night, your brother told me your accountant indicated the business was not profitable. He discovered the safe was empty when he opened it."

Anna's mouth fell agape. "He was going to pay his debt to you from the company safe?"

"Yes, as we saw the numerous capital withdrawals, so I assume it is a habit of his."

"Even though the evidence may be clear, we're still unable to draw a solid conclusion." Anna sighed as she petted Barret on the head.

Douglas smiled as he looked at the dog and entertained a change in subject. "You can't whistle?"

Anna refused to look at him as she admitted, "No." She continued to stroke the dog's head before daring to meet his eyes and shook her head slightly.

"Come now, everyone can whistle." He teased as he sat forward in his seat.

"Not everyone." Anna grinned. "I've tried many times over, yet I cannot produce a sound."

"Perhaps you are doing it incorrectly. Place your tongue against your bottom front teeth, purse your lips, and blow as if you are extinguishing a candle."

Following each step of his instruction meticulously, Anna failed to produce a sound. She shrugged her shoulders.

Douglas tilted his head to the side in disbelief. He momentarily stood and sat down next to her. "Try again."

Anna turned in her seat to face him, recalled each instruction, and failed again.

He watched as she concentrated, pursed her lips, and blew. He looked into her emerald eyes. "If I may be so bold, Miss Stewart, I find your lips quite desirable even though you have failed once again to whistle. May I kiss you?"

Anna blinked, as if taken back by his request. "I've never kissed anyone before." She admitted.

"Then may I have the honor of being the first?" He inched his body closer to her, removed her hood, and lifted her chin with the knuckle of his index finger as he lowered his lips to hers.

The coach came to a stop. Douglas looked at Anna's eyes as he ended the kiss. They remained closed, and her lips slightly puckered. He glanced out the window to see the cottage and watched as Anna's eyes slowly opened. He grinned as he placed her hood on her head.

The driver opened the door and stood aside for Barret to pass.

Douglas motioned for Anna to exit, and he followed. "I will be just a moment." He instructed the driver.

"Aye, sir."

"I promise you, Anna, we will get to the bottom of this," Douglas said as he walked Anna to the door.

She turned as she reached the front door and looked up into his hazel eyes as he took a step toward her, drawing near.

Douglas stared into her emerald orbs. He leaned toward her, his face mere inches from hers. The temptation to kiss her again was overwhelming, but he resisted and smiled. "Goodnight, Anna."

Her smile faded. "You don't want to come in?"

Barret scratched the door, impatient to assume his spot before the warm fire.

"The hour is late, and I have to call on your brother tomorrow to return his keys. With any luck, we will learn the answers to the questions we have raised tonight."

She tilted her head to the side in a slight nod of agreement. "Goodnight, Mr. MacEwan."

He leaned toward her ear and whispered. "Douglas. My first name is Douglas."

His breath caressed her cheek. She looked into his hazel eyes, his face nearly touching hers. "Goodnight, Douglas."

Chapter 24

Douglas was confident he had remembered the location of the Stewart house. He climbed the steps and knocked on the front door. He turned around and spoke to Martin and John, who stood one step below him. "Now remember, if you recognize this man's voice as the one you talked with in the pub, I want you to show no facial recognition."

"No facial recognition?" John looked up at Douglas. His quizzical expression indicated he did not understand.

"He means don't give yourself away. Just keep quiet, like a secret." Martin explained.

John nodded as his mouth formed a silent 'oh.'

Douglas turned toward the sound of the door squeaking open.

"May I help you, sir." Helen looked up at the tall, handsome gentleman before looking past him at the two men standing on the step below.

"Yes, I need to speak with Mr. Lachlan Stewart."

"For what purpose?"

"I have something that belongs to him, and I want to ensure it is returned into his hands."

"Just a moment, please." Helen shut the door. With Lachlan's sour mood as of lately, she wanted to ensure he would receive the visitors.

Douglas admired the stone architecture of the house. The two-story residence was sandwiched between several others on the block, all similar in build. The door opened again, drawing his attention.

"Come this way, please." Helen motioned for them to enter. When the three men were in the foyer, she closed the door and offered to take their coats and hats.

"Thank you, but we won't be staying long." Douglas declined.

"Very well." She led them to the study.

Lachlan closed the morning paper, angered by the interruption. He stood as he heard footsteps drawing near and tossed the newspaper onto the chair's seat. "Gentlemen, what can I do for you?" He took a step forward and stared at the tall man, who was vaguely familiar.

"Good day, Mr. Stewart. I came to return these to you." Douglas withdrew the ring of keys from his pocket and held them before Lachlan. Martin and John stood near the entrance of the room. As instructed, they remained silent.

Lachlan looked at the keys as he grasped them and stared at the man's face. "I'm sorry, but how did you come by them?"

"Ah, you and I were playing poker at the pub. I won the last hand, and you offered to pay your debt. However, when we arrived at your shipping company's office, you discovered the safe empty and passed out on the floor. Unable to carry you to the coach, I left, locking the door on my way out. I apologize for the delay in returning them. It took me a day to locate your residence." Douglas watched as Lachlan put his hand to his forehead as if searching his memory.

"I'm sorry, I don't seem to recall much of that evening. I do remember waking in the office, though." He admitted as he turned away, his face flushed with embarrassment.

"Yes, so there is still the loose end of settling your gambling debt." Douglas reminded him.

Lachlan's heart began to race. He turned toward Douglas. "You said the safe was empty?"

"Yes, quite."

"I'll have to check with my accountant and get back with you. Give me a day or two."

Douglas nodded. "Very well. I'll return tomorrow for my winnings. That should be enough time for you to gather the funds." He turned to leave the room.

Lachlan's stomach fluttered; his heartbeat increased. "If you don't mind me asking, how much do I owe you?"

Douglas stopped and turned to face the young man. He could forgive Anna's brother's debt but thought the truth may curtail Lachlan from ever gambling again. "One hundred twenty-six pounds."

Lachlan's eyes enlarged. He coughed, giving his mind a moment to comprehend the enormous amount. How could he have been so foolish? If the safe was empty the night before last, any income received for one day might not be enough to cover his debt. Had Corbin collected from the accounts of the last shipment? "There must be an oversight. I will speak with my accountant and should have the money by tomorrow."

"Very well. Until tomorrow then." Douglas tipped his hat with a quick nod. The maid opened the door for the visitors to leave.

Once the trio walked several houses out of earshot, Douglas stopped and turned toward his employees. "Well, did his voice sound familiar?"

"No." John shook his head.

"No, sir," Martin confirmed. "He's not the same one we met with at the pub."

Douglas sighed, both frustrated and relieved. He turned his head away from the pair as he placed a fisted hand on each hip.

Martin continued. "We have no money to throw away on cards, so if that's where he spent his time while in the pub, our paths wouldn't have crossed."

"Aye, he's a stranger to us, sir," John confirmed. "We best be getting back to work."

Douglas looked at the men, nodded, dismissing them to return to their assigned ship.

~

Helen stood in the doorway of the study, watching Lachlan pace, obviously deep in thought. "Is there something troubling you, sir?"

Surprised to hear her voice, he turned abruptly and looked at the doorway. "No." Shaking his head.

Persisting, she took a step forward. "Is there anything you need?"

Lachlan muttered under his breath as he turned away from her. "A hundred twenty-six pounds."

"Sir?" The maid tilted her head to one side.

He looked back at her concerned face. "No, Helen. Nothing at all." Even though the clock had yet to strike midday, Lachlan poured himself a drink, hoping to discover the solution to his problem at the bottom of his empty glass.

~

"Here, let me do that."

Anna looked at the open palm poised before her in midair, followed the arm upward, and saw Douglas standing beside her in the garden. She handed him the shovel. "Haggadah has kept the potatoes covered with straw, so we can harvest them throughout the winter." She squatted to gather the exposed vegetable with her gloved hands and put them into a basket.

"I called on your brother today." Douglas overturned the dirt with the shovel.

Anna paused, looking up at his face. She stood with a potato in each hand. "What did he say?"

"It's what he didn't say. I had Martin and John with me. They are quite certain he wasn't the man they met in the pub, but that doesn't mean he didn't employ someone to kill you."

"So, what do we do now?" She dropped the potatoes in the basket.

"We keep you hidden until it's safe." He pressed his foot on the edge of the shovel, driving it deep into the soil, overturned the dirt, and exposed more potatoes.

~

"Where are the entries for the latest shipment?" Lachlan stared at the threatening negative balance in the ledger.

"There are only a few invoices to enter." Corbin pointed to the tray on his desk containing several pieces of paper. "It may be enough to show an increase in profit once entered, but I fear, not by much."

"Enter them now, ye ken." Lachlan went to the safe and opened it. As conveyed by Mr. MacEwan, it was empty.

Corban watched the young owner from the corner of his eye as he dipped his pen into the ink, jotted down the entries, and calculated the balance.

Lachlan shut the safe and rotated the dial. He stood and looked at the accountant. "Well?"

Corbin sighed as he set aside the last invoice. "The balance has only increased a wee bit. Even though the invoices have been recorded, the money has yet to be collected."

Lachlan went to the account's desk and stared at the ledger's balance. Even if the money was collected, it was not enough to cover his debt. "Now, what do I do?" He muttered to himself as he turned away and placed the palm of his hand on his forehead for a moment to think.

"If you don't mind me saying so, Mr. Stewart, your interests seem elsewhere other than running this company."

Lachlan had to admit, the accountant was perceptive. He cared little for the shipping business, the confining small office, and the salty, damp air. "Being the only son, Dad insisted I take over the business. He deprived me of a future of my choosing." He sighed, somewhat conceding. "Perhaps you're correct. It might be better if I sold the Stewart Mercantile Shipping Company."

Corbin set down his pen and closed the inkwell. "Shall I search for a buyer? I'm quite certain I can find one easily."

Lachlan looked at the accountant. The thought of seeking employment had never crossed his mind. He had no intention of doing so. "No, not yet. It's my only income."

~

The day turned to dusk. John's eyes scanned the kirkyard for wayward spirits. "Why are we here, sir?"

Douglas looked at John's face. Its color had turned ghostly white. "I need you to listen to the guard's voice and see if he is the man you spoke with at the pub." He passed through the iron gate as the guard exited the tower and walked toward them.

Angus paused as he saw the three men. "No more visitors. I'm locking the gates for the night."

"Nice to see you again, Angus." Douglas greeted. "I wonder if you can be of any assistance to us. Can you recall anything else about the man who paid you to look the other way when Anna Stewart's body was dug up from the grave?"

Angus looked at the two men standing behind Douglas. One was tall, the other short. The short one seemed skittish, glancing from headstone to headstone as if he expected a spirit to appear. "As I have told you and McLeary before, he had on a black hat like yours, so I couldn't see his face. He paid me a handsome sum, so he must have money."

"Were there any visitors to Anna's grave today?"

"None that I know of."

"Thank you, Angus. You have been most helpful. Goodnight." Douglas turned toward the gate. John nearly ran as he hurried to the gate.

Once the trio walked a block away from the kirkyard, Douglas posed the question. "Well, gentlemen?"

"Not him, sir," Martin confirmed.

"I agree, not him." John nodded.

Douglas posed another option that had haunted his mind. "Do you think she could have been a victim of Burke and Hare?"

John shrugged his shoulders.

Martin shook his head. "Not likely. From what I understand, they killed their victims but never put them in the ground. They took them directly to the college to collect the bounty."

Douglas nodded in agreement. "Your logic is sound. What about the doctors at the college? Could they be a suspect?"

"No, they let someone else do the dirty work. They just pay them for the body." John looked through the iron fence of the kirkyard, eager to be on his way.

Douglas sighed. He had reached another dead end in his line of suspects.

"Stop twitching, John." Martin knew his friend was afraid of the dark. "Mr. MacEwan, if there isn't anything else you need help with, then we should get back to the ship."

The men climbed into an awaiting coach, which stopped long enough for Douglas to pay the driver as he disembarked at the street leading to Haggadah's cottage and continued to the harbor to drop off the crewmen.

~

Douglas walked briskly through the chilly autumn night. Before long, he was standing at the cottage door. As expected, three plates were on the table. After greeting everyone, including Barret, he hung up his overcoat and hat and joined the women at the table.

"Well, Angus, the guard at the kirkyard, can be eliminated from our list of suspects," Douglas informed as he cut a slice of bread from the loaf and spread it with a thick layer of butter.

Anna's eyebrows raised. "We have a list?"

"Even though the resurrectionists say Lachlan wasn't the man they met at the pub, he may have hired the man. I say you lay all the cards on the table, so to speak. Question Lachlan directly." Haggadah broke her buttered bread in half. "He still owes you money from your poker game."

"True. I told Lachlan I would return tomorrow to collect his debt." He pulled a piece of chicken from the cooked breast.

"Then he will be expecting you." Haggadah bit into the soft bread."

"He likes to avoid his responsibilities," Anna added. "So, he may be away when you call, hiding in a pub."

"Maybe it's time to curtail his frivolous ways." Douglas displayed a devious grin.

Anna scowled. "Douglas, what do you have in mind?"

Chapter 25

Helen dusted the marble tabletop and gently replaced the crystal vase in its spot. She rearranged several of the flowers, mostly greenery at this time of year, to fill the holes left by the wilted cuttings she removed. With Lachlan still in bed at the midmorning hour, she was able to rush through her cleaning and hoped to find a few moments to relax before he rose.

Helen looked toward the front door as a knock demanded her immediate attention. Sighing, she wondered who could be calling. Hurrying to the kitchen, she tossed the dusty rag onto a stool just inside the door, brushed her white apron to rid it of any wrinkles, and opened the door. The man who had visited Lachlan yesterday stood on the stoop. He was accompanied by two uniformed constables. Wondering what possible trouble had fallen onto the household now caused her to momentarily forget her manners. She took a deep breath to compose herself. "May I help you?"

Douglas tapped his walking stick on the stone stoop. "Yes, we are here to see Lachlan Stewart immediately."

"I do apologize, sir." The maid formed her excuse. "He has yet to rise from bed."

"Wake him. We will wait in the study." Douglas ordered as the maid stepped aside and allowed the men to enter.

Helen closed the door and ushered the men to the study. Sensing trouble was a brew, she thought it best to be as hospitable as possible. "May I get you something to drink while you wait?"

"No, thank you." Douglas set his jaw, indicating the severity of the issue at hand. "Please tell Mr. Stewart that Mr. MacEwan and the authorities are waiting to see him."

Helen glanced at the two officers, nodded to the men before leaving the room, and ran up the stairs. She knocked on Lachlan's bedroom door. "Mr. Stewart. . .Mr. Stewart, three men, wish to see you."

Lachlan rolled over in his bed, forced his eyelids to open a mere crack and looked at the door. Heavy with sleep, his eyes fell shut. He recalled arriving home well after midnight and stumbling up to his room. Ignoring the maid, Lachlan began to drift back to sleep.

"Mr. Stewart, are you awake?" Helen glanced at the stairway, fearing the men below would become impatient. She worried Lachlan would not rise and began to compose an excuse in her mind.

Lachlan exhaled, reluctant to rise from bed. "Aye, Helen, I'm awake."

"Then your presence is requested in the study."

"By whom?"

"Mr. MacEwan and a pair of constables."

Lachlan's eyes popped open. "Constables?"

"Aye, sir."

"Tell them I'll be right down." Lachlan tossed aside the covers, swung his feet to the floor, and sat on the edge of the bed. He waited for the fog to clear from his mind.

"Very well, sir." Helen returned to the study to see the men standing together in whispered conversation. "Excuse me, Mr. Stewart will be down shortly."

Douglas looked at the maid and nodded once. "Thank you."

Heavy footsteps echoed from behind the maid. She turned to see Lachlan enter the room. He ran his hand through his messed hair to right it and tucked his wrinkled shirt into his pants. It was easy to assume he had slept in both. She dismissed herself to the hallway but lingered to eavesdrop on the ensuing conversation.

"Gentlemen, what do I owe this honor?" Lachlan met the inquisitive stares of the three men.

One of the officers stepped forward. "We have a few questions on several matters that involve you."

"Oh, which matters?" Lachlan sat in the chair the officer motioned toward.

"We understand you owe Mr. MacEwan a sum of money on a badly placed bet during a poker game." The officer placed both hands behind his back as he paced.

"Aye, a bet I do not recall because I was drunk. But I perceive Mr. MacEwan is an honest man, and if he says I owe him money, then I owe him money."

"Several others who were present in the room can attest that you do indeed owe him money. One hundred twenty-six pounds, to be exact."

Lachlan shrugged his shoulders. "Fine."

"There is also the matter of your sister's death." The constable continued.

"Anna?" He tilted his head to the side and scowled.

"Her body has disappeared, dug up by resurrectionists."

"When?" Lachlan sat forward in the chair. "This is the first that I'm hearing of it."

"What can you tell us about the night she died?"

Lachlan shrugged one shoulder. "Not much. She left the house on an errand. The next thing I knew, we were informed Anna was dead. We buried her the next day."

"What errand?" The constable stopped pacing and stared.

"Mum wanted her to go to the store and purchase some items on a list."

"So, your mum gave her the list?"

"No, I did."

"How do you know your mum wanted her to go on the errand?"

"I didn't. Helen, our maid, gave me the list and told me Mum wanted Anna to get the items."

"I need to question the maid. Please call her." The constable insisted.

"Certainly. Helen?" Lachlan sighed, hoping the maid could clear up the matter at hand.

Soft footsteps could be heard before she appeared in the doorway. "Aye, sir?"

"The officer would like to ask you a question."

Helen looked at the officer.

"Helen, you gave Lachlan the list of items for Anna to purchase on the night she was killed."

"Aye." Helen nodded once.

"Where did you get the list?"

"From Mrs. Stewart's desk." The maid explained.

"You found it and gave it to Lachlan?"

"No, Mrs. Stewart told me where it was and asked me to give it to Lachlan. He was to give it to Anna."

"Why didn't you give it to Anna?"

Helen paused momentarily. "Because I did what Mrs. Stewart instructed. She wanted Lachlan to give it to her."

"Did she indicate when Anna was to retrieve the items on the list?"

The maid entwined her fingers as she tried to recall the tiny detail accurately.

The officer pressed. "Miss, did she specify the task could have waited until morning?"

Helen shook her head. "She didn't specify a time, just to give it to Mr. Stewart."

The officer looked at the maid and then Lachlan. "Didn't either one of you think it was out of the ordinary to send Anna out into the night on an errand? We all know crime in the city is running rampant. It isn't safe for a young lass to be out after dark."

Helen looked at Lachlan. "I'm a loyal maid, sir, and simply followed directions."

Lachlan looked at the constable. "It never crossed my mind."

The constable exhaled. "That is all, Helen."

"Aye, sir." The maid resumed her spot in the hallway and continued to listen. She sensed the issue of Anna's death was more than she once thought. Helen knew of the young lass's curse, but was Lachlan somehow involved in her demise?

The officer turned to Lachlan. "Is it true, Mr. Stewart, you have recently had your mum committed to an asylum?"

"Aye, my sister's death was tough on her. She was mad with grief."

"Quite convenient to have your sister and mum out of the way." The constable insinuated.

"What are you suggesting, sir?" Lachlan stood, taking offense to the accusation.

"With your sister deceased and your mum committed, you became the sole owner of the Stewart Mercantile Shipping Company. A devious plan, indeed."

Lachlan's mouth dropped open. "What? I didn't murder my sister, and my mum needed help."

The constable continued. "How do we know you didn't employ someone to kill Anna? Is your mum genuinely grieving, gone mad, or as many men do, have you just locked her away for convenience? After all, with them both out of the house, it gave you the freedom to do as you pleased; drink, gamble, and even sell the shipping business."

Lachlan clenched his teeth as he spat his words through them. "I didn't kill my sister nor hire anyone to do so. Everyone knows Anna was cursed. Many blamed her for Dad's death. She probably brought it upon herself."

"Well, we have further investigating to do, and until this matter can be sorted out, we are taking you into custody as a suspect. We don't want you leaving on one of your ships, now do we?" The constable nodded to his partner. They grabbed Lachlan's arms and escorted him out of the room.

Helen stepped forward and opened the door.

Seeing the maid, Lachlan yelled over his shoulder. "Helen, contact my lawyer and let Mr. Heywood know I've been taken into custody."

"Aye, sir."

"Good day, Helen." Douglas tipped his hat at the maid as he followed the constables out the door. He was more than willing to sacrifice the gambling debt to keep Anna safe. After dropping off Lachlan at headquarters, he hoped their next visit would shed some light on the questionable bookkeeping of the Stewart Mercantile Shipping Company.

"Good day." She closed the door, wondering who to notify first.

~

Martin and John carried thickly coiled hemp ropes over their right shoulders as they walked along the shipyard. Flags on masks snapped in the gust of wind.

"When do you think we'll be fully loaded and on our way to Virginia?" John looked at the grand ship with its crew loading cargo up the ramp.

"Do you think I'm privileged to the ship's schedule? I doubt Mr. Townsend or any of the captains know for sure. You'll have to ask Mr. MacEwan."

"There will be no ships leaving today. Not with this wicked wind. I bet there's a storm blowing in." John grabbed his hat as a gust of wind nearly removed it from his head. "I'm looking forward to seeing Virginia. It's a new start for us, ye ken. We have jobs, money, and can afford food in our stomachs."

"Aye, hard work, but nothing that will bust our backs, and we have a place to lay our heads every night. If truth, I'm mighty thankful for the turn in our lives." Martin dodged a large barrel rolling toward the ramp of a ship. He looked at the name on the bow and did not recognize it as one belonging to Mr. MacEwan, who currently had three in port.

Dark gray clouds hung low in the sky. Even under the threat of rain, it was a hectic day in the shipyard. There were many people and passengers on the waterfront and workers darting in and out between them.

Martin spotted Douglas walking with a constable. "There's Mr. MacEwan now. You can ask him when we're leaving port." He pointed at Douglas as he disappeared into an office.

John hurried toward Douglas with Martin trailing behind. The office door, caught by the wind, failed to latch shut and swung open partially.

John stepped in the doorway and quickly backed out, bumping into Martin. He flattened himself against the building.

"What are you doing?" Martin stood beside him.

"Ssshhh. . . listen."

Martin leaned over his friend and pressed his ear as close to the opening of the doorway as possible. His eyes widened as he listened. He looked down at John, who was looking up at him.

~

"Mr. Stewart lost a significant amount of money during a hand of poker. I came to collect what is due." Douglas stared at the accountant.

Corbin withdrew the account book. "Mr. Stewart has yet to report to the office today. You might want to call on him at his residence."

"We have. Mr. Stewart is not there either." The constable added, keeping the reason for Lachlan's absence to himself.

"As you can see," Corbin opened the ledger and turned it for the men to examine, "the account is bare. I'm afraid Mr. Stewart spends the company funds frivolously. Perhaps you should return later when he is in, and you can request your payment from him directly."

"And who are you, sir?" Douglas wanted to ensure they were interviewing the company accountant.

"I'm Corbin Heywood, the accountant for the Stewart Mercantile Shipping Company." He announced, lifting his chin with pride.

"Have you been employed by the company very long?" The officer inquired.

"Since the passing of Mr. Oliver Stewart."

"And you were given the job by Mr. Lachlan Stewart?" Douglas pressed to see if the accountant would tell the truth.

"No, Mrs. Evelyn Stewart secured my employment."

"Well, we won't take up any more of your time, Mr. Heywood. Thank you, and we will call again if we are unable to contact Mr. Stewart." The officer turned toward the door.

"Good day," Corbin smirked, realizing Lachlan had finally gotten himself into trouble that he could not resolve.

"And to you as well," Douglas called over his shoulder as he left the office.

~

With the conversation concluded, John and Martin took several steps away from the building and masked their faces with a look of innocence.

They watched as Douglas and the constables exited.

"Mr. MacEwan, imagine running into you." John smiled sheepishly.

"John," Martin interjected, "why don't you ask Mr. MacEwan the question you have wanted to ask him."

John opened his mouth to speak.

Martin elbowed his friend. "In private." He looked at the officers. "If you don't mind, constables, sirs."

The constables nodded once before walking toward the edge of the water to admire a ship's operations and its efficient crew.

John inhaled. "Sir, when do we leave port?"

"Not that question." Martin looked skyward. "What we just overheard."

"Oh, aye." John connected the dots of his partner's train of thought and looked at Douglas. "The man we met in the pub is inside that office." He nodded his head once at the door.

Douglas's eyebrows raised, and his eyes widened. "Are you certain it's him?"

Both men nodded their heads.

"Quite certain," Martin confirmed.

"It's him, all right." John continued to nod as he hoisted the heavy rope higher onto his shoulder.

"Well, the only other person who could identify him is Angus. I'll speak to the chief inspector about this matter. Don't tell anyone else, for Anna's sake."

"Aye, sir." Martin nudged John.

"Aye." John walked to the ship with his friend following but turned around abruptly. "Oh, sir, when do we leave port for Virginia?"

"Soon." Douglas was uncertain of the exact date. "Once Mr. Townsend indicates the ships are fully loaded,

I'll make the final decision." He would delay the departure if necessary.

~

Lachlan sat in the cold, dank cell among the riffraff of thieves, tax evaders, and whatever else they had committed. He wet his lips with his tongue, wishing he had a drink, and wondered how long he would be retained. He thought of the brighter side of his dire situation. Those he was indebted to could not reach him. Without his constant withdrawals from the company safe, he hoped a stack of money would be in it to pay off his debts once he was released.

He watched one of the men relieve himself in a nearly overflowing bucket of excrement. Its stench, rather unpleasant, made his eyes water. Several men itched their scalps. Lice, he assumed. He wondered how long he could endure the confinement.

~

Douglas rejoined the constables at the water's edge. "I've just learned of some interesting news."

Recognizing the concerned tone in Douglas's voice, the constable looked up and down the crowded waterfront and suggested, "Perhaps we should return to the station, give Chief Inspector McLeary an update, and discuss your information privately."

They took a coach to headquarters and were joined by McLeary in a small office.

"I understand there is an update in this case." McLeary sat behind the table with a pen, ink, and an open folder with several papers inside. He looked at the constables and Douglas seated across from him.

The constable looked at Douglas and nodded for him to begin.

"Martin and John, who are now my employees, identified the man who persuaded them to exhume Anna Stewart's body. By happenchance, the constables and I questioned him at the Stewart Mercantile Shipping Company, a Mr. Corbin Heywood, the accountant."

McLeary looked down at a paper in the file and picked it up. "According to this report, they couldn't see his face. How did they know it was him?"

"They recognized his voice."

"They were inside the office with you?"

"No, they were waiting outside to ask me a question. Eavesdropping, so to say." Douglas went on. "If Mr. Heywood is the person who paid off Angus, perhaps he can collaborate Martin and John's claim."

McLeary scribbled the information onto a paper in the file. "A magistrate may not believe the word of two resurrectionists. Since Angus was paid off, he may not be credible either. We need to follow up with him, though."

"Also," Douglas continued, "I believe this may be of importance. After a poker game, Lachlan and I went to the company office. He planned to pay his debt from the safe. However, once he opened it, it was empty. He encouraged me to look at the company ledger. I went to retrieve the ledger from the accountant's desk, and I discovered two ledgers. One ledger has a profitable balance, while the other ledger's balance was close to negative. Miss Stewart and I used a set of keys to go into the office the following night and reexamined the ledgers. She identified her father's entries in the ledger showing a profit. There were no entries in her dad's hand in the other ledger, and its first entry was made shortly after his death."

McLeary looked up from his file after recording the information. "Sounds to me as if Mr. Heywood is up to no good."

Douglas expressed his most significant concern. "If Martin and John have correctly identified Mr. Heywood as the man in the pub, then he knows Anna is alive."

McLeary exhaled. "I suggest we post a plain-clothed constable near the shipping office. He will trail

Heywood's every move and watch for anyone entering and exiting the office." He looked at Douglas. "Will it be necessary to post a constable where Miss Stewart is currently residing?"

Douglas knew she was well hidden, and Barret usually by her side. "I believe she is safe for now."

Chapter 26

A constable leaned against a barrel on the waterfront. He was dressed like a crewman but kept a watchful eye on the door of the Stewart Mercantile Shipping Company.

McLeary nodded to the undercover officer before opening the door and entering the office. "Mr. Heywood."

Corbin looked over the rim of his glasses at the officer.

"I'm Chief Inspector McLeary. I assume, since Mr. Stewart is a vital part of this company, you may want to know he has been located."

The accountant returned his pen to the inkwell. "That's good news." He went to the dying embers of the fireplace and added several logs even though the tiny office was a comfortable temperature. He sneezed, pulled his handkerchief from his pocket, and blew his nose.

McLeary watched the accountant's face for any reaction as he clarified Lachlan's location. "He's in jail."

Corbin stared at the officer as he returned his handkerchief to his pocket. "I assume drunk and disorderly were the charges?"

"Suspicion of killing his sister, Anna Stewart."

Corbin put his palm on his chest and opened his mouth as if shocked by the news. "Has he been formally charged?

"Not yet. We're still gathering evidence. Mr. Stewart will remain in our custody until we have completed our investigation."

"Thank you, officer. Keep me posted of any further developments."

"Good day." McLeary nodded at the accountant as he left, looked at the undercover officer, and winked as he walked away.

~

It was just past midday when Douglas arrived at the cottage. He waited in the coach until a woman seeking Haggadah's advice left with her remedy and turned onto a side street, disappearing.

Haggadah watched as Barret went to the door. His tail wagged like a loose shutter blowing in the wind. "Anna, I believe Mr. MacEwan is here."

To avoid Haggadah's inquisitive stare, Anna looked down at the bread dough she was kneading to conceal the grin extending across her face.

The old witch opened the door before Douglas was able to knock. "Hello, Mr. MacEwan. Were you able to collect your debt from Lachlan?" She stepped aside, allowing him to enter.

Douglas glanced at Anna as he petted Barret. "No, he is short funds, has been taken into custody, and is in jail."

Haggadah returned to the apothecary and began putting herbs used for the remedy in their proper places.

Anna scowled, her hands stilled, and her mouth dropped open as she looked at Douglas. "In jail? For not paying a gambling debt?"

He stood at the working table, opposite Anna. "A debt I would gladly forgive. However, Chief Inspector McLeary suspects he may have an ulterior motive and will hold him in jail until his questions are answered."

Anna nodded as she returned to kneading the dough.

Douglas continued. "Martin and John have identified the person who encouraged them to unearth your body."

Haggadah turned and looked at Douglas's back. "Mr. Heywood."

Anna stilled her hands once again.

Douglas turned and stared in disbelief at the old witch, who replaced the top on a jar and set it on its proper shelf.

Anna looked from Douglas to her godmother and back to Douglas. "Is she right?"

He ignored Anna's question. "How did you know, Haggadah?"

She sighed and shrugged her shoulder. "I didn't. It just came to me. It's an advantage in my profession at times."

Anna raised her eyebrows and looked at Douglas. "So, she's right. They identified Mr. Heywood?"

Douglas nodded. "Yes. He is the mysterious man in the black hat."

"He's the one who tried to kill me?" She stared at him for a moment before rolling under the edge of the dough to shape the loaf, placed it in a greased bowl to rise, and covered it with a clean cloth.

"We don't know that for certain. All we know is Mr. Heywood instructed Martin and John to exhume your body. Unfortunately, he also knows that you're alive, so we must remain vigilant and keep you hidden, now more than ever." He sighed. "I must go to the harbor and get an update from my assistant. I'm certain the crew are eager to leave port as soon as possible."

Anna looked at Douglas, her smile fading. "You aren't staying for dinner?"

He reached across the table and clasped her flour-covered hand. "For you, my dearest, I will return." He smiled as he winked. "After all, I'm eager to taste a slice of your freshly baked bread." He touched his fingertip to the brim of his hat and exited the cottage.

~

Corbin sneezed as he withdrew both ledgers and opened them to the last entry. He glanced from one to the other and back again, comparing balances. His body ached and shivered. He blamed the damp, cold office for his ailments, pulled his handkerchief from his pants pocket, and blew his chapped red nose.

The accountant retrieved a piece of paper and jotted down the necessary information he wished to convey. He folded the message and sealed it with wax. The door of the office opened, and a worker from one of the ships stepped inside.

"Good day, Corbin. I thought you would like an update."

The accountant addressed the note before looking up at the shipman. "Good day." He returned his pen to the inkwell.

"We are waiting for cargo to finish loading, and then we will set sail tomorrow morning."

"As scheduled," he replied dryly.

"Aye." The crewman turned to leave.

"Could you hand this to a messenger on your way back to the ship?" Corbin reached into his pocket, withdrew a coin, and placed both into the palm of the shipman. "Thank you."

"You're welcome."

Corbin paced the office as he realized the web of his plan had a snag, one that needed to be untangled. With Mrs. Stewart in the asylum and Anna presumed dead by many, Lachlan possessed power of attorney, and he was in jail.

Corbin grinned as a devious solution developed in his mind. He closed the ledger books, returned them to the drawer, and locked the office door as he left to pay a visit to a trusted friend.

~

The constable watched the crewman leave the shipping office. He failed to notice the sealed note in the man's hand when the door opened again, distracting him. The undercover officer became suspicious as a man dressed in a black overcoat and top hat, locked the door, and walked away with a determined gait. Assuming no one was inside the office, he followed at a distance.

~

A nurse walked into the large patient room. She smiled at Evelyn. "How are you feeling today, Mrs. Stewart."

Evelyn looked up from the book she was reading. "Never better, thank you."

The nurse took a note from the pocket of her overskirt. "While I was in the office, a lad delivered it. It's for you. I thought you may want to read it."

"Thank you." Evelyn broke the seal and began to read as the nurse went to aid another patient. Her heartbeat increased and breathing labored as she continued to read. Unable to contain her displeasure, Evelyn threw off the covers, got out of bed, and began to pace. "No! No! No!"

Doctor Esmond and several nurses went to her bedside.

"Mrs. Stewart, let's get you back into bed." He coaxed.

Evelyn continued to pace as if she had not heard the doctor's suggestion. She placed the palm of her hand over her mouth, lowered her other hand to her side, and let the note drop to the floor.

"Mrs. Stewart, please return to bed." Doctor Esmond persisted. He placed his hand on her arm, which she pushed away.

"No! How can this be?" A wildness appeared in her eyes as she looked about the room, searching for an answer.

"Mrs. Stewart, please, let's have you lay down." A nurse stepped forward and guided her toward her bed.

Evelyn pushed the young woman, who fell to the floor.

The doctor and several nurses wrestled her into bed. Evelyn's jaw was forced open, and a nurse poured a sedative into her mouth. They continued to hold their patient until the drug took effect, and she calmed.

"What caused the outburst?" One of the nurses stood from the bed. She straightened her uniform and skewed cap on her head.

"Maybe this." Doctor Esmond picked up the note from the floor and read it. He looked at Evelyn, taken back by the obscure message. "If she wakes and resumes her hysteria, administer the sedative again."

"Aye, Doctor." The nurse watched as the doctor left the room with the note in his hand.

~

He kept his black hat tilted over his eyes as he stood behind the doctor, who dropped what he assumed was a human organ into a large clear glass vessel. "I need something to put in a drink that will cause an eternal sleep, a dirt nap, so to speak."

Dr. Knox poured a clear liquid over the organ, submerging it completely. He did not turn around. He knew who was behind him. "Eternal sleep. I've heard hemlock is quite lethal." Knox placed the top on the specimen jar, set it on a shelf, and left the room without making eye contact with his visitor.

Corbin sneezed. He searched the various bottles on the shelves. Spotting the indicated poison, he took the bottle, dropped it into his pocket, and left.

Chapter 27

Chief Inspector McLeary entered the asylum. A shiver ran up his spine every time he passed through the doors of the building. This time was no different. His body quivered as he stepped into the hallway and went directly to the office.

The receptionist looked up from the open file on her desk. "Hello, Chief Inspector McLeary."

"Good day, Rose. I've been summoned by Dr. Esmond. The messenger indicated it was most urgent, so I've come post-haste."

"Aye, please seat yourself, sir, while I let the doctor know you've arrived." She disappeared out the door.

He was not in the mood to sit. McLeary listened to the short gait of Rose's fading footsteps as she hurried down the hallway. Always observant, he admired the neatness of the receptionist's desk. The occasional cry of a patient echoing from somewhere in the asylum haunted his very soul. McLeary vowed he would never become a resident of the godforsaken place. He turned toward the open doorway as he heard footsteps.

Doctor Esmond paused in the doorway "Rose, we will need to use your office for a few minutes."

"Aye, Doctor." The receptionist sat on a bench against a wall in the hallway.

"Hello, Henry." McLeary greeted as the doctor entered the small office, closing the door behind him, and the men shook hands.

"Roger. I know you're a busy man, so let me get straight to the issue." Doctor Esmond produced the note from his white overcoat pocket and gave it to the officer. "I normally keep my patients' correspondence confidential, but when Mrs. Stewart read this, she became agitated, quite agitated." Esmond sighed. "Even though its meaning is unclear to me, I thought you should see it."

McLeary accepted the note, turned away from the doctor as he unfolded it, and began to read. His eyebrows raised at keywords that were a cause for concern. He turned back to the doctor and looked at him. "May I keep this?" He refolded the paper.

"Certainly. I doubt Mrs. Stewart, in her sedated state, will realize that it's missing."

~

"I understand my employer, Lachlan Stewart, is being held in a cell. I'd like to visit with him."

The sergeant looked down at Corbin from the elevated desk. "And who are you?"

"The accountant for the Stewart Mercantile Shipping Company. I need to see him on company business."

"Very well." The sergeant turned to the constable behind him. "Escort him to the cell."

A door opened to the side of the desk and the officer ushered Corbin to the jail cell where Lachlan was being held. "Make it short," the constable ordered as he left the two to converse through the iron bars.

"Well, hello, Corbin. What do I owe the pleasure of your visit in this fine establishment?" The sarcasm was as thick as cream in Lachlan's voice as he rose from a bench and spread his arms wide, giving a small, guided tour. He approached the iron bars.

"I came to offer my advice and hoped to persuade you to sell the company while there is a smidgeon of profitability left in the account." Corbin urged.

"Auch, I refuse to sell. It's the only income I have, ye ken."

"You have drained the account dry. It's time to sell."

"No, I will not sell. Not today, not ever."

"Very well." The accountant looked down the hall at the guard, who had his back turned toward him. "I know of your fondness for whisky and assumed you could use this to wet your whistle until you are released." Corbin reached into his coat pocket and handed his former boss a flask.

Lachlan glanced at the guard and tucked the flask into his arms as he folded them. "Thank you, kindly, Corbin."

"You're welcome, Mr. Stewart." The accountant sneezed. He ignored the shiver that caused his body to tremble and gooseflesh to rise on his skin. Corbin turned and joined the officer, gladly leaving the jail and its occupants behind.

~

Evelyn blinked her eyes several times, trying to clear her blurred vision and the fog in her mind. She struggled to sit upright in bed, recalling the reason she had been drugged once again. "The note," she muttered to herself. It was no longer in her hand. She scanned the bed covers and lifted them to search beneath.

"How are you feeling, Mrs. Stewart?"

Evelyn looked into the concerned eyes of the nurse, who straightened the covers and adjusted. "Better, much better, thank you."

"Good. Is there anything I can get you?"

"Aye, paper, pen, and ink. I would like to send a note." She watched as the nurse gathered the items, placed them on a bed table, and set them before her as she sat up. The nurse adjusted her pillow, and she leaned against the headboard.

"Thank you." Evelyn waited until the nurse turned away before opening the ink bottle, dipping the pen, and scribbled her concerns on the paper. When finished, she fanned the ink to dry it. "Nurse."

The nurse went to Evelyn's bedside and watched as she folded the note. "Finished writing already?"

"Aye." Evelyn wrote the name on the folded note and address. "Could you have a messenger deliver this post-haste?"

The nurse closed the lid on the inkwell and nodded. "Certainly, Mrs. Stewart." She accepted the folded message and slipped it into the pocket of her skirt before lifting the bed table and walking away. Returning the ink and pen to their proper place, she began to leave the room but paused at the end of a bed, pretending to straighten a bedsheet. Without making eye contact, she kept the volume of her voice low. "Doctor Esmond, may I have a word with you in the hallway?" She continued to the double doors without waiting for his reply.

The doctor finished with his patient before joining her in the corridor. "What is it?"

The nurse pulled the note from her pocket. "I assume this is a reply to the correspondence Mrs. Stewart received earlier. I thought you should see it."

Doctor Esmond opened the note, scanned it quickly, and refolded it. "Thank you for bringing this to my attention. Well done."

~

Feverish and shivering, Corbin tried to swallow, but his throat was painfully raw as if it had open sores. Wincing as he forced saliva down his throat, he instructed the coach driver to take him to the town witch, hoping she could concoct a remedy for what ailed him.

~

As the afternoon waned, Haggadah went to the garden to dig up carrots. Barret followed behind the old witch for some needed fresh air.

Anna set the table for the evening meal. Her thoughts strayed away from the mundane task to Douglas, his kindness, his charming smile, and her first kiss.

A knock sounded upon the door. Nearly giddy with anticipation of Douglas's arrival, Anna hurriedly opening it, froze, and stared into the eyes of Mr. Corbin Heywood. Her smile faded.

The accountant took a step backward as he stared at the young woman. She could ruin his plans, his years of scheming. He would not allow the truth to be known. Corbin's eyebrows drew together in a scowl and his face reddened with anger. He took a determined step forward, his hands balling into fists. "So, this is where you've been hiding," he spat her name through his clenched teeth, "Anna."

Anna sensed something was terribly wrong. The accountant's raspy voice sounded like the devil himself coming to claim her soul. Grasping the edge of the door, she slammed it shut, pushing with every bit of strength in her body.

The door was nearly closed before Corbin rammed it with his shoulder, making it impossible for Anna to latch it securely. The impact caused the hinges to pull away from the old doorframe. The oak door hung askew. Corbin rolled his body toward the opposite side, planted his feet, and pushed. The door pivoted open, forcing Anna backward as it crashed to the floor of the cottage.

Anna's heart skipped a beat as she stared down at the door, then watched as Corbin methodically stepped inside. The accountant breathed heavily, catching his breath as he returned her stare. She ran to the far side of the table, defensively keeping it between herself and the intruder, reading his intent to make her death permanent this time. "Mr. Heywood . . ." she began, but he kept advancing toward her.

Corbin went to the opposite side of the table. Each time he lunged in one direction or the other, Anna did the opposite. They mimicked a pair of boxers dancing around the ring, with each trying to determine when to throw the first punch.

Growling in frustration, Corbin's patience had reached its end. He grabbed the edge of the table and flipped it upward. It crashed to the floor as it tipped onto its side. Corbin charged at Anna, whose only escape was the open front door. She darted toward it.

~

Barret perked his ears and stared at the back door of the cottage. He took a step forward, listened, and heard another thud. He darted to Haggadah, circled around her, and ran to the door.

Haggadah had paused in digging carrots and looked toward the door too. She wondered if her old ears were wrong, but her ever-faithful canine indicated otherwise. She dropped a handful of carrots into the basket and looked at her dog. "Barret, there is something amiss." With her shovel in hand, she assumed Anna may have dropped a plate, but her intuition told her it was something much worse.

~

Nero woke from his sound sleep on Haggadah's bed, hissed, and darted beneath it.

The accountant stretched his arms as he charged, grabbing Anna by her hair, pulling her away from the open door as her foot crossed the threshold. Yanking her close to his body, he wrapped his hands around her neck and squeezed. She tried to yell, but his grip tightened before she could utter a sound. Anna gasped for air as she pulled one of his fingers toward his wrist, but her effort was futile as her strength drained from her body.

Corbin sneered as he watched her face reddened. He knew she would lose consciousness soon. "I should have hit you harder with the shovel."

Chapter 28

Douglas stared at the open cottage door as he stepped down from the coach. He scowled, knowing Haggadah kept it securely closed, especially for Anna's safety. Barret's growl echoed from the doorway. Without hesitation, Douglas rushed through the portal.

The accountant's hands were clamped around Anna's throat and the canine's powerful jowls locked on Corbin's leg, trying to pull him away from Anna.

Anna's eyes looked heavenward as they rolled back toward her hairline, and her limp body began to crumble to the floor.

With a large, determined stride, Douglas fisted his hand and punched Corbin in the face. The dazed accountant released his hands and dropped to the floor. Barret unsympathetically dragged Corbin's body to the other side of the room while the accountant screamed in pain.

Douglas caught Anna before she fell to the floor. He scooped her into his arms, gently holding her like a fragile porcelain doll, uncertain what to do to help her.

Haggadah entered, the shovel still in her hand. Her goddaughter was cradled in Douglas's arms. "Mr. MacEwan, I think Anna would be more comfortable on my bed where I can attend to her." She looked at the stranger Barret had well in hand. "I assume the authorities need to be informed." Haggadah went to the withering man as he screamed, begging for help. "Here, let me ease your pain." She slammed the shovel against Corbin's head, knocking him unconscious. "Barret, come, let the man sleep for now." She leaned the shovel against the apothecary.

Douglas laid Anna on the bed. He brushed her hair away from her eyes, placed his fingers beneath her nose, and felt her exhale. "She's alive." He stood at the head of the bed as Haggadah approached.

"I'm concerned about the swelling from the trauma." The old witch went to the bedside, sat on its edge, and touched the quickly bruising marks on her goddaughter's neck.

Anna's eyes snapped open and welled with tears. She coughed as she sat up and gasped for air.

Douglas knelt on one knee on the mattress and placed his hands on Anna's back as she teetered. "Shhh, you're safe." He glanced over his shoulder at the unconscious accountant.

The old witch chuckled. "He'll probably have quite a headache when he wakes."

Douglas grinned as he looked back at the old witch. "Will the two of you be fine while I hail a coach and escort Mr. Heywood to the authorities?"

"Aye, I'll give Anna something to combat the swelling. She just needs to catch her breath and rest a bit." Haggadah confirmed.

Douglas propped up the pillow against the headboard and eased Anna backward to rest. He clasped her hand in his, brought it to his lips, and kissed it gently. "I'll return as soon as possible." He wiped away a tear cascading down her cheek as the traumatic shock began to overtake her body.

Anna opened her mouth to speak, but no sound came forth, so she nodded, conveying she understood.

Haggadah, acutely aware of her goddaughter's distress, covered her body with a quilt. Anna began to shake uncontrollably, the color drained from her face, and her hands became cold.

Douglas left the cottage, only to return moments later with a coach driver. He looked at Anna, who was still shaking, tears cascading down her cheeks. He went to her, cupped her face in his hand. "Shhh, I'll be back soon."

Anna nodded.

Haggadah pulled jars from the apothecary. "She will soon be as right as rain, ye ken. I'll make her a cup of tea."

Together the two men dragged Corbin out the front doorway, with Barret trailing closely behind.

~

"What do we have here?" The sergeant stood and peered over the edge of his desk at Douglas, Corbin, the coach driver, and Barret.

"I found this man, Corbin Heywood, accosting a young woman." Douglas and the driver dropped Corbin on the floor.

"I assume the dog is a witness?" The sergeant added sarcastically.

"Aye, he apprehended him. You will find evidence of the canine's arrest on his leg." Douglas confirmed. He looked at Corbin, who remained unconscious.

"Get him off the floor." The sergeant ordered. There was only one constable in the headquarters at the time. "Mr. MacEwan, if you would be so kind as to help the officer take Mr. Heywood to a cell, it would be appreciated."

"Certainly." Douglas instructed the driver to wait by the coach.

The door to the left of the desk opened. A constable and Douglas lifted Corbin by his arms and dragged his body down the hallway. Barret followed curiously.

The officer stopped before a rather crowded cell and unlocked the barred door. "Inside you go."

They placed Corbin on the floor near the door and returned to the hallway.

"Officer," one of the prisoners said.

"What do you want?" The constable paused before shutting the door.

"You may want to check on that lad. I think he's dead."

Douglas peered between the bars to see Lachlan on the stone floor, unmoving, with a flask in his hand. "That's Lachlan Stewart."

"Everyone back against the wall," the constable ordered. He withdrew his baton before he entered the cell. Barret stepped into the doorway, curiously sniffing the rancid odor. The prisoners stared at the intimidating canine, afraid to move or aggravate the beast.

The constable placed his foot on Lachlan's hip, pushed, and shook the prisoner's body. Receiving no physical or verbal reaction, he touched Lachlan's hand. It was cold. The prisoner's chest did not rise or fall. "Aye, he's dead." The officer twisted the flask from his hand, knowing the alcohol was not permitted in the cell. "I wonder where he got this?" He sniffed the rancid fragrance, wrinkling his nose. "Smells like mouse urine."

"He got it from that man." A prisoner pointed at Corbin. "I saw him give it to him when he came to visit earlier today. The way he withered and died in pain; it's probably laced with poison."

The officer turned to Corbin, who had yet to wake. "Assaulting a lass and poisoning a man to death. I wonder how much more there is to your story?"

~

The sergeant dipped his pen in the inkwell and entered the admittance of the prisoner in the daily log sheet. A tall man approached his desk. He ignored him until he finished the entry, returned his pen to the inkwell, and looked at the man who had unbuttoned his ebony overcoat to reveal a white medical uniform beneath. "May I help you?" He assumed the man's occupation. "Doctor?"

"I need to speak with Chief Inspector McLeary." Dr. Esmond informed.

"For what purpose?" The sergeant glanced at the door to his left and watched Douglas and Barret exit.

"I have obtained a correspondence between Mrs. Evelyn Stewart and a Mr. Corbin Heywood that implicates wrongdoings. It must be brought to his attention immediately."

Upon hearing the pair of familiar names, Douglas glanced at the man standing before the front desk and waited to see what else he may learn. He reached down and patted Barret's shoulder as the canine brushed against his leg.

The constable leaned toward the sergeant. "Lachlan Stewart is face down in the cell, dead. One of the prisoners is a witness and claims Corbin Heywood gave him this." He held up the flask. "The witness said Lachlan withered in pain as he died. I could smell whisky, but it reeks of something else too."

The sergeant looked at Dr. Esmond and Douglas. He rose from his desk and sighed. "I think both of you need to meet with McLeary. Through the door, please."

The constable opened the door allowing the men and the dog to enter. He escorted them to a small office. "The Chief Inspector will be with you soon."

They seated themselves at the available chairs and waited. Barret sat next to Douglas, who patted his shoulder. "Good boy."

The door opened, and McLeary entered with the constable. "What do we have now?"

The doctor nodded toward Douglas, conveying him to speak.

Douglas began. "When I arrived at Haggadah's house...."

"The old witch? Why were you there? Are you ill?" McLeary began.

"No. Haggadah hid Anna in her cottage. You see, the old witch is her godmother."

McLeary nodded.

"As I was saying, when I arrived, the front door had been knocked from its hinges. I went inside and found Corbin Heywood attempting to strangle Anna. Her face was red, and she was close to fainting. Mr. Heywood was screaming in pain because Barret," he petted the dog, "had him by the leg and was attempting to drag him away from Anna. I did what was necessary to loosen his grip from her neck."

"Do you know what provoked his attack?"

Douglas shook his head. "No. Anna was unable to speak afterward. Quite understandably, she was in shock too."

"I know why Mr. Heywood attacked Anna Stewart." Dr. Esmond retrieved the note from his pocket. "I believe this will explain his motive." He handed McLeary the note.

Douglas glanced at the doctor and stared at McLeary.

"Another note. Let's hope this one is a little more specific." The chief inspector opened the paper but paused before reading it. He looked at Douglas to explain earlier developments. "Mr. MacEwan, Doctor Esmond obtained a note earlier today. The message was vague and unsigned, but apparently, Mrs. Stewart understood its meaning because she became visibly upset and had to be sedated." The detective looked at the doctor and then at Douglas before reading the note in his hand. "This implicates her in the attempted murder of Anna and as Corbin Heywood's accomplice in forcing Lachlan to sell the shipping business to Mr. Heywood. She signed it 'your loving wife.'"

Douglas's eyes widened. "They're married?"

McLeary handed the note to Douglas. "Perhaps secretly. It looks as if the two of them were trying to eliminate Anna and Lachlan and become the sole proprietors of the shipping company."

Douglas scanned the message between the husband and wife. "I can only surmise they worked together to kill Anna. They tried to convince Lachlan the business was worthless to purchase it for a low price. Ah, that's why Mr. Heywood kept two ledgers."

Doctor Esmond spoke up. "Mrs. Stewart gave her power of attorney to Lachlan, a condition of the asylum."

"Yes, but Mr. Heywood allegedly poisoned Mr. Stewart, thus killing him. With Lachlan out of their way and everyone believing Anna was dead too, Mrs. Stewart, ah, Heywood, would inherit the Stewart Mercantile Shipping Company upon leaving the asylum. However, if Lachlan would have sold the company to Mr. Heywood, he would own it outright. Whether or not he would have told Mrs. Heywood or left her in the asylum for the remainder of her life, well, I guess we will never know." Douglas confirmed.

McLeary looked at Dr. Esmond. "Henry, I would like your medical opinion on the mental status of Mrs. Stewart . . .Heywood."

Dr. Esmond took a deep breath, gathering his thoughts. "She appeared quite distraught when submitted. Other than her reaction to the previous note she received the other day . . ."

McLeary interrupted. "Aye, I have it on file as evidence."

"Aye, she has displayed utter calmness and kindness toward the staff. I would say she is of sound mind."

Douglas was compelled to add his opinion. "From what I understand, she could leave the asylum at any time?"

Dr. Esmond looked at Douglas. "Aye, she was free to release herself whenever she decided to leave."

Douglas proposed a motive. "Since Mrs. Heywood told her maid to retrieve the list of items from her desk and give it to Lachlan to give to Anna, do you believe, Chief, she is guilty of planning the murder of her daughter? Could she have been hiding in the asylum until Mr. Heywood could purchase the shipping company and then release herself to avoid the conviction of a crime?"

McLeary rose from his chair. "Both Mr. and Mrs. Heywood will be questioned thoroughly. With the present evidence in hand, Anna will obtain total control of her family shipping business."

Douglas stood. "I'll inform her of such." He extended his hand containing the folded note.

"I'll stop by a bit later and inquire about Anna's recovery." McLeary accepted the note to place in the file.

"Until then, Chief Inspector. Good day." Douglas left the headquarters with Barret. He was eager to return to the cottage, and to Anna.

Chapter 29

Douglas stepped down from the coach. Staring at the open door as Barret trotted toward it, he vowed to assign a few men from the ship's crew to make the repair. "Please wait," he said to the driver. Douglas followed the canine into the cottage.

Anna sat at the table with a blanket over her shoulders and one on her lap. Haggadah was pouring hot water into a teacup.

"How are you feeling, Anna?" He sat next to her.

She nodded her head and grinned.

The old witch placed the teacup in front of her goddaughter. "It's a bit chilly with the unhinged door, so we have kept the fire blazing to keep us warm."

"I'll have it repaired before nightfall." He stared into Anna's eyes. The color had returned to her face. He peeked into her teacup and saw a golden liquid with bits of green leaves floating on top. "Does Haggadah have you as right as rain yet?"

"Nearly," Anna replied, her voice the volume of a raspy whisper. She sipped her tea.

"Auch, she's fine. Anna just needs time to rest." Haggadah refilled the teapot from the cauldron hanging over the flames, set it on the table, and joined the couple. "Oh, I'm an improper hostess, Mr. MacEwan, would you like a cup of tea?"

"Perhaps later. Now that I've seen for myself that Anna is doing much better, I'll address the issue of repairing your door." He stood and looked at Anna. The news of her mother, brother, and Mr. Heywood could wait. First and foremost, he would make the arrangements for Lachlan's burial.

"That would be lovely, thank you." Haggadah looked at Anna's half-empty teacup. "Keep drinking, my dear."

"I'll return soon." He squeezed Anna's arm gently before leaving, entered the coach, and asked the driver to take him back to the headquarters. He organized the list of items he needed to address in his mind.

Arriving at the headquarters, Douglas approached the sergeant, who peered down at him.

"Back so soon, Mr. MacEwan?"

"Yes, I need to make arrangements for Lachlan Stewart's body to be taken to Saint Cuthbert for burial. I also need his personal effects."

"Aye, we will transport the body to the kirkyard. Do you have any request for the burial?"

Douglas was puzzled by the clarification. "Such as?"

"Plot placement? Mortsafe?"

"Yes, if the plot next to his father is available, place his body there. And yes, a mortsafe."

"The church charges for the rental of the mortsafe." The sergeant explained.

"I will pay the fee before his service, which I assume is tomorrow morning."

"Aye." The sergeant turned toward the cupboard and withdrew a small wooden box with Lachlan's name on it. He tipped it upside down on his desk and looked at Douglas. "His personal effects, sir."

Douglas placed his hand beneath the edge of the desk and pulled the items into his open palm. "Thank you. Good day." He looked down into his hand to see a set of keys and a few coins as he went to the coach. "The waterfront," he ordered the driver.

337

As the coach stopped before the waterfront, Douglas instructed the driver to wait once again. He fumbled with the keys to the Stewart Mercantile Shipping Company.

"Mr. MacEwan."

He looked up to see Martin. "Yes."

"Mr. Townsend sent me to tell you that we are ready to cast off." He turned toward the ship and pointed to the assistant standing at the railing.

Mr. Townsend waved. Douglas gave a single nod.

He scanned the harbor. There were several ships waiting to dock. "We will cast off tomorrow at noon. Send a few men to Haggadah's cottage to repair the door that was knocked off its hinges. Take a plank or two of wood, tools, and whatever else you need to make the repairs."

"The old witch's house?" Martin's eyebrows raised.

"Yes, the old witch's house."

"Aye, sir."

Douglas unlocked the door and entered the small office. He took both sets of books from the accountant's desk and locked the door as he left. Taking time to meet with the captain of Anna's ships, Douglas informed him of the new owner.

"Auch, that's why the office has been closed. We're ready to cast off and have been waiting for confirmation to do so," the captain informed.

"My ships will cast off tomorrow at noon. You and the other two will join us as we cross the Atlantic."

"You have the authority to give the order, sir?"

"I'm speaking on behalf of Miss Stewart. Noon tomorrow."

"Aye, sir."

Douglas boarded the coach once again and ordered the driver to go to the Stewart's house. He sighed as the coach came to a halt. Douglas climbed the steps to the front door, knocked, and wondered how much information he should tell the maid.

Helen opened the door. "Mr. MacEwan, how may I help you?"

"I need a moment of your time. May I speak with you inside?"

"Aye, come in."

Once inside the foyer, Douglas waited as the maid closed the door before he began. "I will not divulge every detail of the current events but must inform you of the following. Mr. Lachlan Stewart is dead. Mrs. Evelyn Stewart is still in the asylum." He paused as he took a deep breath. "This house belongs solely to Anna Stewart."

Helen shook her head, grinning slightly. "Mr. MacEwan, Miss Stewart is dead."

Douglas sighed. "Her body was exhumed by resurrectionists, and she was found alive."

The maid's eyes nearly popped out of her head as her mouth dropped open.

"Until Miss Stewart returns to reside within the house, please keep its maintenance."

"Of course, sir." She nodded once.

"Thank you."

Helen opened the door and watched as Douglas descended the stairs and boarded the coach before closing the door. The maid ran to the kitchen to tell the cook what she knew.

Douglas breathed a sigh of relief as he sat, and the driver headed to Haggadah's cottage. He searched his mind to find the words to gently break the news to Anna.

The driver reined the horse to a stop before the gate of the aged dwelling. Several men were working. Douglas was confident the door would be back in working order soon.

"Mr. MacEwan," the men greeted Douglas, who touched the brim of his hat as he passed by them and entered the cottage through the open door. With the ledgers tucked under his arm, Douglas inhaled the aroma of chicken. "Preparing dinner?"

Haggadah looked up from the pot she was stirring. "Aye, a lovely chicken soup with barley, onions, potatoes, and carrots."

"And we have freshly baked cinnamon raisin bread," Anna added as she placed the loaf on a cutting board and set it on the table.

"Sounds delicious." Douglas became silent, uncertain of where to begin. "Anna, I need you to sit for a moment. I have rather grim news I must convey to you."

Anna looked at her godmother, who nodded once. She pulled out a chair, sat as requested, and looked at Douglas.

He stared down at his shoes before finding the words he must convey, then looked into her emerald eyes. "The man who tried to murder you was indeed Mr. Heywood. His plot was finally revealed through two correspondences with your mother."

"My mum?"

"Yes, she was secretly married to Mr. Heywood."

"Married?" She became saucer-eyed and glanced at Haggadah. "To Mr. Heywood?"

"Yes, they plotted to kill you and have Lachlan sell the company to Mr. Heywood at a low price, thus the reason for the two ledgers. Lachlan refused, so Mr. Heywood gave your brother a flask laced with poison while he was in jail. He died."

"Lachlan is dead?" Anna's eyes welled with tears.

Douglas glanced at Haggadah before continuing. "Yes, I'm sorry. I've taken the liberty to make funeral arrangements with Saint Cuthbert's kirkyard. He is to be buried tomorrow morning."

"What will happen to Mum?"

Chief Inspector McLeary stood in the doorway. "Her case will be heard by a magistrate. He will decide her fate." He stepped into the cottage. "Miss Stewart, I came to see how you are recovering from your attack."

Haggadah rose from the stool, went to her goddaughter, and stood behind her chair. "She is recovering nicely, sir. Thank you for your kind interest in her welfare."

McLeary continued. "That's good to hear. Miss Stewart, I'm to inform you that you are the sole proprietor of the Stewart Mercantile Shipping Company."

Anna wiped away a tear from the corner of her eye. "I'm what? I don't know much about the shipping business, nor do I know how to run it."

The front door opened and closed several times to test it was operational. One of the men poked his head inside the cabin. "It's as good as new, Mr. MacEwan."

"Well done. Thank you." Douglas nodded.

Haggadah grinned as she looked at Douglas. "Mr. MacEwan has the situation well in hand, don't you, Mr. MacEwan?"

Douglas sighed before displaying a slight grin. "I've talked with the captain of one of your ships and have instructed him to cast off at noon tomorrow. My ships will be casting off at the same time."

"You're leaving?" Anna stood. Weakened with anxiety, her legs barely supporting her slight weight. Douglas wrapped his arm around her waist, offering his strength.

"I must leave when my ships depart. However, I've delayed their departure until after I've attended your brother's funeral." He paused. "My fondest wish is that you will accompany me to Virginia. Will you consider it?

Chapter 30

Anna, Douglas, Haggadah, and Barret stood silently beside the grave as the priest finished the short sermon the following morning.

"Rest assured, Anna, I insisted a bell was put in your brother's hand before his casket was closed." Douglas confided as the priest walked away.

"Thank you." Anna looked at the grave next to where Lachlan's body would lie in rest. It eased her mind knowing her brother would remain beside her father's grave, untouched and safe. "He is at peace." She stated bluntly as the casket protected by an iron mortsafe was lowered into the grave. Anna looked at Douglas. "And what of Mr. Heywood?"

Douglas adjusted his top hat as a gust of wind threatened to topple it. "McLeary said he'll be tried for the murder of your brother and the attempted murder of you, hung, and his body given to the college for dissection in the anatomy theater."

"And Mum?"

"Doctor Esmond has stated she is of sound mind. It was all a ruse to distance herself from the crimes." Douglas offered his bent arm to Anna and Haggadah as they turned toward the gate entrance. "The evidence against her is weaker since she was merely an accomplice. The most the magistrate may do is have her committed to a convict ship and exiled for a given length of time."

Haggadah glanced at the profile of Douglas's face. She gazed into the distance and grinned, knowing Anna would be happy with the kind gentleman by her side. "You'll be off to Virginia."

Anna smiled at Douglas before looking at her godmother. "I've always wanted to see it, but I dread the thought of leaving you alone, Haggadah."

"My place is here, where I'm needed. You will always have your home to return to when visiting the city. After all, you have a shipping business to manage, with the help of Mr. MacEwan, that is. Nero, Barret, and I will be fine, and we look forward to your visits in the future."

~

Shortly after midday, the last trunk was carried by two crewmen up the loading ramp to the ship. Haggadah insisted the Book of Shadows, the Triple Goddess statue, candles, the MacEwan tartan, and an apothecary containing small bottles of nearly every herb and spice accompanied her goddaughter.

Anna looked over the ship's railing at the waterfront where her godmother and Barret stood. They had said their goodbyes at the cottage, but Haggadah insisted on seeing her off properly. Thankfully, Douglas employed a coach to return her and Barret home safely. She looked at the crewmen carrying her trunk as they stepped onto the deck. "Take it to my quarters, gentlemen."

"Aye, Miss Stewart."

Anna waved to her godmother, who returned her wave of farewell.

Douglas came up from below deck and went to Anna's side. He waved to the old witch and her dog.

Martin stood on deck just behind the couple. "Mr. MacEwan, Miss Stewart." They turned toward him. "Mr. Townsend has had quite a time going over the list of cargo and assures me all is in order. All six ships are fully loaded and ready to cast off sir, miss." Martin reported as he looked at Douglas and Anna for their approval.

Anna stared at the resurrectionist. She saw John on the deck standing behind his friend.

Douglas nodded. "Very good. Tell the captain to cast off."

"Aye, sir." Martin hurried to Captain Williams to relay the message. John followed.

Douglas and Anna turned to face the waterfront once again.

Anna grinned as she looked at Douglas. "You hired the resurrectionists?"

Douglas gazed into Anna's emerald eyes. "Yes. I told them I would take care of them if they cooperated. They did, so I employed them. They have a job and a steady income for as long as they wish to work." He smiled. "It was the least I could do. After all, they brought you back to life, which pleases me immensely." He clasped her hand, lifted it from the railing, and kissed the back of it gently. "Many accuse you of being a witch. I believe it's true because you have truly bewitched me as no other woman could. Will you do me the honor of becoming my wife?"

Anna smiled. "Aye, I would like nothing more."

He drew her near, wrapping his arms around her waist, and lowered his lips to hers. She cared little who was watching as she threaded her arms around his neck while the whooping hollers of the crew announced the romance.

Douglas ended the kiss and touched his forehead to hers. "Lucky us, we just happen to have a captain on board to perform the ceremony." He smiled.

Haggadah nodded her approval. "Time to go home, Barret." With her cane in hand, she and her faithful canine climbed into the coach, knowing her goddaughter would return to see her again someday.

Thank you for reading

The Cursed Witch

If you have a moment, please post your
review at the store where you bought it.

For additional information about the author,
signings, and her books, please visit

www.BrendaHasseBooks.com

To sign-up for the author's newsletter,
please visit

www.BrendaHasseBooks.com/newsletter-sign-up

9 781734 778663